THIS GUY WALKS INTO A BAR

a novel of unrelenting suspense

WILLIAM J. GOYETTE

OTHER BOOKS BY WILLIAM J. GOYETTE

Jake Hawksworth Series

In Our Blood

To request permissions, contact the publisher at projectcoordinator@dragonalchemypublishing.com.

Paperback: 979-8-9864784-0-1
eBook: 979-8-9864784-1-8

Library of Congress Number: 20229413449

First eBook edition August 2022
First Paperback edition August 2022

Printed by Ingram in the USA.

Cover By: Jessica Beaver

Dragon Alchemy Publishing
Frederick, MD 21701

Dragonalchemypublishing.com

For my father and brother, Frank Sr. and Frank Jr.
I think you guys would have really liked this one.

ACKNOWLEDGMENTS

Although *This Guy Walks Into a Bar* is a work of fiction, its inspiration came from a real-life experience I had many years ago. Like Joe Campbell, I was offered the opportunity to ghostwrite a novel by the mistress of one of America's most notorious crime bosses. Unlike Joe, I turned down the offer, mainly out of fear for my family. But every once in a while, I ask myself, *What if?*

I would like to thank the team at Dragon Alchemy Publishing for taking a chance on me. I am also grateful to James Caffarella for your legal expertise and sound advice. To my early readers: Anne Antonellis, Sharon and Tom Cronin, Jennifer Garbuzinski, Michelle Goyette, John Jagielski, and Elaine and Bob Postler, thanks for your support and feedback. I also owe gratitude to the mystery woman who almost convinced me to tell her story one cold, rainy night many moons ago. Almost.

Lastly, I want to thank my wife and partner in crime, Sue, and my two amazing daughters, Christie and Lexi. You three have inspired me to be a better man and pushed me to finish what I started. I also want to thank my girls for bringing two amazing young men, Alex Hawksworth and Matt Cibotti, into our family. I am truly blessed to have you all in my life.

So, this guy walks into a bar. It hurt like hell.

Don't like that one? Okay, how about this one.

This guy walks into a bar after playing a round of golf. He turns to the leggy blonde sitting to his left and says, "What's a nice girl like you doing in a place like this?" She smiles and says, "I'm a hooker." The guy replies, "Try turning your hands on the shaft a little bit to the left."

Come on—don't you get it?
See, the guy's a golfer and—never mind.

Okay, I've got it. You're gonna love this one!

So, this guy walks into a bar...
and everyone inside
is dead.

PART ONE

Confessions of a Goomah

CHAPTER ONE

T*he story eating at my insides has to be told before it kills me.*
      That's how the letter requesting a ghostwriter began.
Somewhat intriguing, if a bit sinister. Even more intriguing was
that it had been formally written on fine stationery rather than
through today's more impersonal electronic channels. An old-
fashioned kind of gal, perhaps?

    His first instinct had been to pawn her off on someone else.
After all, he'd been referred to her by his wife Kate, who said
she'd been referred by a friend of a friend of a friend (and who
knows, maybe a couple of second cousins sandwiched in there
too), so why not continue this game of Pass the Buck? But she'd
said the magic word. Money. And money was something he
could really use right about now.

    Kate had practically pushed Joe out the door, saying how
he'd always wanted to write a novel and could now actually get
paid to do it. Sure, his dream was to write a best-selling book

that would influence generation after generation. Hemingway. Steinbeck. Kerouac. Campbell.

Campbell. Joe Campbell. Didn't exactly sound like the voice of a generation. It sounded *average*. Like everything about his life. Average job. Average height. Average looks. Even his name was average. Just your regular old Average Joe.

Kate was right—well, half right. He wanted to write a novel, but *his* novel, not some anonymous piece of drivel from a Patricia WhatsHerName who just had to get the story inside her out. If Kate were so gung-ho about it, why'd she pass it off on him? Though Joe hated to admit it, his better half was a better writer. He'd known it since reading the first line of her first assignment for a creative writing workshop she'd roped him into taking with her. Except for one thing. She had no drive.

With Kate on indefinite sabbatical (and, who was he kidding, not planning on going back to work any time soon), their live-beyond-their-means lifestyle was about to come to a screeching halt. Factor in a Range Rover and a mortgage the size of Texas, and you had yourself one big cluster-fuck.

That's why good old Average Joe Campbell was sitting outside a ramshackle bar on a Tuesday night at 7:44 in an epic rainstorm. For the money. And maybe something else. The idea —no, the hope—that on the other side of that door was a life less ordinary. A life less average.

Joe Campbell pulled on the hood of his overpriced Brooks Brothers rain slicker, pushed open the door of his exorbitant silver Range Rover Sport, and made a mad dash for a battered old bar called Griffin's.

CHAPTER TWO

Griffin's had all the amenities one might expect from a top-notch dive bar. Threadbare décor highlighted by assorted kitsch splashed the walls in garish splendor. The quintessential barfly nursed a drink on the corner stool. A boorish looking bartender scrolled with disinterest through his phone. *Griffin, maybe?* The lighting was hazy enough to obscure the grit and grime that no doubt shellacked every surface. The melancholy vocals of Aimee Mann, arguably one of music's most underrated talents, drifted from the shadows.

Joe approached the bartender with trepidation, wishing the guy were on a leash. An intricate landscape of black and green obliterated any indication of skin on the heavily veined arms. The body ink crept across the guy's neckline and snaked up the tightly shorn skull, which resembled a skinned watermelon.

"Excuse me. I'm here to meet someone." Joe avoided eye contact with Griffin, scanning the room for his mystery date. Only two of the dozen or so tables were occupied. At one, an obese man gnawed feverishly on a plate of grease Joe guessed to be meat in one form or another. At the other, a heavily mascaraed woman with high hair played coyly with the thinning hair of a probably married, probably *working late*, middle-aged man. The man's suit looked bespoke, the drab tie's double Windsor knot cranked a bit too tightly to his protruding Adam's apple.

"Isn't everybody?" the surly bartender replied in a bored, yet slightly hostile tone.

Joe laughed. Louder than he meant to. The obese guy glanced up from his gourmet meal, grunted, and resumed his feeding. "No, it's not like that."

"Never is." It was Griffin's turn to laugh. "But always is."

"Listen, I think I made a mistake. I'm just going to—"

"Joe? Joe Campbell?" A gravelly voice called out from his right. The barfly. Perfect. Just perfect.

"Have a nice time, Joe," Griffin said. Then added, "You'll need a drink, or ten, with that one."

Joe smirked and made his way to the end of the bar, where the Queen of All Barflies sat proudly perched on her throne. "Patricia?" he asked more incredulously than he intended.

"In the flesh. And, please, call me Patty. Only my mother called me Patricia. God rest her pathetic soul." Patty extended a deeply tanned, snap-in-two hand, which Joe shook with care. "Thought that might be you. You look like a writer."

Joe laughed at the absurdity of the comment. "What does a writer look like?"

Patty Quigley smiled and said, "You. Looks like you." Joe was about to feign an emergency so he could get the hell out of Dodge, but Patty tugged at his still-damp slicker and said, "Pull up a stool."

Patty motioned to the bartender. "Hey, Rufus, bring me another and—what'll it be, Cowboy?"

Rufus? So much for Joe's Griffin theory. "Whatever cold lager you have on tap, Rufus." Joe stifled a laugh. *Rufus? Man, his parents must've hated him.* Probably had the shit beat out of him all through school. And probably why he looked like he did now, muscle regenerating from muscle.

Patty expelled a rattly cough and said, "Throw in a coupla belts of Jameson too."

"None for me, thanks."

Patty laughed, the maraca rattling in her throat again. "Who said they were for you?"

Joe chuckled along with her, not sure if he was laughing at a joke or the absurdity of the situation he suddenly felt trapped in.

"You okay, Cowboy?" Patty leaned in close enough for Joe to take in the intense mix of alcohol and nicotine, topped off with a hint of nondescript perfume probably purchased from the same corner store where she bought her cigarettes.

"Listen, Patty," Joe said, "I'm not sure I'm the right person for this project."

Patty's face sucked up into itself. Her hard eyes got harder. "But you ain't even heard my story."

"It's just that—"

"You don't think I can pay you, do you?" Patty's voice shot up a few octaves, took on a sinister edge. "Do you, you arrogant sonuvabitch?"

They had a captive audience. Rufus and his third-rate cast of characters gazed in their direction. "Listen, Patty, it's not that, it's just..." *What, Joe? How are you going to get yourself out of this one?* "It's just, I don't know, I don't know if I'm good enough to tell your story." *Nice recovery, ace. Puts the onus on you. Softens the blow.*

Patty Quigley eyeballed him, those steely eyes cutting right through him. Then they softened and disappeared into the sunbaked, weather-beaten face Joe suspected had once been stunning, before that triple threat of booze, butts, and sun did their number. She gazed at him some more, the way an art connoisseur might study a painting, searching its surface for depth and comprehension.

A delicate hand brushed his forearm. Joe's instinct was to recoil. He didn't. This mystery woman was too unpredictable and likely short of a few cards from the deck. He forced a smile.

Long, well-manicured fingernails *tap-tapped* his skin, sending a minor shock up his arm. He was swept up in a memory of his high school crush, the kind an adolescent boy never really gets over. Miss Mayhew, in that clingy red dress that displayed a body destined for the pages of Playboy (which, Joe found out years later, it was) and those fuck-me heels that *click-clacked* as she strutted her stuff before the class. But it was those nails that no student, male or female, would ever forget. Blood-red daggers gripped the chalk with a mix of tenderness and aggression as they danced across the blackboard, spewing algebraic nonsense Joe would never use in real life. With every $a + b$ and $x = y$, the class held a collective breath, waiting for one of those glossy daggers to connect with the cloudy slate, unleashing a screech so spine-chilling—

"You with me, Cowboy?" A voice far more offensive than fingers to a chalkboard repeated the question.

"Huh...yeah, yeah. Sorry."

"Thought I lost you for a sec," Patty squealed. "Anyway, as I was saying, sorry I got so defensive."

"No worries."

Patty, clearly pleased to have him back in her good graces, cracked a broad smile that, like the fingernails, was meticulously maintained. Rufus slammed down their drinks, told them to "enjoy" with zero conviction, and went back to his post.

Defeated, Joe snatched up the Jameson, savored the warmth of the fiery liquid as it made its way down his throat, and said, "So, what is this story you just have to tell?"

Patty downed her shot and said, "Hold onto your hat, Cowboy. This story? It's gonna blow you away."

CHAPTER THREE

"You want to call it *what?*"

"Confessions of a Goomah."

"You mean like in *The Sopranos?*"

"Good for you, Cowboy."

"Why do you keep calling me Cowboy?"

"You look like a cowboy."

"I thought I looked like a writer?"

"You look like a cowboy who writes."

Joe took a long swig of his piss-warm beer. "So, let me get this straight. You're saying you're the girlfriend of a, what, mob guy?"

"Was," Patty replied pointedly. She downed another shot —*how many is that?*—and said, "Ain't that a hoot?"

"You're serious."

"As a heart attack."

The lady's nuts. Bonkers. "So, let's say you are. Whose goomah are—I mean—were you?"

"I'd tell you. But then I'd have to kill you." Her face turned to stone, unblinking eyes laser-beaming him.

Joe laughed the way one would when their boss has told a totally inappropriate joke while conducting a job performance review.

"I'm just fuckin' with ya!" This time when Patty laughed, Joe expected to see a blackened set of lungs pop out of her mouth right into the bowl of stale pretzels before her. She finally composed herself and, with all vital organs seemingly intact, added, "Sorry, industry humor."

Joe wore his annoyance on his sleeve. "Yeah...I got it."

Patty frowned. "Sorry, just tryin' to break the ice." She reached into the threadbare shoulder bag riding shotgun on the barstool beside her, produced a thick hardcover book, and plunked it face down on the table. "Him."

Joe's pulse quickened. The grainy image smiled amicably at him. But the eyes conveyed something else. Ruthlessness. Brutality. Evil. These were the eyes of Dominic "The Skinner" Guierriero.

"You look like you've seen a ghost, Cowboy."

Her voice sounded as though she were underwater. Joe's heartbeat thrummed in his ears. Patty came in and out of focus. *Dominic "The Skinner" Guierriero.*

"Hey, Cowboy, you okay?"

Patty zoomed back into focus. Joe noticed a slight tremor in his hands. Tried to regulate his breathing the way his chiropractor had taught him. When his tongue tethered itself back to his brain he said, "You were Dominic Guierriero's goomah?"

Patty smirked. "Well, we weren't exactly exclusive or nothin' but, yeah, I guess you could say that."

"And you want me to write a book about *him*?"

"Kinda, but not really. It's gonna be through my eyes, ya see? Dom will be in it, of course. But it's about me. My life."

This whack job was out of her mind. How did he even know she was telling the truth? Big deal, she had a book about the guy. So did millions of others. It sat atop the New York Times Best Sellers List for almost a year. Probably picked up a copy on her way over here.

Patty grimaced, apparently sensing what was banging around in Joe's head. She produced a ragged manila envelope and tossed it in front of him. Half a dozen poor quality photos slid out. Trembling fingers picked up a snapshot of good old Patty in a tight embrace with The Skinner.

"Believe me now?" she crowed, looking pleased with herself.

Joe gazed at the photo. Maybe it was photoshopped. But it looked pretty real. Too fucking real. He was aware of his mouth agape, Patty eyeing him curiously.

"What's wrong with you?" Patty said harshly.

The dank walls closed in around him. Patty went in and out of focus again. His mouth tasted of copper. He felt the onset of a panic attack creeping up, something he'd kept at bay for over a year. The signs were all there. The beads of perspiration he could almost hear *pop-popping* on his forehead. The heart doing laps inside his constricting chest. The sense of hollow dread closing in, crushing him in its blackness.

At last, he rose, pulled some bills from his wallet, plunked them down and said, "It was nice meeting you, Patty, but I've got to run." He shot a glance at Rufus, bee-lined it to the door, and charged out into the lingering rain.

CHAPTER FOUR

"What do you mean, you *left?*"

"I left."

"Why?" Kate Campbell's lovely gaze scorched him.

"Why?" Joe said incredulously. "Did you not hear me? We're talking about Dominic "The Skinner" Guierriero. Do you even know how he got that nickname?"

Kate rolled those beautiful baby blues. "Why don't you enlighten me?"

"You really want to know? I'll tell you. This Guierriero dude makes Ted Bundy look like a Boy Scout. Word is that he slowly, and I mean very slowly, flays his victims. First an arm, then a leg, then a—"

"Okay, I get it," Kate interrupted. "You don't have to get so graphic."

Joe expelled an angry laugh. "Considering you want me to get into bed with the guy, I think I do."

"Well, these so-called victims were probably all criminals

themselves," Kate shot back. "Besides, he's never been convicted, so maybe he's innocent."

"Innocent? The reason he's never been convicted is because no juror who values his life would ever vote to convict that guy."

Kate rolled her eyes again. "You're being a bit dramatic, don't you think? So, you're saying that every time he's faced a jury, he's scared them into submission?"

"Would you vote to convict him? I know I wouldn't." Joe sighed and let out a long puff of air. "Listen, if this is about money, there are other ways I can drum up some freelance."

Now it was Kate's turn to sigh. "Baby, it's not about the money. I'm thinking about your dream. To be a published author."

Joe snapped open the fridge and grabbed a cold one. He downed half the bottle, then turned to his wife of six months. "I just don't want to put us in danger."

Kate's features softened. "Of course you don't, babe. Neither do I. But you haven't even heard the woman out." Her fingers danced playfully in his hair. "Besides, if this is a work of fiction, you can change the names, the places. Nobody will ever connect it to this Guierriero guy." Her gaze steeled. "It *is* a work of fiction, isn't it?"

Joe shrugged. "Yeah. I think so."

"You *think* so?"

He lied. "No, I mean it is fiction. Definitely."

Kate ruffled his longish hair and planted a loud kiss on his forehead. "Good. Now let's get you out of those wet clothes." She tugged coquettishly at his shirt, ran a hand across his increasing hardness. It had been weeks since they'd last made love. The loving and adventurous spirit Joe had fallen in love with had recently done a one-eighty. Dark undertones singed the edges of Kate's demeanor, and these days she seemed to be sick, tired, depressed, or all of the above.

Wondering if he could be the cause of her drastic mood change, Joe had brought up the subject on several occasions. Kate brushed it off as *nothing* or *just having a bad day*. And when the topic of kids came up, she withdrew further into her cocoon. This set off alarms in Joe, as Kate had talked incessantly about starting a family immediately after the wedding, if you could call it that.

The event was hardly standing room only. Kate had no family, aside from a couple of estranged aunts and uncles. When she was a teenager, her parents and younger sister had perished in a terrible fire, something she refused to talk about with anyone, including her husband.

Joe's family, on the other hand, was alive and well—*well* being a bit of a stretch. Dear Old Mom and Dad had finally, after years of both physical and verbal abuse, decided to cut their losses. Those severed ties included Joe and his five-years-senior brother Glen (named after a country star Joe's mother had idolized during her pre-abuse days). Dolores Campbell, never the motherly type, kissed her boys goodbye one day, told them to have a nice life, and moved out West to "start living." Tom Campbell, on the other hand, found himself a new punching bag, younger than his own two sons, and hoofed it down to Florida. Joe had invited his father to the nuptials. Tom accepted, then backed out in the eleventh hour. Three weeks later, Joe received a Hallmark card with a *Congrats, Son!* and a torn twenty-dollar bill.

So, on The Big Day, Joe and Kate, along with Glen and a rent-a-priest, vowed to honor one another in good times and in bad, in sickness and health, until death do them part.

Kate unzipped Joe's damp Banana Republic khakis and slid them stealthily down his legs. He eagerly stepped out of them, rock hard and ready to go. As he moved in for the kill, Kate planted a determined hand on his bare chest and pushed away.

"It's late," she said, gathering up Joe's soggy clothes. She kissed him tenderly on the cheek, whispered "maybe tomorrow," and disappeared, leaving Joe and his quickly deflating ego exposed and bare.

CHAPTER FIVE

"You wanted to see me, Shea?"

Shea Gilfoy eased back in her ergonomic leather office chair and planted ten ringless, unmanicured fingers on the highly polished mahogany desk. She lifted a mannish hand to her roundish chin. Joe watched the fingerprints defog from the glossy surface, then brought his eyes to meet Shea's. Shea gazed out the window toward the silvery skyline. Not a good sign.

"Come on, Shea," Joe demanded. "Spill it."

Shea shifted her weight, and the pricey leather emitted a noise that would have any adolescent boy rolling in the aisles. "It's about the position." She looked toward the skyline again. "They're giving it to Mitch."

Joe slammed a fist on the perfectly arranged desk. A hand-made mug proudly touting #1 AUNT toppled, spilling an assortment of pens and perfectly sharpened pencils across the slick surface. *Who the hell even uses pencils anymore?*

"Joe, what the hell—"

"No, Shea. More like what the *fuck*," Joe said. "You and I both know Mitch is no Creative Director. In fact, he's barely what I'd call creative."

Shea snatched up a rogue pencil as it rolled toward the desk's precipice and snapped it in two with her meaty paw. "You're way out of line, Campbell! Now get the hell out of my office before you say something you're really going to regret."

Joe turned to leave. In the bullpen, a couple of twenty-something interns peeked sheepishly over their lattes and laptops. Joe returned to the desk, looked directly into his boss's heated eyes, and said, "The only thing I regret is not taking that position I was offered over at McManus last month."

As the door crashed open, the two interns dissolved into their laptops. The words *You're fired!* never left Shea's lips as Joe made his grand exit. Or maybe they did and the blood thrumming in Joe's ears had blocked them out. He was now out of a job or reporting to the talentless Mitch Wasserman. Either way, his days there were numbered. Either way, he was fucked.

He walked with purpose, gliding through crowds of suits and trendy messenger bags, sidestepping poor homeless souls stretched across the concrete pathway, ignoring the blares of angry motorists as he cut a swath through a steady stream of traffic, daring them to go on and mow him down.

The chaos of the daily rush dissolved into white noise as Joe made his way into Boston Public Garden. He sprawled out on a well-shaded bench and loosened his stifling tie. A frail woman dressed in layer upon layer of soiled rags on this unseasonably warm spring day shuffled past, pushing a baby stroller brimming with treasures she'd collected on her journey. She paused, sized Joe up, and smiled weakly. A decaying smile. A hopeful smile.

Joe dug out a few rumpled bills and tucked them into the

woman's treasure trove. The woman, with kind eyes and a world-weary face, nodded and continued on her treasure hunt. Joe pulled out his cell, scrolled through his contacts, and jabbed an angry finger on the name.

The inimitable voice of Patty Quigley answered on the first ring.

"What made you change your mind, Cowboy?"

Joe lied. "I think your story has a lot of potential." *And I could really use the cash.* "So, before we get started—"

Patty slammed a thick envelope down in front of him. "Didn't think I'd put my money where my mouth is, didya? How's five grand for starters?" Joe turned the hefty envelope over in his hands. "It's all there. Count it if you like." Joe opened his mouth to speak, but Patty cut him off at the knees. "Thought you'd like it in smaller denominations. Tens and twenties okay?"

Joe nodded dumbly. *Is it untraceable?* he thought to say, then decided he'd rather not know.

Patty smiled her million-dollar smile and added, "There's plenty more where that came from. So, when do we get started?"

CHAPTER SIX

I t was the summer of 1987 when I first met Dimitri Giacomo. I was nineteen and had a killer body back then. A body meant for working. That was how I landed the gig at Foxy, a gentlemen's club in Chicago's South Side. The pay was good, the drinks free, and the no-touch policy an added bonus. Life was good. Until that night.

My girlfriend Charlene Nivens (not her real name) and I had just finished up our set. It had been a rough night. The drunks and perverts were out in full force that evening. Those, I could handle. It was those damn frat boys I thought I could. I was wrong.

There were three of them. Ralph Lauren poster boys, dripping of Daddy's money. And that money was being put to good use on the other girls and me. At first it was all harmless fun. Boys being boys. Rude catcalls. Suggestive gestures. Until Jock #1 decided to cop a feel. I brushed him off with a nice "No touching the merchandise," as Vic had always instructed us to do. Jock #1 figured those rules didn't apply to him. And when Jock #2 decided to join in on the fun, that's when things went to shit.

A couple of broken tables and broken egos later, the Greek boys were sent packing, along with a lifetime ban. Charlene and I were pretty shaken up, but otherwise unharmed. As we walked arm-in-arm to catch the train, that's when he called out to us.

"No hard feelings, ladies?" a very drunk Jock #1 hollered. As we turned, we found ourselves surrounded by the man-boys.

I was terrified. Charlene gripped my arm like a vise. I remained calm. "No hard feelings, boys," I replied in a soft voice. "Now, why don't you run on back to campus and sleep it off." Wrong thing to say.

The boys converged on us like a pack of feral wolves, a mix of whiskey and musky cologne wafting in the humid late-night air. "Not 'til we get what you owe us, bitch," said Jock #2, a tough guy with a military bearing and a linebacker's build. "We paid you well, and we're here to cash in."

This is when all reason went out the door and panic set in. Charlene made to run, but the combination of five-inch heels and grime-slick alley sent her sprawling. Jock #3, whose milquetoast appearance defied the rage inside, was on top of Charlene, clawing clumsily at her clothes. Charlene's a pretty tough girl and was holding her own with the guy until Jock #2 jumped to his brother's aid and pinned her down.

I made my move. Stiletto as my weapon, I charged them. My head snapped back violently. Jock #1 twisted a meaty fist around my hair, forcing me to my knees. With his other hand, he fumbled drunkenly with his zipper. "Time to earn your money."

That's when Dimitri Giacomo entered my life. This larger-than-life man tossed my attacker aside like a rag doll and offered me his hand. "Are you okay, Miss?" he asked. After that, everything else was a blur. I woke up the next morning safe in my bed, how I don't know. But I knew one thing—this man was my savior, my knight in shining armor.

A couple of days later, I heard that some frat boys from the local university were mugged and beaten severely, one so badly that his foot-

ball-playing days were over. None of the boys would describe their attackers, saying they couldn't remember. But I knew better.

"I love it," Patty Quigley squealed, glancing up from the printout. "You really bring it to life. And I love the big words, too! What's a milquetoast?"

Joe laughed, then said, "Glad you like it."

Patty frowned. "I still don't know why you couldn't use Dom's real name."

"We talked about this. It's supposed to be a complete work of fiction. Remember?"

Patty released a loud puff of breath. "I know, I know," she whined like that kid in the supermarket checkout line who didn't get that candy bar she'd been eyeballing. "I just know if we asked that he'd be fine with it," she said. "He'd probably give you cart blank."

"I think you mean carte blanche."

"Sure," Patty said, "whatever you say, Mister Writerman."

"Those were the rules," Joe said. "Guierriero isn't exactly the kind of guy I want to cross."

"And why does it have to take place in Chicago? I ain't never even been to Chicago. What about New York?"

"Because Chicago is further away from Boston," Joe said. "Remember, we don't want any connection to Guierriero or the East Coast."

"Of course," Patty crowed. She showed her lovely smile. It was almost becoming endearing. How she kept those pearly whites so pearly white with the constant barrage of nicotine was as enigmatic as the woman herself. She rose abruptly and said, "Well, gotta run, Cowboy. Hot date tonight. But keep 'em coming. I'll have some more stories for you in a couple of days."

As Patty breezed out of Griffin's, Joe was overcome by a sense of dread. What had he gotten himself into? And what secrets did Patty's future stories hold? He slumped into the tattered seat in the darkest corner of this bar that was starting to feel like his new home. Rufus, his new best friend, threw a quick wave from behind the bar. Just Your Regular Old Average Joe's ordinary life had suddenly become a little less ordinary.

CHAPTER SEVEN

The agency was abuzz with deadlines looming on both the Samsonite and Mermaid Cruise Lines accounts. Joe had come in with his tail between his legs this morning, wondering if he was still on the payroll after last week's rift with his boss. Shea had shot him a terse glance as he passed her office, then returned to her laptop.

Joe sucked down his coffee like it was water and cranked out enticing descriptions of exotic island destinations, but Patty Quigley and Dominic "The Skinner" Guierriero kept creeping into the landscapes. He was filled with a gnawing sense of dread, the kind that nestles deep inside, cowering in fear, all the while knowing something horrific is lurking just around the corner. He'd painted himself into a corner, one he wasn't sure he could dodge without making one big, sloppy mess.

"Campbell." The deep, anchorman-like voice of Mitch Wasserman shook him from his reverie. Joe glanced up. Mitch even looked like an anchorman. The hackneyed spray tan. The ridiculously thick and shiny hundred-dollar haircut. And those teeth. Those impossibly white fucking teeth.

"Mitch," he said, unable to mask the surprise and disdain in his voice. "I thought you were taking the day off."

Mitch tossed his thick mane, all movie-star-like, and said primly, "I was. Shea asked me to stick around to make sure we're on point with the campaign."

Joe ignored the fire rising in his face and leaned back casually, feigning indifference. "We're on point, Mitch. So, no worries. Enjoy your time off." He turned back to the beckoning laptop.

Hot, coffee-tinged breath brushed his cheek. Mitch threw any notion of personal space out the window and said insolently, "Shea is concerned that we aren't. So why don't we regroup in the war room in, say, forty-five minutes?" Mitch turned and sauntered away, his newfound power leaving a trail of arrogance as he left.

The meeting went as planned. Mitch red-penciled Joe's brilliant editorial, pooh-poohed the design, panned more than half the photos. This meant rewrites, redesign, reshoots. It also meant late nights and weekends for Joe and his hapless team.

After reassuring his staff that it had nothing to do with their abilities and was simply a "change in direction," Joe took to the busy city streets. The blaring horns and hurried murmurs of passing automatons, in a stark mix of starched-shirt suits and too-casual-for-work attire, with cell phones cemented to their ears were welcome distractions from the hellish two hours spent taking lashes from a far inferior competitor.

He texted Kate, told her not to hold dinner, then remembered he had a meeting with Patty to pick up her latest stories for him to decipher into some form of English. Joe had suggested emailing the notes to save them both time and inconvenience, but Patty went off on a rant about how much she detested today's technology and longed for the simpler days of rotary phones and typewriters.

The train was full of the usual cast of characters, any of whom could make for a novel of their own. There was the Goth couple—*was that still a trend?*—pushing the legal limit on PDA. The guy with the face tattoo that may as well say DON'T HIRE ME. The college students toting trendy backpacks and absorbed in pretentious paperbacks, flaunting their Ivy League status. And, of course, the myriad of lost souls who rode the train simply because they had nowhere else to be.

Joe exited the train and made his way past rows of ramshackle triple-deckers, their sagging facades bearing the weight of the downtrodden occupants inside. A withered young mother and her grimy toddler sat dejectedly on the stoop of a dreary washed-out-yellow structure. The woman eyed Joe with either interest or disgust, he couldn't be sure. Maybe both. Probably calculating how many months of rent she could get from Joe's navy herringbone suit from Barneys and overpriced messenger bag Kate felt every future Creative Director had to have. Shame washed over him. He glanced down at the crumbling concrete, at a rust-colored smear—*is that blood?*—then quickened his pace until he reached Griffin's. His sleek Tag Heuer watch, another must-have accessory for any burgeoning adman, told him he was nearly an hour late. Which meant Punctual Patty was not going to be happy.

Rufus shot Joe a boy-are-you-in-trouble smirk and motioned to the dank corner where Joe could already feel Patty's gaze cutting deep.

"Listen, Patty, I'm sorry. I got tied up at the office."

"Don't bullshit a bullshitter, Cowboy." Patty slammed her drink down. "Just cuz I don't wear fancy clothes and go to a fancy job, don't mean my time ain't valuable."

"Of course it doesn't," Joe said in the sympathetic tone he'd mastered over countless apologies to Kate. The stony expression staring back at him told him he was playing to a tougher crowd.

A fat manila envelope landed with a dull thud. Thicker than her last. "Here you go. Read it and weep." Patty downed the last drop from her glass and stood abruptly. "Any questions, call my secretary and leave a message."

"Come on, Patty," Joe said. "I said I was sorry."

Patty's eyes scorched him. She blazed past, leaving a trail of rage in her wake. The maraca-tinged voice spoke to the back of Joe's head. "The story's about to get interesting. Oh, and I included pictures this time. Enjoy." When he turned, she was already gone.

CHAPTER EIGHT

I t was after ten when Joe got home. He turned off the ignition and stared in silence at his ostentatious abode. One big enough for a host of children. Joe would settle for just one. The first floor was shrouded in darkness. A yellowish glow flickered in a second story window. Kate was no doubt in bed watching one of a dozen home improvement shows she followed religiously.

Joe ran a hand over the thick packet riding shotgun. All afternoon, he'd been thinking about it, and what Patty had said. *The story's about to get interesting.* The past couple of weeks had been mainly backstory, how Patty had met Giacomo (aka Guierriero), how she'd been accepted into The Family, the relationships with her gal pals Charlene and Vixen, and her deep feelings for The Skinner.

The house was quiet and dark, as if it had been dipped in a vat of thick black tar. It felt as suffocating too. Joe fumbled for a lamp, nearly toppling it in the process. He tossed his jacket, bag, and the mystery package onto the overstuffed couch and poured himself a double shot of Chivas. He shed the tie and shoes and eased back into the couch, tossing back the whiskey, letting his eyes adjust to the diffused lighting.

The room was immaculate. Too immaculate. More like a museum than a place to kick back and feel at home. He imagined toys scattered about. The gleeful sounds of children racing around. A spirited dog bounding behind. A loving wife sprawled across the couch, the heat of her body warming his. This was the life he imagined. A life that seemed to grow more distant with each passing day.

"Okay, let's see what we've got here," he said to the silent room. He unclasped the envelope. Pages of handwritten notes and several snapshots spilled out. Funny, even though Patty's writing was riddled with typos, incomplete thoughts and grammatical no-nos, her handwriting, like her manicure and teeth, was meticulous.

Joe picked up one of the photos. Patty appeared young and radiant. What had those years with The Skinner done to her? Her arms were draped affectionately over the shoulders of the two women bookending her. One was heavyset and unfashionable. She wore a half smile that looked forced. The other woman donned a tight tank top and short denim skirt that accentuated her shapely torso and legs. She had a healthy glow and brilliant smile, but oversized sunglasses obscured half her face. From Patty's earlier notes, Joe guessed this woman to be Charlene.

Charlene had been Patty's most loyal friend and was with her on the fateful night in the alley. A natural beauty (if the hidden face matched the rest of the package), it was easy to see how a sleazy strip joint like The Landing Strip had snatched up a catch like Charlene. A lustrous mane of reddish hair brushed her shoulders. Her body was the stuff of wet dreams. How, Joe wondered, had a girl like that ended up dancing for drunken businessmen and testosterone-fueled frat boys?

When Joe had asked Patty what became of Charlene, her eyes had brimmed over, her face a mask of grief. Her reply had been blunt. "She's dead. And I really don't want to discuss it any further."

Joe hadn't pushed, just as he hadn't pushed when Patty had hinted that she'd once had a daughter who died a traumatic death. He supposed she would tell him in due time. He flipped over the photo and there was Patty's immaculate penmanship, not quite feminine or masculine. Efficient was the word that came to mind. Scrawled neatly across the matte paper was *Charlene, Me & Vixen—summer 2002 Castle Island.*

Ah, so that was Vixen. Didn't quite live up to the name. Maybe there was a story there. Maybe it was in the stack of notes perched by Joe's side.

Joe yawned, the weight of the day, and the Chivas, kicking in. He should probably pack it in. The notes could wait one more day. He was collecting them into a neat pile when something jumped off one of the pages. Six words. Written in looser handwriting. Angry handwriting. *I'm going to kill that sunovabitch!*

Joe nursed the piss-warm beer that he'd actually grown accustomed to and shot Rufus a *what the fuck?* look. Rufus shrugged and went back to his job of doing absolutely nothing. Joe glanced at his watch for the fifth or sixth time. 12:23. He'd said noon sharp. And Patty was never late. He tried her cell again, but it went straight to voicemail. He took one last hit off the beer and rose to leave.

Patty stormed in, a jolt of electricity cracking the silence. Arms flailing, glitzy, oversized earrings dancing like fireflies in the shadowy room. "Sorry, sorry, sorry!" she sang out on her approach. She slumped heavily into the booth, exhaled dramatically, and repeated, "Sorry."

"Listen, Patty, I'm busy and can't just sit around waiting until you decide to show up."

"I said I was sorry, Cowboy," she interjected, anger tingeing each word. "I recall someone else showing up an hour late recently." *Touché.* "And you know those damn buses. Oh, wait, you wouldn't know. Besides, you're the one who called this emergency meeting, saying we had a problem." Her face softened. "So, Joe Campbell, what happened? Did you go and kill someone cuz they cut you in line at Starbucks or put a scratch in your precious little SUV?"

Joe snatched up his notebook and said, "You know what? Never mind, I've got better ways to waste my time."

Patty reached out a bony arm. "Down, boy. I was just fuckin' with ya. I really am sorry I was late. Now sit back down and tell big, bad Patty what this emergency is."

Joe sighed heavily and plunked down in the booth. Patty being Patty again. "Alright, listen," he said, "I can't work with you on this project anymore." There, he'd said it.

Patty's eyes locked in on his, her mouth a giant O. Finally, the frozen mouth thawed and said, "Why the fuck not?"

Joe flipped open the binder containing Patty's signature handwriting. "Because of these. You threaten to kill Dominic Guierriero. Dominic-the-fucking-Skinner-Guierriero!" Rufus shot them a curious glance, then returned to his phone.

Patty laughed. "Oh, c'mon, you can't think I'm serious?"

"As a heart attack, as the great Patty Quigley once said." Joe rifled through the rumpled pages. "And you never mentioned anything about Charlene—or whatever her real name is—being murdered."

Patty placed an icy hand on Joe's, sending a shock up his arm. "Calm it down, Cowboy. Nobody's been murdered."

Joe shoved one of the pages in her face. "Oh, no? Then explain this!" He read the neatly written words that seemed to come alive on the paper. *I'm going to kill Dominic Guierriero. I'm going to kill that sunovabitch! He killed the only woman I've ever loved. He killed Charlene Nivens in cold blood and now's he going to pay for it!*

Joe tossed the paper at her. "So, is this real or is it more of your bullshit lies?"

Patty blinked away tears. Joe wasn't sure if they were genuine or more manufactured fiction. "I can explain," she said, her voice barely audible. "You see, Charlene and I had this bond. We'd both been through so much heartache and shit together. And nobody ever gave a damn about either one of us. Except us to each other." Patty lowered her head and her body convulsed.

Joe almost caved. Almost. "You said nobody's been murdered. So, did Guierriero murder her or not?"

"Not exactly."

"How do you not exactly murder someone?"

Patty rolled her eyes. "He told her that I was his and he didn't share anything. And then he told her if he ever saw her near me again, he'd make her disappear. So, that night, she got high as a kite and threw herself in front of a commuter train. The same train that used to take us back and forth to The Landing Strip."

That's when it dawned on him. Patty and Charlene were probably lovers. For all Patty's bullshit, Joe sensed genuine grief and pain. "Sorry. I didn't know." Patty gently brushed away a tear as it journeyed down the coarse roadmap of her weathered face. "Did you mean what you said, about killing Guierriero?"

Patty smiled weakly and caressed his hand. "Of course not. That part was fiction. Look at me. Could little ol' me kill anyone, let alone Dominic "The Skinner" Guierriero?"

She laughed and Joe joined in. "So, you were venting?" he said.

"Venting, fantasizing, whatever you wanna call it. Are we good now?"

"Hold on."

"What's wrong, Cowboy?"

"You said that Charlene committed suicide, correct?"

"Yeah."

"But in your notes here, it says he killed her in cold blood— these are your words. See?" He underlined the words with his finger.

Patty stared at the paper, seemingly confused by her own words. Then she laughed and said, "Confession time. I might have, how do you say, *embellisized* a bit. I threw it in for a little excitement. After all, it is a book about the mafia."

"Yeah, that's what I want to talk to you about next. You're right, this is the mafia. The *real* mafia. Which is why this needs to be a work of fiction. We change the names, we change the location, we even change the fucking decade. When someone reads this, I don't want Guierriero's name to enter their brain for even one second. Got it?"

Patty sat bolt upright and saluted Joe. "Aye, aye, captain!" She waggled Joe's glass toward Rufus.

Joe took the glass and placed it between them. "No, I can't stay."

Patty's lower lip protruded. "Aww, can't we have one little drink to celebrate? Now that it's all made up, we can *embellisize* whatever we want! Cart blank, right?"

Joe laughed. This woman was insane. And he was back in bed with her. "Yep, cart blank to do whatever we want," he said. "But I really do have to run. I'll draft up the next few chapters and give you a call."

Patty beamed. "Ooh, this is so exciting," she purred. "I'll start thinking up some more scenarios for you. This is gonna be the best mafia book ever! Step aside, Mario Putzio."

"It's Puzo. Mario Puzo. And don't go dissing my all-time favorite movie."

Patty raised her arms in surrender. "My, my, Mister Campbell," she said in a formidable Southern impersonation. "Please accept my sincerest apology."

Joe chuckled and gathered his things. "Okay, Miss Scarlett, I've got to go."

Patty bounced out of her seat. "Wait, I forgot something. I brought you a gift." She placed a neatly wrapped box on the table.

"Patty, that really isn't necess—"

"I wanted to. To say thanks. Please, just open it."

Joe sighed. What the hell. He was already late for his meeting anyway. He sat down and pulled the box close. "It's heavy. What's in there, a dead body?"

Patty feigned shock. "My, my, Joe Campbell, I do declare," she said, keeping the Scarlett O'Hara gag going. They both laughed. Maybe this partnership would work out after all.

"See, I can do mafia humor too," Joe said.

Patty wriggled like a schoolgirl pining over her first crush. "Well, are you gonna open it or what?"

Joe tore gingerly at the shiny gold paper. He flipped open the lid of a cardboard box and fished through the mounds of tissue paper. His hand touched something cold. And hard. He glanced up at Patty, still all eager beaver. "What the—" He gripped the object and tore it from the box. There was a moment when he thought it wasn't real. But it was. It fell from jelly fingers and clanged loudly as it hit the table.

"Everything okay over there?" Rufus said without emotion.

Joe wiped his shaky hand on his jacket, as if he'd just touched death. Was he hallucinating, like Lady Macbeth sleepwalking though the castle? *Out, damned spot!* But it was no hallucination. His eyes narrowed. "What is this?'

Patty frowned, apparently displeased with his reaction. "What does it look like? It's a gun."

"I know it's a fucking gun!" Joe said in an Irish whisper. Rufus glanced over. Joe lowered his head and his voice. "I know it's a gun. The question is, why are you giving me a gun?"

Patty's bottom lip jutted out. "I thought it would be good inspiration." Her eyes hardened. "I thought you'd appreciate it."

Joe stared at the hunk of shiny metal. It looked even more ominous in the room's endless shadows. "It's just that I've never touched one. Hell, I've never even seen one up close." Curious eyes inspected it. "Is this what they really use?"

Patty tossed her head back and released a guttural sound. "If by they, you mean gangsters, then yes. What were you expecting, an Uzi or something?"

"It just looks smaller than I pictured. What kind is it?"

Patty pushed it closer to him. "It's a Smith & Wesson 9-millimeter. Compact enough, but gets the job done. Pick it up."

Joe blinked and whispered, "What?"

"I can tell by the way you're drooling that you're dying to. Go on, it won't bite. In fact, it ain't even loaded."

Joe brushed a finger to the cold steel and recoiled.

"Oh, for chrissakes, Cowboy. How ya gonna write a book about the mafia if you're too chicken shit to even hold an unloaded gun?"

Heat burned his cheeks. Partly out of embarrassment. But in reality, more out of excitement. Patty's eyes bored through him. He picked up the gun, wrapped it tightly in his grip.

Patty clapped, a slow mocking clap. "Feels good, don't it? Powerful."

It *did* feel powerful. For once, he didn't feel like the pushover. The guy who works his ass off only to be passed over by lesser talent. The guy who gets cuts off in line at Starbucks by some dickhead in a power suit. The son who strives for acceptance. The browbeaten husband who can never quite rise up to expectation.

No. At this moment, Joe Campbell was not just your Average Joe. He was a force to be reckoned with. He could feel the power in his cold fingers, running up his tensed forearm, rocketing through his veins, beating soundly in his heart.

He looked at Patty and said, "It feels fucking great."

CHAPTER NINE

E lectricity still surged through Joe's fingers as he made his way through the midday bustle. He'd wanted to take the piece with him, but Patty logically suggested that she hold on to it. After all, how would it look for an upstanding member of the community to be caught with a 9-millimeter in his messenger bag?

Even without the gun on his physical person, he felt renewed and energized. His stride had purpose, his usual slouched posture ramrod straight. He was late for his meeting, and he didn't give a damn. Those fuckers could wait for a change.

He passed by the elevators and charged up the stairwell, two steps at a time. By the time he hit the twentieth floor, his chest was pounding, his brow damp and clammy. And yet, he felt like he could take on the world. He swiped away the sweat and swaggered into the conference room. Shea, Mitch, and their pathetic drones looked up from their mundane notes.

"You're late," Mitch said with venom.

"Am I?" Joe said. "Guess I lost track of the time." He plunked down next to Adrian, a twenty-something intern who hadn't quite nailed the hipster look. He eyed the steaming cup of coffee in front of Adrian, steam coiling around them in an erratic dance. "Hey, Adrian. Any of that coffee left?" Adrian nodded and Joe started to rise.

Adrian beat him to the punch. "I'll get it for you, Mr. Campbell."

"Thanks, Adrian," Joe said. "That's very kind of you. It's nice to see we have some real team players here." Mitch turned three shades of crimson. Shea wore her typical look of indifference.

"Adrian?" Joe said. Adrian spun around, nearly toppling an easel displaying precious Samsonite storyboards. "Light cream, shaken not stirred." Adrian opened his mouth to speak, then exited, leaving a trail of confusion in his wake.

"Joe, what's up with you?" Shea barked, her severe haircut and boxy suit enhancing her stiff, all-business demeanor. "Are you feeling okay?"

"I feel great," Joe replied and leaned back into the cushy leather-look chair. "Just thought a cup of joe might get Joe's old creative juices pumping."

Mitch Wasserman pushed back his chair, stood, and said, "If Mr. Campbell is ready to start working, may we please continue?" He shot Joe daggers, daggers that would have shredded him any other day. Any day but today.

"Aye aye, Cap'n."

Mitch's face flushed. At last, he regained his composure and directed the team to the flat screen. It displayed the Mermaid Cruise Lines logo, a sensual blonde mermaid cradling a cruise ship in her arms. "As I was saying before the interruption, we thought we'd take an even more whimsical approach to our campaign," Mitch began. "We open with a mother, father, and their two young children—a boy and a girl, of course—sitting on a beach, looking bored and restless. Suddenly, a beautiful mermaid rises from the ocean, beckoning them to sail away with her on Mermaid Cruise Lines. They—"

The ever-graceful Adrian stumbled through the door. "Mr. Campbell," he whispered, "I didn't quite understand when you said to shake it, not stir it, so I did both." Adrian, clearly not a Bond fan, pushed the thick black frames up on his blotched, birdlike nose.

"Good man, Adrian." Joe turned his gaze to Mitch. "Mitch —I can still call you that, can't I? I was thinking we should take a different approach."

Mitch crossed his arms in defiance. "Oh, you were, were you? And what direction would that be?"

Joe stood and moved to the alpha position. "Sex," he said.

Adrian the wannabe hipster giggled. Shea sat in stunned silence. Mitch made a move in Joe's direction. "Sex? Have you completely lost your mind? We're talking about a family cruise line here."

Joe moved closer, this time invading Mitch's personal space. "That's the thing, Mitch," he said. "If you had done your research, you'd know that the percentage of families booking on Mermaid has dropped nearly fifty percent over the past nine months. You would have also learned that the percentage of twenty-something singles has increased tenfold in the past six months. Looks like our cutesy, whimsical approach may be a little off brand. Wouldn't you agree, Shea?"

Shea cocked her head to one side like a confused puppy. "Mitch, are those stats accurate?"

Mitch Wasserman, all clenched teeth and balled-up fists, looking more pit bull than puppy, said, "He's making this shit up. He's trying to sabotage me!"

Joe casually took a sip of coffee. He turned to Adrian. "Nice cup of joe, Adrian. Correct me if I'm wrong, but don't you handle research for us?"

Adrian pushed the thick frames back up his ski slope and said proudly, "Yeah, that and a bunch of other stuff."

Mitch snorted. "Like fetching coffee for your superiors?"

"Mitch, that'll be enough," Shea said, though her delivery lacked any semblance of conviction.

Joe paced the room like a ruthless lawyer delivering a crushing closing argument. "Adrian, you seem like a smart guy. So, in your research, have you seen any statistics that back up my claims?" Adrian glanced first at Mitch, then at Shea. Joe placed a soft hand on Adrian's shoulder. "Adrian, nobody's going to crucify you for being honest. Are they, Shea?"

Shea ran nervous fingers across her doughy chin. "Adrian, tell us what you think."

Adrian beamed. Probably the first time anyone had ever looked to him for an opinion on anything. "Well," he said with trepidation, "I believe Mr. Campbell's assessment of things to be pretty accurate."

"How dare you!" Mitch screeched. "What do *you* know?" He spun his attention to Shea, a shock of that perfect hair flopping across his forehead. "Shea, are you going to let an intern determine how we run things around here?"

Shea, suddenly looking old and feeble, dropped her gaze to her lap. Her minions followed suit. Except for Adrian. Confidence oozed from his acne-scarred face.

Mitch gathered up his things and stormed from the room like an F5 hurricane.

Joe patted Adrian's shoulder, then moved to the door. As he walked out, he turned and said, "Hey Shea, looks like our friend Adrian here deserves a raise."

CHAPTER TEN

The first time I experienced love was at a 7-Eleven. That was also the same place I first experienced death.

Let's start with the good memory. I remember it like it was yesterday. I was sixteen. I'd stolen the change from the bottom of my mother's handbag, figuring she'd never miss it anyway. Then Ruthie, Andrea, and I hoofed it off to the 7-Eleven down on Main Street.

Tommy Packer and his crew were hanging outside as usual, smoking and talking shit to one another. Tommy had the most amazing eyes. And that hair. The way it just slightly brushed the edges of his eyes. He was the epitome of cool.

"There he is," Andrea murmured, nudging me in the arm.

I brushed by Tommy, pretending not to notice his awesomeness, and let out a puff of air as I passed. We got our Slurpees, cherry of course, and headed out into the steamy August air. My eyes locked with Tommy's. He smiled. I quickly dropped my gaze to the cracked pavement, my body feeling strange, tingly. I quickened my pace.

"Hey, Patty." He'd said my name.

I turned, a flash of heat tickling my face. "Hi, Tommy," I managed to stutter, nearly dropping my Slurpee. Ruthie and Andrea giggled.

He dropped his smoke, crushed it on the sidewalk, and sauntered over. He looked even more beautiful up close. That strange electricity ran through my body again. "I got a proposition for you ladies," he said. "Let's see who can drink the longest before getting brain freeze." His boys in the background chuckled but my sole focus was on Tommy. "You ladies game?"

Ruthie shrugged the way she always did when someone asked her a question. Andrea muttered, "I dunno." Tommy glared at me, his eyes taunting. "Sure," I said.

Tommy clapped his hands together sharply. His posse gathered round. "Alright," he said, excitement building in his voice, "when I count to three, start slurping. Last man—I mean woman—standing wins. Ready?"

Ruthie and Andrea didn't seem up for the challenge, but I was. On "three" the competition was underway. Ruthie gave up after about five seconds. Andrea lasted a little longer until she screeched, "Brain freeze!" But I just kept on going, even though my head throbbed. It was excruciatingly painful yet strangely exhilarating.

I never saw Tommy again after that day. Someone said he moved away. Someone else insisted he'd gone to jail. I never did find out what became of that boy. After all, back in those days you couldn't just Google somebody. But ever since that day, I've never been able to fully enjoy the sensation of pleasure unless it also involved pain.

Now for the bad memory. I had run to the 7-Eleven to grab a pack of smokes because Charlene had scoffed my last one. It was midday and the place was empty, aside from an elderly couple and two teenaged boys ogling the Slurpee machine.

It had been ages since I'd had one of those, so I figured, why the hell not? I waited impatiently as the teenagers went back and forth, trying to decide on a flavor, as if it was the most important decision in their pathetic lives. The taller of the two slightly resembled Tommy Packer, minus the cool factor.

My patience hit the wall. "Excuse me, boys," I said, trying to curb my usual sarcasm. "Mind if I sneak in there while you decide?"

The Tommy lookalike snarled and said, "Yeah, lady, I do fucking mind."

I was about to go off on him when a scream interrupted us. The old woman. We all turned. The elderly gentleman, who moments ago had nodded and smiled at me, was writhing on the ground like an epileptic snake. The young woman behind the counter was already on the phone, frantically calling 9-1-1.

"Shit, man," one of the boys said.

"Help him, please!" the old woman screamed, her tired eyes wild with horror. I could have. I'd been trained in CPR, after all. And yet, I just stood there, watching with fascination as the writhing man slowly wound down. When at last he stopped, the old woman fell on top of her husband's lifeless body and wailed. The cashier held a hand to her mouth. And the Tommy lookalike cried like a baby, his tough guy act a sham.

It was the first time I saw someone die. And I felt nothing. Nothing at all.

The second time was a bit different. Hell, who am I kidding? It was a lot different. Dimitri and I had gone out to dinner and dancing. Dimitri loved to dance. It was on the dance floor that he let his guard down, exposing a softer side, a side very few people ever saw.

I was on a high as we climbed into the back of the Town Car. We were starting to get intimate when Dimitri's car phone rang. After a brief, somewhat cryptic discussion, he instructed Gino, his driver and one of his oldest friends, to change direction.

"What's going on, babe," I said. "Where are we going?"

Dimitri, no longer in a touchy-feely mood, said, "I have some quick business to take care of."

I thought to ask what kind of business, but Dimitri didn't take kindly to questions of any kind, from anyone. Instead, I sat in silence, gazing out at the Chicago skyline, at once breathtaking and sinister. Dimitri stared straight ahead, all business. The heat of his anger was electric.

The city lights dissolved into blackness. I had no idea where we were or where we were heading. It was the first time I didn't feel safe in Dimitri's presence. I could feel my pulse quickening, hoped it went undetected.

At last, the car slowed. A deserted building loomed before us. An old factory, perhaps? Through the haze of the headlights, I spotted a black sedan. Two tall men stood beside it. My fear kicked up a notch. Who were these men and why were we in the middle of nowhere? I shot a glance at Dimitri. His face was a mask of evil.

I knew something bad was going to happen. My instinct was to run. I didn't. The two men walked toward the car, their features blurred by the glowering headlights and the stark night sky. As they reached the car, Gino slid down the front passenger window.

"Hop in," Dimitri said. His voice was pleasant, a contrast to the rage etched in his face. A man slid into the front seat, shut the door. The other man walked back to the black sedan.

"Hello, Marco," Dimitri said. No hint of trouble in his voice. And yet, I was terrified. I stared at the back of Marco's head, thick black hair and broad shoulders all that was visible in the mournful shadows of the car.

"Evening, Boss," he said. His voice was deep, amiable. "You wanted to see me?"

Dimitri shifted slightly, the rage in his face intensifying. I dared not speak or move. "Marco," he said, "tell me, where were you earlier this afternoon?"

Marco's shoulders stiffened. His head pivoted, then stopped. He faced forward and said, "This afternoon?" His voice cracked. Dimitri shifted again. "I'm not sure what you mean, Boss."

Something glinted in the darkened interior. I glanced down. A gun. "I think you know exactly what I mean, Marco," Dimitri said. Coldness crept into the edges of his voice. "I warned you to stay away from Maria."

Maria. Dimitri's baby sister. A stunner beyond words.

Marco's voice was now dripping in two coats of fear. "Honest, Boss, I haven't seen her. You have to believe me." The broad shoulders quivered, accompanied by strangled sobs.

Dimitri gripped the gun. I was petrified. And yet, a sense of excitement washed over me. It felt exhilarating, like my Slurpee brain freeze.

Dimitri's voice reached a crescendo. "Are you calling me a liar? I watched you and my sister enter that hotel, and watched you exit two hours later! So, tell me again, where were you this afternoon?"

Marco turned, opening his mouth to speak. It was my first glimpse of his face. A face as stunning as Maria's. Until it exploded in a blur of red. The impact sent his body into the windshield, the echo resounding for what felt like hours. Then silence.

Dimitri touched my hand. Instinctively, I recoiled. "I'm sorry you had to see that, love," he said as tenderly as he had upon our first encounter.

I reached for his hand, expecting it to be trembling. It wasn't. Neither was mine.

I smiled and took his face in my hands, ignoring the carnage before us. "It's okay, Dimitri," I said softly.

It was the second time I saw someone die. And I felt nothing. Nothing but excitement. Nothing but alive.

Joe sat back, satisfied with the latest chapter. Patty was one sick puppy, that was for sure. But it did make for great reading. He closed the file, powered down the laptop and smiled. It was starting to come together. *Confessions of a Goomah* may not be Shakespeare, but he was pretty sure it was going to appeal to the masses. And that was good enough for him.

He raised his glass of gin and toasted the room. "You may be the best thing that's ever happened to me, Patty Quigley," he said to the average looking guy toasting in unison with him through the reflection of the window.

CHAPTER ELEVEN

The voicemail from Patty was hectic and puzzling. Her breathless voice told Joe that their meeting at Griffin's had to be pushed back from 9 pm to 11:30. Strange. The bar usually closed at 11. Thinking it was probably a simple error on her part, Joe returned her call, only to be met with her raspy, yet cheery voice to leave a message and she'd return it "whenever the hell I feel like it."

After half a dozen failed attempts to reach her, he decided to swing by Griffin's at 11:30. It was later than he'd planned, and he was dead tired. But he was also excited about the progress he was making and the direction the story was going in. Fuck it, he may as well go. Kate had her monthly book club, which was really just a glorified cover for her and her girlfriends to put back the wine and put down their significant others.

Joe heated up a leftover lump of pasta, clicked on the end of a Red Sox-Yankees double header. He stared blankly at the flickering screen and was roused from his stupor when the crack of a bat ended the game in extra innings. He clicked off the TV, listened to the deafening silence for a moment, and hefted himself off the couch. The time was 11:12.

A light drizzle *tap-tapped* the windshield as Joe edged up to the curb. Something felt wrong. The neon Budweiser beacon that customarily summoned Griffin's patrons was silent. And the bleak interior looked bleaker than usual. No movement, no sign of life. An icy chill tickled his spine. Instinct told him to leave. He shifted into Drive and pulled away. He braked. Maybe he was overreacting. But better to be cautious. He maneuvered the Rover down a dark side street, stepped out into the raw drizzle and jogged toward the bar.

The door handle was cold and damp. He turned the knob, not expecting it to budge. It did. A rush of warmth hit him as he entered the bar. And a foreign, acrid odor. Rufus was absent from his perch behind the bar and the lighting was dimmer than its usual foggy grey. Something else hung heavy in the air. The smell of dread.

Joe inched forward. His instincts told him to turn and run but his body had other plans. He took another step forward.

Then he saw them. Two of them. Even in the inky shadows, he knew they were dead. He tasted metal in his mouth, was dizzied by the thick, stifling air. Bile rose up in his throat and he swallowed hard to resist upchucking that leftover pasta. One man was slumped facedown on a table. The other was sprawled out across a cheap vinyl booth, eyes wide and wild, mouth agape in a silent scream. Even shrouded in a death mask, Joe recognized the man immediately.

Dominic "The Skinner" Guierriero.

The bile rose fast again, and Joe knew this time he could not stop it. He bolted for the door with the word MENS scrawled haphazardly into it and made a beeline for the first stall. The release was hot and violent. Shaky hands palmed the sides of the metal stall, which were adorned with a variety of obscene words and even more obscene sketches.

He swiped at his mouth with his sleeve and stood on jelly legs. Exiting the stall, he glimpsed a ghastly reflection in a cracked mirror. He doused his face with water and swept rogue strands of hair off a damp forehead. His heart hammered inside his chest, as if searching for a way out of this nightmare. He staggered, caught himself on an unstable sink fixture.

Then he heard it. Voices. And he knew he was not alone.

CHAPTER TWELVE

He was not alone. And he had no escape. Well, there was a window. Which would be fine if he were the size of a preschooler. His eyes scanned the room. Nowhere to hide, except one of three stalls. Maybe that standing-on-the-toilet-behind-a-locked-stall-door trick worked for the little Amish kid in *Witness*, but this was no movie. And there was no Harrison Ford to save the day. No, this was Joe Campbell's no longer ordinary, completely fucked up new life. In stereo.

The voices were loud, angry. *Think, Joe. Think.* He was a sitting duck in here. With his options down to zero, he slid the door open a crack. The voices nearly slammed him in the face.

"Whoever did this is gonna wish they never saw the light of day." The accent was thick, unpolished. And it meant business.

"Hey Dom, come check this out." The accent was similar, but harsher, like the guy was chewing on a mouthful of gravel.

Another Dom? Didn't Guierriero have a son by that name? *Fuck. Is that The Skinner's son?* Joe melted into the shadows and caught a glimpse of the men. They were big. And, no doubt, heavily armed.

"What you got there, Lucio?" the Dom guy said.

Joe saw Lucio point to something on the table between the two corpses.

"This gun don't look like Sal's or your Padre's."

Padre? Shit, it is Guierriero's son. Dominic Guierriero, Jr. Joe was no expert on the Guierriero family, but he'd read enough about them in the papers and in online rants, even caught a documentary a couple of years back. And, according to the media and online trolls, Dom Sr. was bad—but Dom Jr. was even more ruthless than his Dear Old Dad.

Dom Jr. moved into eyeshot. "What the fuck is this?" he said. He picked up something small, black.

Joe strained to see the object in Dom Jr.'s gloved hand. He heard a *click*. It was a miniature tape recorder, like the one Joe kept in his glove compartment should any genius brainchilds pop into his head while enduring a typical traffic jam.

A somewhat familiar voice filled the blackness. *Joe Campbell, what happened? Did you go and kill someone?* Was that Patty's voice? The sound was distorted, as if to disguise the identity of the speaker.

What came next sliced Joe in two. His own voice. Not distorted at all. Crystal fucking clear. *I'm going to kill Dominic Guierriero. I'm going to kill that sunovabitch! He killed the only woman I've ever loved. He killed Charlene Nivens in cold blood and now he's going to pay for it!*

Joe's pulse pounded in his ears. He'd been set up. Patty Quigley had recorded him reciting from her manuscript. And that gun on the table. No doubt the one she'd given him. The one that now had his fingerprints all over it.

Dom Jr.'s voice snapped Joe back to this living nightmare. "Who the fuck is this Joe Campbell and how does he know about Charlene?"

So, Charlene was her real name. And her death was no suicide. Why would Patty set him up? To avenge the death of her lover? The enormity of the situation rattled Joe to the core. He went to steady himself. His foot brushed the bathroom door.

"What the fuck was that?" Dom Jr. spun in Joe's direction. Joe hugged the wall, wishing for the blackness to swallow him up. "You hear something?"

Joe wasn't familiar with guns, but he did know what one sounded like when it was being cocked. The men moved toward him.

Joe heard the front door fly open. He risked stealing a peek. Three men in black charged in, along with a flurry of rain. Dom Jr. and Lucio swung their attention from Joe's hiding spot and aimed their focus, and guns, at the three hulks silhouetted in the faint light of the moon. Joe peered out into the shadowy bar.

"Whoa, easy Dom," said a tall, heavily muscled thug with a shaved head and thick eyebrows. "It's Jimmy C. What are you doing here, brother?"

Dom Jr. moved toward Jimmy C, his gun unwavering. "What am I doing here? What the fuck am I doing here? About a half hour ago, I got an anonymous call saying there was trouble and that I better get over here."

Confusion washed over Jimmy's chiseled face. "Anonymous call? From who?"

"How the fuck should I know!" Dom Jr. screamed. He leveled the gun at Jimmy.

Joe had a pretty good idea who the mystery caller was.

Jimmy raised his hands, gripped his shaven head. "What's with the gun in my face? Where's your Padre?"

"You wanna know where my Padre is?" Dom Jr. waggled the gun toward the carnage. "He's right there, all over the fucking wall, and the table, and the floor!"

Jimmy's face cracked open in horror. "Oh, shit, Dom, you don't think I had any—"

Dom Jr. put the gun back on Jimmy and his sidekicks. "I don't know what the fuck to think! Who's Joe Campbell?"

Jimmy shrugged. "Who? Joe Campbell? Never heard of him."

Dom Jr. played the recording again. "So, who the fuck is this guy? And why would someone leave this behind for me to find?"

"All I know is we were supposed to meet Sal and Dom Sr. to pick up the money," Jimmy said. His eyes scanned the crime scene. "Where's the money?"

Clarity slammed Joe upside the head. Patty had chosen this place for a reason. This was Guierriero's drop spot. Not only had she gotten her vengeance, but she'd also gotten what Joe guessed to be a shitload of cash. And good old Joe Campbell was left holding the proverbial bag, and the murder rap.

It was time to go. He looked to his left. If memory served him right, there was a storage room just down the hallway. And where there was a storage room, there was usually a back way out. He edged along the wall, feeling his way in the darkness. The doorway came into view. He went for it.

"Somebody's back there!" he heard one of the men yell.

Time to hightail it. He pushed through the door, tripped over a keg and went sprawling. Movement down the hallway. He was dead meat. Then he saw it. The word EXIT summoning him. He clambered to his feet and made for the exit. He could feel the heavy footsteps on his tail. The drizzle had turned to a downpour and the rush of cold gave him a renewed energy. He bolted through the alley, dodging empty bottles and trash strewn everywhere.

Joe had been a track star back in the formative years. And though his prowess and speed never earned him any college scholarships, it sure as hell paid off now. He moved liked an Olympian, hurdling obstacles, making distance between him and his competitors—his competitors being five ruthless killers.

Their screams and footfalls became more distant now. Joe silently thanked his high school track coach for pushing him to be the best in state and sidestepped it into an old playground. When he was sure he'd lost them, he slumped against a rusted old seesaw and let the cold rain drum his face. He had no sense of where he was. But he knew if he hung around any longer, he'd be dead come morning one way or another.

CHAPTER THIRTEEN

The rain fell slantwise at an impossible angle, slamming Joe as he moved toward the Range Rover. Luckily, he'd had the foresight to park it down this desolate alley. Still, he approached with caution, in case Dom Jr. and his posse had done a recon of the area. When he was sure it was clear, he made a run for it.

The car's interior enveloped him in warmth. His body was a giant sponge, soaked to the core. He shivered uncontrollably as he turned the ignition and jammed the Rover into gear. The torrent slammed the windshield faster than the wipers could sweep it away, making visibility near impossible.

He headed away from Griffin's, toward home, where he hoped Kate would now be. He'd pack a bag, convince her they had to leave, and get as far away as he could. Then he'd get some cash, maybe a gun.

He slammed on the brakes.

The gun. The gun with his fingerprints all over it, sitting in plain view, bookended by two bloody corpses. He spun the car around and floored it.

Griffin's was dark as Joe rolled up. He stopped a few doors down, killed the headlights. No cops yet. But there was a good chance Dom Jr. and his posse could return at any moment. Time to put those track skills to good use again.

The cold rain sliced at him like razor blades as he bolted along the sidewalk, almost losing his footing twice. He crept around back, entering the same way he had exited only shortly before, but what now felt like hours ago. He stepped inside and closed the door, muffling the torrent slamming the weather-beaten shingles.

An eerie silence followed him as he made his way through the storage room, past the bathrooms, and into the front room. A strong coppery odor hung heavy in the air. He moved toward the crime scene, trying to avoid eye contact with the wide-eyed Dominic Guierriero.

Get the gun and the tape recorder and go!

The gun was front and center on the blood-spattered table. Joe snatched it up. The tape recorder was gone. Joe looked around one more time at the carnage, playing over in his mind what evidence he may have left behind. The bathroom.

He moved quickly, wiping down the bathroom door, the toilet, the stall walls, the sink. Anything he could have touched. When he felt confident that he'd wiped away all traces of himself, he made his way out into the stormy night.

Pulsating red and blue lights exploded in the night sky. Joe dove for cover, hoping he hadn't been spotted. A second cruiser screeched to a halt ten feet from where he lay. The quick response from law enforcement told Joe that a certain someone had, in addition to calling Dom Jr. to the scene, tipped off the cops. As the officers stormed the bar, Joe disappeared into the blackness.

The rain had slowed to a tired drizzle by the time Joe got home. The house was dark, except for the comforting flicker in the upstairs bedroom window. Kate was probably asleep, having dozed off during an episode of House Hunters. Joe wondered if she'd ever stayed awake long enough to see the final outcomes of the hunters' searches.

He bolted up the stairs. He'd shake Kate from her sleep, force her to dress quickly, and grab the necessities. He'd explain why when they were in the car, with some miles between them and Guierriero's posse. He flung open the bedroom door.

The bed was empty, sheets and duvet tossed carelessly to one side. No Kate. The bathroom. She must be in the bathroom.

"Kate," he whispered. He flicked on the light. Again, no Kate. "KATE!" he yelled. His panicked voice echoed through the room. As he turned to leave, an invisible force grabbed him by the ears and spun his gaze back toward the bathroom sink. Spots on the polished marble sink. Red spots. Spots that looked like blood.

He checked the other rooms upstairs, then flung himself down the staircase two steps at a time. After a recon of the first floor showed no evidence of Kate or anybody else, Joe planted his shaky body at the kitchen island, topped by richly grained granite. Maybe she was still out. Then he saw them.

Kate's purse and car keys, on a side counter where she usually left them. And he knew they had her.

CHAPTER FOURTEEN

J oe peeled waterlogged clothes from his body, toweled off, and quickly redressed. He tucked the gun into his waist like they did in the movies, then decided blowing his dick off may not be a good choice if Kate were ever to change her mind about having kids. He gingerly removed it, tucked it into his coat pocket, and made his way out into the raw darkness.

He drove in no particular direction, wondering what his next move was. How was he going to find Kate when he didn't even know where to find Patty? Or whatever the bitch's real name was. And what if Kate was already...

He pushed the thought to the far reaches of his mind and instead recalled one of the last conversations he'd had with Kate.

"What do you mean you don't want kids?"

"*I don't want kids.*"

"*But we talked about this before the wedding. You know I've always wanted—*"

"*Well, I changed my mind,*" Kate had said matter-of-factly. "*Besides, with that fucked up family of yours, why would you even want a family?*"

The jab hurt. But Joe had become used to dodging Kate's uppercuts. "*That's not fair,*" he'd said, though it was a hard argument to dispute. "*Remember how we talked about having a boy and a girl, and a dog? A lab or an Irish Setter, I think we said.*"

"*And the white fucking picket fence, Joe?*" Anger tinged the last word. "*Get over it. I've made up my mind and that's final.*"

Joe had hated his wife in that moment, had even secretly wished he could erase her from his life. And now she was gone, taken, maybe even erased permanently.

He slammed on the brakes, got his bearings, and headed for Griffin's.

An eruption of blue and red flashes disrupted the dead night. Joe cut the lights and watched the buzz of activity through lazy sweeps of the wipers. Officers in rain gear huddled on the sidewalk, while more official looking bodies moved with purpose in and out of the bar.

He searched for any sign of the one man who might be able to help him find Patty. The owner of this joint. Rufus. But unless Rufus had already been contacted about the carnage that had gone down in his place of business, he was most likely sleeping like a baby.

Joe had seen *The Godfather* too many times to count, had

often fantasized about what it would be like to be Michael Corleone. Only now he felt like Michael's ill-fated brother Sonny.

Joe slowly reversed the car. He'd return when the activity died down, when he could get to Rufus, beg for his help. He cut the wheel, heard gravel ping the undercarriage, and put the car in drive. Then he saw him. Huddled in the light mist, tucked into the shadows. Staring at the circus that had rolled into town and pitched its tent right outside his bar.

CHAPTER FIFTEEN

Joe slumped in his seat. Rufus hadn't appeared to notice him, his gaze fixed steadily on the bar. What was he doing? Why hadn't he approached his establishment, demanding to know what was going on? The answer hammered Joe between the eyes.

Rufus was in on it. He and Patty had played Joe like a fiddle, even made him feel at home in their company. Joe was no Michael Corleone. Or Sonny. He was Fredo. The idiot. The stooge.

He sat in the darkness, watching Rufus watch the feds. The rain picked up again. And Rufus was on the move.

Joe backed the car into an empty lot, pulled his hood over a disheveled mop, and hoofed it to catch up with Rufus. He kept distance between them, tucked close to the shadows of the ramshackle row houses, their bleak facades secreting the horrors that lay beyond.

Rufus glided through the torrent with purpose in his step.

Joe moved stealthily through the sleeping streets, keeping watch over his prey. He made a mental note of each left and right. Finally, Rufus stopped in front of a triple-decker that looked like it could be felled with a strong gust. Or a gentle nudge.

Joe dissolved into the shadows, watched as Rufus climbed steep steps and disappeared into the darkened building. Then two inky panes on the third floor came alive, glowing like two devil eyes cutting through Joe's soul. Shadowy figures moved silently behind the shaded windows. Rufus and Patty, no doubt planning their next move.

At last, the eyes blinked and went out. Joe wiped rain from his eyes, patted the steel lump in his pocket. He imagined himself kicking in the door, guns blazing, the shiny knight rescuing the forlorn princess. But, no, that only happened in the movies. In real life, the door didn't shatter into a million slow-motion pieces, and the hero didn't overtake the two-times-his-size villain. In real life, he'd be dead before he even hit the floor.

Joe hurried through the deserted maze, his brain processing the lefts and rights, to the warmth of his car. He gazed at the windshield, mesmerized by the rivulets snaking down the slick surface, and considered his options.

He could turn himself in, hope for the best. No. They'd never believe him. Besides, with Kate in danger, time was of the essence. Who could he turn to? There was always—*no, not a chance.* He needed time to think. Coffee. Maybe a shower. He'd recharge, reassess, then take back his life.

Maybe this Fredo Corleone was Michael Corleone after all.

CHAPTER SIXTEEN

Dominic Guierriero, Jr. stared out at the Boston skyline, the half-dozing buildings dotted with random squares of light. So many windows winking back at him, and behind any one of them could be his father's killer.

Who was this Joe Campbell? Lucio had run a check on all Joe Campbells living in the Greater Boston area. There were around seventy-five men by this name in Massachusetts, and roughly half of those resided in Boston or the surrounding neighborhoods. Narrow that down to guys in their twenties and thirties, which Dom Jr. deduced this guy to be based on his voice and athletic skills, and you were left with around a dozen. A dozen soon-to-be-dead Joe Campbells.

Lucio and the boys were already scoping out the first of the hapless Joes. Dom Jr. would go through them one by one and when he found the sorry son of a bitch, the guy would find out, slowly and painfully, what happens when you cross a Guierriero.

He thought of Ma. The news was going to kill her. This

woman had suffered more heartache than any human should ever have to endure. First Felicia. Then Angelo. And now this. Padre was her rock, her everything. Dom Jr. was now all she had left. And he feared that wouldn't be enough.

A tempest swelled in his chest, churned through his body. His knees trembled, then buckled. He fell to his knees, clawed at the air that was now thick and suffocating. A howl of anguish erupted from his throat. Padre was gone. The man whose footsteps Dom Jr. had eagerly walked in. The man who would lay down his life for his wife and children. The man who was both highly respected and deeply feared by millions. The man whose brains were now splashed across a grease-spattered booth in some shithole.

The buzz of the cell shattered the silence. The screen came alive. Lucio. *We found one.* Dom Jr. swiped away angry tears and rose steadily, newfound strength propelling him forward with a vengeance.

Daybreak on the Charles River. A glorious sight all should experience at some point in their lifetime. The Pru and Hancock, Boston's famous bookends, seemed to rise out of the river, a fiery backdrop casting a mesmerizing reflection on the glassy surface. The postcard-perfect scene was interrupted by a lone kayaker, who glided seamlessly across the murky surface.

Joe watched the kayaker through tired eyes, wondering what motivated someone to rise at such an ungodly hour. The kayaker dissolved into the horizon, leaving Joe with a sense of loss and loneliness, as if he were now the only person on Earth. He closed his eyes, wishing for sleep that he knew would not come. A sharp *rap-rap* on the window. His eyes snapped open.

One of Boston's Finest peered in through the window, which was misted with morning dew. Joe's heart clawed at his chest wall. How had they found him? He must have missed something, some breadcrumb that led them directly to where he now sat, unable to move.

"Sir, please roll down your window," the fresh-faced, buzz-cut officer said.

Joe complied. "Is everything alright, Officer?"

"I might ask you the same thing," the officer said.

Joe could feel the heat rising up in his face, sweat beads forming on his brow. Kate had always said he wore his emotions on his sleeve. Or, more accurately, his face. "I'm sorry, Officer," Joe said, noting the tremor in his voice. "My wife and I had an argument last night and I came out here to clear my head. Must've fallen asleep."

The officer, steady and alert, locked eyes with Joe. "License and registration, please." The four words everyone hates to hear after being pulled over for speeding. Or for leaving the scene of a bloodbath.

Joe smiled weakly, his game face definitely not on its game. "Certainly, Officer," he said in the calmest tone he could muster.

Joe watched the young cop saunter back to his cruiser. They'd somehow linked him to the bar. Did he miss a finger-print? Did he drop something from his pocket? Was there a witness who saw him leave? He contemplated flooring the gas and heading for the border like they did in the movies. Without a license and registration. Brilliant idea.

Then he remembered the gun in his coat pocket and sheer panic took over. What if the cop said those five words everyone hated to hear even more? *Step out of the car.* A flash in the rearview mirror. The burly cop was heading his way. In a single motion, Joe slipped the gun from his pocket and slid it under the driver's seat. His heart slammed against his ribs and his left leg began to spasm.

The officer reappeared. *Just give up, Joe. Tell them the truth and maybe they'll believe you. Maybe they can still save Kate. And maybe pigs will fly by.*

Joe could hear the cop's quickened breath, the distant roar of an airplane departing Logan. A plane he desperately wished he were now on.

"Mr. Campbell." He snapped back to reality and faced his doom. The cop's beefy arm was extended toward him. But it held no gun. Just a license and a registration. "Mr. Campbell," the officer repeated. "Are you okay, sir?"

Joe smiled weakly. "Yes, Officer," he managed to spit out. "Just not feeling very well."

"Well, I suggest you get yourself home and get some rest," the cop said. "Pardon my French, but you look like hell." Joe nodded and accepted the card and paper that floated before him.

He rolled the window up. His heart sank back into place, then leapt from the gate again as another forceful rap exploded in his ear. He unrolled the window, the crisp morning air washing over his sweat-slick face. That's it. He was done. Finished. Kaput. Guilt oozed from his pores. "Officer, I—"

The cop smiled, his resolute eyes softening. "I do hope you and your wife work everything out. You have yourself a good day now." And he was gone.

CHAPTER SEVENTEEN

The lifeless eyes of Joe Campbell gazed at Dominic Guierriero, Jr. But not *the* Joe Campbell. Sure, his size and age looked about right, but this was not Padre's executor. Dom Jr. had seen men ten times as tough as this guy give in to the punishment Lucio had just doled out. This pitiful fuck, or what was left of him, would've caved long before Lucio took out the blowtorch.

Lucio lit up a smoke and shrugged. "What now, Boss?"

Dom Jr. kicked Lucio's workbench of horrors over, sending various implements of pain skittering across the cold concrete. "Find him. Now." Before he left, he added, "And clean up this fucking mess."

"Would you like to hear our specials?" Joe glanced up at the tired face of the waitress, armed with pen and pad. Impatience edged her voice.

"Just coffee, please. Black."

Janice, as her nametag boasted, sighed and shuffled off, no doubt calculating the huge tip she'd be receiving. Joe rubbed his eyes, contemplated his next move.

He knew where they were holding Kate, but he couldn't go to the police for help. And going in there alone was suicide. But who could he trust? The talking head on the television droned on about the recent stock market crisis and how it was affecting local retailers. Joe glanced around the joint. A trio of men wearing matching GREENEST LANDSCAPING polos lined the counter, chatting up Janice, devouring eggs and hash browns, fueling up for their workday. A young hipster couple cozied up to one another in a corner booth, giggling over something on the dude's laptop.

Janice plunked a chipped mug down in front of Joe and said, "No free refills on the coffee unless you order something to eat." Joe nodded and shrugged. Janice shot him a not-so-subtle eyeroll and rejoined her friends at the counter. Joe took a healthy gulp, cringing as the scalding liquid seared his throat.

The coffee was worse than the sludge back at the agency. *Don't have to worry about that refill, Janice.* He was plotting his next move when the talking head with the perfect hair and perfect teeth on the tube ripped him from his reverie. Maybe he could find out more on the Guierriero hit. Surely, that would be the top story.

Joe raised a hand to catch Janice's eyes. Her eyes rolled in annoyance again as she moved toward him, coffee pot in tow. "Another?" she said and added, "Remember, it's not free."

"No, thanks," Joe said. "Would you mind turning the TV up?" Janice sighed, as if the request had been to find the cure for cancer while balancing the economy, then granted his request with an icy gaze.

The talking head turned to her counterpart, he of the same perfect hair stylist and dentist. *"Repeating our top story, police have just identified the body of a man pulled from the Charles River earlier today. He has been identified as thirty-two-year-old Joseph Campbell from Jamaica Plain. Mr. Campbell was last seen..."*

The mouths of the talking heads moved, but their voices were drowned out by the hammers slamming Joe's eardrums. The diner went fuzzy. The hipster couple gazed his way, their smiling faces now stern, their eyes prying.

Coincidence, Joe. That's all it is.

The diner spun like a kitschy kaleidoscope, the voices ebbing and flowing with each spin round. A blur appeared before him, then snapped into sharp focus. Janice.

"Sir, are you alright?" Her bedside manner morphed into one of concern and empathy. "You look like you've seen a ghost, and you're sweating like a dog on the hottest day of summer."

Joe swiped his dampened brow and rose from the booth. His legs collapsed, flinging him back into the cushiony seat.

"Are you on something, sir?" Janice demanded, her newly enriched bedside manner tossed right out the window. "Guys," she said, turning to the men at the counter, their eyes swimming in confusion and curiosity. "Can you give me a hand with this gentleman?"

This time, Joe's legs complied. He stood, threw some bills on the table, and said, "I'm fine." He pushed past Janice, past the beefy trio, past the hipsters, out into the brisk morning air.

He has your name. So don't thousands of other guys. Okay, maybe not that many in Boston. But still, it's a pretty fucking common name. The guy was probably drunk, lost his footing, fell into the river. But why was that the top story? Why weren't they reporting on Guierriero?

Joe knew this coincidence was too coincidental. This guy wasn't dead because he'd had one too many. He was dead because he had been unlucky enough to be blessed with the name Joe Campbell.

CHAPTER EIGHTEEN

I t was nearly noon as Joe entered the agency's pretentious foyer, all sleek and shiny and full of itself. The place, usually rife with the sounds of cutthroat ad execs and creative egos, lay silent in its weekend slumber. Joe entered the bullpen and moved silently through rows of tiny cubicles, typically bustling with activity, now looking like tiny jail cells. Which, in a sense, they were five days out of the week.

He was one of the chosen few to be bestowed with a door, a door he knew he was disdained for, a door coveted by those cubicle-enslaved ladder-climbers thirsty for power. What they didn't know was that, beyond the door they so hungrily craved, there was no brass ring. Only a greater sense of loneliness.

Just get what you need and get out. That was the plan. He padded quickly down the darkened hall, past the war room, past the game room all hip agencies had to have these days, toward his coveted door. He froze. Voices. Muffled, undetectable, coming from his office. Who the hell was here on a Saturday? And what were they doing in his office?

The voices grew louder. Angrier. He crept closer, plastered himself to the wall. A familiar voice. Mitch Wasserman. Why was Mitch in his office? Going through his files, no doubt. Mitch's newsman voice took on a different tone now. Fear.

I already told you, I'm not Joe Campbell.

Then why's it say that on your door?

It's not my office!

Joe edged closer, inches from the office. He caught a quick glimpse inside. Two men. Large men. Guierriero's men. Then he saw Mitch. A bruised and bloodied Mitch.

"I swear I'm not Joe Campbell," Mitch whined. "I don't even like the prick."

Feeling's mutual, buddy.

A Neanderthal with a shaved head and thick neck said, "If you're not him, then where is this prick?"

Mitch turned in Joe's direction. They locked eyes. Joe raised a finger to his lips. Slowly shook his head. *Don't, Mitch.*

"He's right there!" Mitch cried, pointing a shaky finger at the door.

Joe bolted. Heavy footfalls fell in right behind him. He'd never make it down the long corridor to the elevators in time. In desperation, he ditched it into the maze of cubicles. Crouching in the darkness, he listened. Silence. Aside from the heartbeat playing a steady beat in his ears.

He counted to twenty, then slowly rose, peeked over the partition. Despite the wall of windows showcasing the Boston skyline, very little light filtered in through the tempered glass. He crept toward the exit. Stopped. Mitch. Even though the fucker had given him up, it was Joe who'd gotten him into this. He had to make sure he was okay.

The door to his office was ajar. He whispered out to Mitch. Nothing. Again. Only the dull hum of the computer on his desk. He stepped into the doorway, half expecting to find a gun in his face. What he found was worse. Much worse.

Mitch, sprawled across the carpet, resembled a large child making a snow angel. Except for one thing. He wasn't surrounded in white. A blackish red Rorschach pattern blossomed out from his body, ruining the lush carpeting. A crude slash of red glistened on his neck. Glazed eyes stared desperately at the ceiling. Yet, despite Mitch's gruesome appearance, not a hair on his coiffed head was out of place.

"Sorry, man," Joe said aloud, bile rising up in his throat.

Movement from the hallway.

Peering out of his office, Joe saw nothing. *Just your imagination.* Then he spotted them. Two silhouettes moving across the blurred Boston skyline. Slowly, methodically, purpose in their steps.

He had two options. Make a run for the elevators. That would almost certainly be suicide. The other option was to get to the rooftop patio, another amenity all slick agencies had to have. The patio it was. Besides, he could use some fresh air.

The patio, small yet sleek and trendy, jutted out from the main building. The post-drizzle air was sticky, condensation slathering the thickly tufted seat cushions, lacquered grey tables and trendy faux-wood tiles underfoot. The city screamed below, desperate for sunlight, albeit partly cloudy sunlight, after endless days of rain.

Movement beyond the glass wall. They were approaching.

Fast. He scanned the terrace. He was trapped. Nowhere to go but down. Unless...

He grabbed a trendy chaise, hoped it was built as well as it looked, and dragged it to the awning. His heartbeat thrummed in his ears, blocking out the sounds of all the other Average Joes below, going about their mundane lives while this Average Joe was fighting for his. He reached up, clamped a sweaty hand around the slick eave, and heaved himself up. The chaise beneath him let out a grunt and split into pieces. He reached up with his other hand, grasping for purchase. The awning groaned, but it held.

Joe laughed silently, imagining the look on Shea's face when she saw the rooftop patio, her sanctuary, torn to pieces. Then he remembered Mitch and realized the patio would be the last thing on Shea's mind. The sliders slammed open. Joe could feel the energy of the hulking men crashing through.

"There he is!"

It was now or never. And he only had one shot. He swung his body, sinew and muscles working overtime. A gunshot erupted. Pain seared his right bicep as his body arced upward with the grace of a seasoned gymnast.

He landed atop the awning with a dull thud. The awning groaned again, then screamed. Like its friend the chaise, it seemed to have been built more for aesthetics than for holding one-hundred-seventy pounds of skin and bones. He rolled onto the blacktopped roof. A barrage of gunfire shredded the awning.

He stood, assessed his arm, decided it was just a flesh wound, and scanned the area. Once again, he was trapped.

He heard fumbling below as the two lunkheads scraped furniture across the trendy tile. *Good luck with that.* It may take a little effort, but Joe knew it wouldn't be long before they made their way up. *Think, Joe. Think.*

He had a thought. It was a stupid thought. An insane one, in fact. But it was all he had left. And they were coming fast.

It's the NCAA Division I Track and Field Championship. Long jump finals. It's your last attempt. You need to nail this. You can do this.

Though you're average in almost every aspect of your life, you're not average here. On the track, running, jumping, you're anything but average. You know you'll never match Mike Powell's world record jump of twenty-nine feet and change, but you can come close. And that's much better than average. This is your stage. And you're the leading man.

Electricity runs through the crowd. That girl you've been trying to impress all semester long is somewhere in that crowd, watching, waiting to see if you're just another Average Joe, as her friends have all likely whispered into her delicate ear.

This is your chance to show her. Show her you're not average. Because you know she isn't. Never has been. She is...perfection.

You scan the faces one last time, hoping to glimpse that vision of beauty. But it's nowhere to be found among the pumping fists, the gaping mouths, the snarling teeth.

You propel your body forward. You're a rocket, unstoppable, moving at the speed of light, the crowd now a blur as you make your approach. Your stride is long, lithe. Perfection. You gradually accelerate, your speed increasing as you approach your mark. Your brain checks off all the boxes your coach drilled into it. You focus on the crucial long-short rhythm of the last two steps. You plant your takeoff foot and push up and out.

You hear a loud crack. A lightning jolt of pain slices through your ankle to your brain. The crowd gasps. Sand mixes with saliva. The stadium spins around you. Faces, some concerned, some angry, silently screaming. Then you see her. That vision of beauty. Her face doesn't convey concern or anger. It conveys something else. Something much worse. Disappointment. And then she's gone.

Joe accelerated. He could hear the heaving and cursing of the lunkheads as they cleared the awning, stumbling to their feet. He erased them from his mind, focused solely on that rooftop, one he had estimated was within the twenty-nine foot and change distance that Mike Powell conquered. Give or take a few feet.

What his body lacked in pure stamina and strength since those good old college days, his mind made up for in sheer determination. Propelled by fear. He pumped his arms, body arched perfectly, legs moving like a well-oiled locomotive. Perfection.

He approached his mark, the mark being the edge of a very tall building, prepared for takeoff. Planting his left foot firmly, he propelled his body forward. He was airborne. The world around him stood still.

You need to increase your air time, Campbell. Coach Costello's gravelly voice resounded in his head. *Like I showed you. Remember the hitch-kick?*

Yes, Coach, I remember.

And not too high.

Got it.

Go get 'em, Campbell.

The hitch-kick, a technique favored by many long jumpers, involves a series of rapid-fire steps. *Punch-punch-press.* Punch with the left knee, then punch with the right. Then bring both legs out in front of you, reach for the skies, and press your knees to your chest. All there is to it.

Nothing to it, Joe.

The movement went off without a hitch, just enough propulsion, just enough height.

Now you just need to nail the landing.

The gunshots whizzing around him were background noise now. His only focus was on the rooftop closing in. *Feet first, then butt. The rooftop is made of sand. Soft, cushiony sand.*

He realized with sudden horror that he wasn't going to make it. Not enough momentum. He pumped his arms and legs wildly, willing his body forward. He imagined the two Neanderthals pointing and laughing at the absurdity of it. Some Michael Corleone he was. More like Groucho Marx.

The building was coming in fast. In a last-ditch effort, he reached out for a rusty old antenna that dangled precariously from the building's edge. His fingers made contact, and he gripped the steel rod with everything he had left in him, which wasn't much. It held. For a second. Gravity pulled him and the rusty contraption downward. So that was it.

He pictured Mike Powell and Coach Costello, shaking their heads in disappointment, offering up their color commentary on the whole sorry affair.

Well, I thought he had it there for a minute, Coach.

Too much height. If I've told him once, I've told him a thousand times, not too much height. Nothing special about that.

I'm with you, Coach. Looked pretty average to me.

Average. Like everything else in his sorry-ass life, Mike. What say we go grab a beer?

A sudden jolt snapped Joe up, slamming him into the building's weathered brick façade. The rusty old heap had held. Pure adrenaline rocketed his body up, up and over, rolling onto the rooftop as gunfire shredded the roof around him. Chunks of gravel kicked up, one catching him just below the left eye, burrowing into his cheek. But all he felt was determination. Pure determination. To get the fuck off this roof. To save his wife. To take his average life back.

As he ditched it into a doorway, he laughed as he thought what pathetic shots these two thugs were and why one of the most ruthless criminals in the country had their sorry asses on his payroll.

CHAPTER NINETEEN

Faneuil Hall Marketplace was bustling with activity, the gloomy morning having given way to a cloudless afternoon sky. Weekend revelers shuffled past, some in a hurry, others with all the time in the world. Time. That was a commodity Joe did not have on his side.

Every minute that ticked by was another minute Kate was suffering, if she were even still alive. He had to make a move fast, or they'd both be dead. He spotted a police officer standing watch up ahead. He could just come clean. Maybe the law could save the day, along with his wife. But he'd seen enough movies and crime shows to know how that would go.

What if they'd already linked him to Griffin's? Would anyone believe his crazy story about Patty Quigley, which probably wasn't even her real name? He had no proof the woman even existed, other than the envelope containing snapshots of Patty, Guierriero, Charlene, and Vixen. The envelope he'd had the good sense to hide away for safekeeping. Taped to the underside of his desk. The desk in the office where his rival now lay bleeding out all over the carpet.

Originally, he'd stashed the envelope in the bottom of his toolbox, high up on a shelf in the garage. But something made him uneasy about keeping it under the roof he and his wife shared. The office seemed like a better option at the time. He'd never fully trusted Patty and were she to renege on their deal, the snapshots were the only real evidence that he and Patty had ever connected. He now wished he'd stuck with the toolbox.

If the photos were to be found, they would link him to Guierriero, which would undoubtedly make him a suspect in the bloodbath at Griffin's. Not to mention the bloodbath in his office. But going back there was suicide. He'd just have to hope that the detectives working the crime scene were as incompetent as Guierriero's goons were with their aim.

He grabbed a coffee, making sure to pay cash, and moved aimlessly through the marketplace, the festive air around him white noise. Street musicians, magicians, and performers captivated their audiences, occasionally throwing in not-so-subtle reminders of the tips they were expecting for a job well done.

His thoughts turned to Kate. Although she'd never been overly affectionate, in recent weeks she seemed more distant than usual. Joe had even suspected she was having an affair. Nothing concrete, more a feeling. And her change of heart about wanting a family had floored him. Or maybe it wasn't a change of heart after all. Maybe that had been her intention all along. Maybe he really didn't know the woman he'd fallen in love with at all.

Yet, for all his resentment, he still loved her. And would do whatever it took to get her back alive.

"How the fuck did you let him get away?" Dominic Guierriero, Jr. threw a pricey bottle of Cognac across the room. The two men seated before him flinched as the bottle exploded in a showy display of liquid and glass.

At last, one of the men, who looked like a body double for Vin Diesel, spoke. "Boss, the guy is superhuman. You should've seen him jump—"

Dom Jr. shot up a hand, silencing the Diesel doppelganger. Then he laughed. "So, what you bozos are telling me is that we're dealing with Spiderman here?"

Vin-lookalike and his equally brawny sidekick laughed along with him. A gun leveled at their faces abruptly ceased the merriment. Dom Jr. waggled the gun back and forth. "Eeny, meeny, miny, moe..."

"Please, Boss," Vin-lookalike said, "just give us another chance and we'll—"

"Catch a moron by his toe..."

The men cringed as the gun wavered from one to the other.

"If he hollers let him go..."

"Boss, don't do this! I swear on my mother's grave, we'll get the fucker!"

Dom Jr. held his expressionless gaze. "Eeny, meeny, miny, moe." The last thing Vin-lookalike saw before his head was blown apart was the face of Dominic Guierriero, Jr. as it morphed into a sinister smirk.

Blood, sinew, and bone fragments splashed across the other man's face. He stumbled back, gazing in horror at the convulsing body without a face. He instinctively raised his hands to his own face. "Pl-ea-se, Boss," he stuttered, his hulking frame shaking spasmodically.

Dom Jr. raised the gun to the hulk's face. Then he smiled an awful Grinch-like grin. He lowered the gun and said, "You beat the odds on that one, T-Bone. One more chance. One more fucking chance. You got that?"

T-Bone, awash in his friend's brains, unable to speak, simply nodded.

Dom Jr. lit up a cigar, took a long drag off it, and said, "Now get out of my sight before I change my mind."

CHAPTER TWENTY

mbulance chasers milled about, speaking in hushed voices, a few capturing the scene on their phones, hoping for anything that might boost their social media following. The caravan of police cruisers and a dozen or more boys in blue were evidence that something big was happening inside the granite and glass skyscraper.

Detective Mickey MacAvoy pushed through the looky-loos, sidestepped a lingering rain puddle, and entered the building. A boyish officer motioned him toward a row of highly polished stainless-steel elevator doors. The honed marble floor and walls lent a stark sense of austerity to the vast foyer.

His reflection frowned back at him as he waited for his ride. Three-day stubble dotted a wan complexion. Thick dark hair desperately in need of barbering shot out in a million directions. A drab grey sport coat hung listlessly on its sagging frame, the wrinkled shirt beneath boasting a fresh coffee stain. At just thirty-five years of age, Detective Mickey MacAvoy, or Mick-

Mac as he was known to most, had already hit rock bottom. And it showed.

Maybe it was because he simply didn't give a shit anymore. About his appearance. His job. His pathetic life. The once model officer, all shiny and clean-cut, had worked his ass off to get out from behind the desk and on the streets where the real action was. Promises of advancement in the ranks came and were dashed, the latest hit being the most devastating blow.

He and Eddie had come up through the academy together, forming an instant bond. The brother he'd never had. The brother he trusted with his life. The brother who screwed him out of the promotion he had so justly earned. Sergeant Detective Edward Diaz. His superior. His brother. His nemesis.

The shiny doors slid open, erasing the stranger staring back at him. He rode the elevator to the top, encased in more of that honed marble, the one-two punch of acrophobia and claustrophobia clawing at his chest. At last, the doors opened, spitting him out into a still pretentious, yet more inviting space. He mopped the sweat from his brow, collected himself, and headed toward the action he'd once craved, and now simply endured.

He pushed through the sea of crime techs buzzing about, followed the breadcrumbs to the main event. And there was the ringmaster.

"Mick-Mac, you get lost on the way over here?" Eddie Diaz called out in his trademark snarky tone. Eddie was all slick and professional in his tailored sport coat and tie, crew cut razor-sharp and intimidating. He looked like he'd put on a few pounds, and not in a good way.

"Hey, Eddie," was all Mick-Mac could muster. He gazed at the gruesome sight sprawled out before him. The guy looked like one of those pretty-boys Mick-Mac detested. Aside from the not-so-pretty gash that ravaged his neck. "I take it this is Joe Campbell?"

Eddie's eyes narrowed, the wrinkles in his forehead became more pronounced. "Joe who? Oh, the nametag outside the door. No, our vic appears to be a Mitch Wasserman, co-worker of said Joe Campbell."

Mick-Mac spotted a photo on the desk. A young couple in a loving embrace. "Is this Campbell?"

Eddie rolled his eyes. "Brilliant deduction, Sherlock." The two techs sniffing around sniggered. Once again, good old Eddie had made Mick-Mac out to be the incompetent fool, the class dunce.

"Hey, Sarge, come take a look at this," a voice called from down the hall.

Diaz tossed a pair of blue latex gloves at Mick-Mac. "Here, put these on before you fuck up my crime scene." They fell short, landing dangerously close to the lifeless, perfectly coiffed head of Pretty-Boy.

"Nice catch, Buckner," Eddie snorted, referencing the former Red Sox first baseman whose accomplished career was marred by one single error—the passing of a ball between his legs during Game 6 of the 1986 World Series, giving the New York Mets the win and, ultimately, the Series. Mick-Mac had always thought Buckner deserved better than the wrath imposed upon him by rabid fans. These days, he felt an awful lot like the former All-Star.

Mick-Mac silently cursed his superior and knelt to retrieve the discarded gloves, careful to avoid contact with Pretty-Boy. He snatched up the gloves and began to rise. Something caught his eye. An envelope. Taped to the underside of the desk.

"Hey Gina," he said to the lone tech still working the room. "You mind if I have the room for a sec?"

Gina, a perky twenty-something with a keen eye for detail, shrugged and said, "Sure, Mick."

Mick-Mac worked quickly, removed the envelope and tucked it safely under his threadbare sport coat. Who knew, maybe it held the key to solving this bizarre case. Maybe it would gain him back the respect he deserved. Maybe this was his ball-between-the-legs moment. And unlike Mr. Buckner, he wasn't letting this one slip by.

CHAPTER TWENTY-ONE

Joe tucked himself into the shadows, keeping watch over the building where he hoped his wife was still being held captive. No life breathed from the decaying triple-decker, its tattered shell and grime-slicked windows secreting the misdeeds that lay beyond. The late afternoon sun punched its timecard, calling it a day. Streetlights flickered on, the grating hum of their fluorescent glow fashioning an ominous soundtrack to the nightmarish landscape.

A large SUV, blackish in color, rolled up to the building. For a minute it idled, the engine playing in cadence with the buzz of the streetlights. Joe was lulled by the sound until a blaring horn shook him from his stupor. Moments later, Rufus appeared in the building's doorway, followed by a much smaller figure. A woman, head down, features shrouded by a hooded jacket. The two figures descended the building's precarious staircase.

The driver of the SUV emerged. Patty. Rufus and the other woman appeared beside her. The woman lifted her head and peeled off the hood. Kate! Joe felt a rush of relief. She was alive. Patty's mouth moved, and Kate nodded in return. Funny, Kate didn't appear to be frightened or distraught. In fact, she appeared to be smiling.

What happened next nearly brought Joe to his knees. The two women embraced, like old friends reuniting. Then Kate laughed. The laugh Joe had found so endearing during their early days together, the laugh that now reverberated through the sordid, trash-strewn neighborhood. The trio then boarded the SUV. Before Rufus closed the rear passenger door, he leaned in and kissed Kate. Her manicured fingers softly caressed his big, fat watermelon head. Rufus climbed aboard and the SUV lurched forward, dissolving into the darkening night.

Joe stared at the spot where, moments before, the woman he loved, who he thought loved him back, had given him the proverbial slap in the face. A sense of sorrow and hopelessness washed over him. *Wake up, Joe. The joke's been on you all this time.* Then anger kicked in. How long had this betrayal been going on? Had it been a setup from the day they'd first met?

Their first encounter took place at some watering hole he couldn't even remember the name of. Vintage license plates boasting clever, six-digit innuendos plastered the wall behind the highly polished oak bar. Rows of pool tables, their surfaces tattered and beer-stained, entertained locals in flannels and ball caps. The aroma of French fries and onions hung heavy in the air. Minimal light filtered in through sparingly placed transom windows, giving the dive a cavernous sense of dread.

Joe nursed his gin and tonic, licking his wounds from today's disaster of a presentation. Maybe it was time to move on. New job. Maybe even a new city. Then she walked in.

Definitely not a local. In fact, she was as conspicuous as a rose among weeds. Words couldn't do justice to the exquisite face making its way toward him. A face that left him, to use another tired cliché, speechless.

She hesitated, then touched the stool to Joe's right and said, "Excuse me, is this seat taken?" Joe erupted in laughter, a move he quickly regretted. The woman furrowed her brow. "I'm sorry, did I say something funny?"

A rush of heat dashed across his face. *Smooth move, Joe.* Not that it mattered. She was, since today seemed to be the day for worn-out clichés, way out of his league.

The woman frowned and turned to leave. "Wait..." Joe said.

She turned slowly, the frown dissolving into a slight smile.

"I didn't mean to laugh," Joe said, pointing past the woman. "It's just that I'm looking at an empty bar with about twenty empty stools. So, I guess the answer to your question is, no, this, nor any other stool in this fine establishment, is currently occupied."

Her smile broadened, then she laughed. A laugh that was one part cloying, two parts endearing. "Well, in that case, do you mind if I join you?"

She signaled for the bartender. "I'll have a Sidecar, please. And whatever this gentleman here is drinking." The bartender, laps ahead of Joe in brawn and good looks, nodded coyly at this mysterious woman and turned away.

He returned quickly and placed the orangey drink in front of the woman and a fresh gin and tonic before Joe. "Enjoy," the man said. Joe was sure he winked at the woman.

Elegant fingers gripped the stem of the delicate glass with the colorful concoction and said, "Cheers."

Joe returned the gesture, then said, "Do you mind my asking what a Sidecar is?"

Now it was the woman's turn to laugh. "It's Cognac with orange liqueur and lemon juice. I've never been much of a Chardonnay girl." She pushed the glass toward Joe. "Here, give it a try."

The woman's fingers brushed Joe's as he took the elegant glass. The velvety liquid was soothing, sensual. Like the lips that now wrapped themselves on the rim of the glass. And the hand that now rested on Joe's thigh.

She glanced around at the sparse midweek crowd bent over pool cues. "So, what brings a guy like you into a place like this?"

Joe was suddenly aware of his disheveled appearance. The wrinkled, half-tucked shirt. The hastily loosened tie that hung limply from his neck. "Well," he said, "let's just say I had a rough day at the office."

She shifted on her seat, edging closer. "Rough isn't always bad," she said, her manicure spidering up his leg, stopping just short of his stirring manhood. "And what type of work constitutes such roughness?"

Joe smirked. "I'm a writer. Advertising."

"So, you write fiction, then?" She let out that lovely laugh again. Joe joined her.

"The name is Joe. Joe Campbell." He thrust out a hand, hoping she didn't notice the slight quiver.

"Kate." With that, she took his hand and moved it between her legs.

How was this happening? Joe Campbell, the guy who had to practically beg to get a prom date in high school, the guy who went through most of his college years a virgin, the guy who had a better chance at winning the lottery than he did getting laid. So how was it that this beautiful mystery woman had suddenly entered his life and had him literally by the balls right now?

She released her grip on him and gave him a come-with gesture. Their lovemaking was fast and feral. The bathroom stall was a petri dish, slathered in god-knows-what germs and diseases. But Joe was oblivious to it all. With each thrust, he imagined away the faint odor of stale urine, the droning of the overhead fluorescents, the *click-clacking* of the loosening lock on the stall door.

They hastily pulled themselves together and made their way back to the bar, most seats now occupied by off-the-clock laborers in soiled work clothes and too-old women in too-short skirts cozying up beside them.

Joe pointed to a quiet booth tucked neatly away from the action. Kate nodded, and they made their way to the darkened corner.

"Well, this is much better," Joe said to the mystery woman seated across from him. "I can hear myself think." He ordered Kate another Sidecar, then told the waitress, who looked much too young to be serving them, to make it two. He considered asking Mandy, as her nametag stated, if he could see some ID, then decided she didn't seem the joking type.

They made small talk, softball questions like "Do you come here often?" and "Where did you grow up?" but when Joe raised the topic of family, Kate's demeanor took a one-eighty. She withdrew into her colorful drink, eyes wandering anywhere but in Joe's direction. "I'm sorry," Joe said. "Did I say something to upset you?"

Kate shook her head slowly, still evading Joe. Then she said,

"I lost my family in an accident long ago and I'd really rather not talk about it." Her eyes met his. Then they brightened. "Besides, I'd much rather hear about you, Joe Campbell."

Joe proceeded to regale her with tales from his not-so-stellar childhood. The mother who abandoned him. The father who was either drunk, absent, or both. The brother who had been his rock and only true friend until he, too, drifted from his life.

"So, how did you wind up in advertising?" Kate asked.

"Well," Joe said, "I just kind of fell into it. Growing up, whenever my parents would fly into one of their fits of rage, which was most of the time, Glen and I would slip out of the house to escape the madness, even if just for a while. We'd make our way down to Old Man McCready's farm and sprawl out in his field, gazing up at the stars, dreaming of how we'd make our great escape."

Kate placed a tender hand on Joe's, sending a mild shock-wave through his body. "That's so sad," she said.

Joe laughed. "No, they were actually the best memories I have of my childhood. Just me and Glen and a billion stars, each one signifying a new place we'd explore on our journey around the world together. Glen appointed me tour guide, prodding me to describe all the exotic places we'd travel to." Joe stopped. "I'm sorry, if I'm boring you—"

"Not at all," Kate said in a willowy voice that made something stir deep inside him. "Please, go on."

"Well, you see, it turns out I was a bit of a geography nerd. When I was around ten, my grandmother gave me one of those cheapo globes of the earth that spins on a plastic axis. I remember Tom—that's my dad—rolling his eyes and berating his mother for giving me such a worthless piece of crap. But, you know, it was the best gift I'd ever received. And by the time

I was ten, I had pretty much memorized every continent, country, ocean, gulf, every damn inch of the planet."

"Quite the man of the world," Kate said.

"Well, not exactly," Joe said. "In fact, before I graduated college, I'd never even been on an airplane. But I could describe a place as if I'd been there a thousand times. As we'd stretch out under the blanket of stars on a hot summer night, the fireflies buzzing all around us, Glen would name a country and off I'd go, spinning yarns of our adventures—climbing the Matterhorn, roughing it in the Outback, running with the bulls in Pamplona. Glen used to call me the world's greatest storyteller, saying I could make you believe anything was possible. And that's what led me to advertising—slinging the bullshit and selling the fantasy."

Kate laughed. "Well, you've certainly sold me. So, where did you go—you and your brother, I mean?

Joe felt a pang of regret and shame wash across him. "Nowhere," he said sadly. "So much for the great storyteller, huh?"

Kate leaned in close, her mystical scent invading his senses. "Why not?" she asked. "What stopped you?"

Joe shook his head. "After the folks flew the coop, Glen and I just kind of drifted apart. And before you know it, we were barely speaking to one another." He shrugged and let out a forlorn sigh. "And to think that I'd actually bought into my own fantasy."

"What fantasy?"

Joe shook his head again. "Forget it. It was just the foolish dream of a very foolish young man."

Kate brushed a tender hand across his arm. "Well, I'd really like to hear it."

Joe recoiled, slumped in the booth, and felt a wave of loss wash over him. "Glen had this crazy idea that we'd move to some faraway exotic island, start our own chartered boat business—you know, guided tours of the island to tourists. Said all I had to do was choose the place, and he'd be packed and ready to go." Joe smiled weakly. "Like I said, a foolish dream from a foolish young man."

"I don't think it sounds foolish at all," Kate said. "I think it sounds wonderful. So, where did you choose—to go, I mean?"

Joe rolled his eyes. "I don't know. Maybe Bali. Or Mykonos."

"Mykonos?"

"Mykonos, Greece," Joe said.

"Why there?" Kate said, genuine interest in her eyes.

Joe shrugged, feeling a rush of heat wash over his face. "I don't know. I saw something about the place on TV one time—a documentary, I think—and I was fascinated by its culture and natural wonder." He glanced up, locking gazes with the beauty before him. "Did you know that according to Greek mythology, this is where Zeus battled the Titans?" Kate shook her head. "Of course, why would you know that?" Joe said. "Only a total loser like me would know something as obscure as that." He rose abruptly. "We should go. I appreciate you humoring me as long as you have, but I'm sure you have much better things to do than listen to me ramble on about places I've never seen and probably never will."

Kate grasped his arm. "I think it's fascinating." She paused. "I think you're fascinating. Now, please, sit down. I'd love to hear more about this magical place."

Two hours later, as they made their way to the exit, giddy from the effects of that sultry orange potion, Joe said, "Want to hear a joke?"

"Sure," Kate said, her slightly mussed hair and makeup making her only more potent, more genuine. "Lay it on me."

"So, this guy walks into a bar..." Joe began.

Kate smiled. "And?"

"And he meets the woman of his dreams."

CHAPTER TWENTY-TWO

Ten minutes after the SUV pulled away, Joe was breaking into the third-floor slum, a skill his big brother had taught him during his reckless teen years. The lock clicked. He was in. *Thanks, Bro.*

Joe hadn't been expecting much, but the conditions inside this rattrap were far worse than he could have imagined. The walls were coated in blackish streaks, maybe soot, maybe mold, probably both. Threadbare, mismatched seating was placed haphazardly, the remaining furnishings a dog's breakfast of pressed wood and chipped plastic. Beyond the living room was a makeshift kitchen boasting a creatively improvised assortment of cabinets and fifties-chic laminate flooring that, having long overserved its utility, curled up in lazy surrender. But the crowning touch was the ancient Coldspot refrigerator, its once lustrous coating dinged and rusted. It bore a remarkable resemblance to the one that adorned the Campbell kitchen before

Dear Old Mom flew the coop and Dear Old Dad fell deeper into the seemingly endless bottle.

Beyond the kitchen was a murky hallway like the kind seen in countless slasher films, where countless scantily clad teenagers decide to investigate the eerie sound despite the shrieks of the audience begging them not to.

A filmy darkness crept from every sinister corner, the grime-slicked and shaded windows allowing in minimal illumination from those buzzing streetlights. Joe sidestepped balled up clothing and hastily discarded trash, at last reaching a lamp. Clicked it on. No wonder they kept the place dark.

The Kate he knew wouldn't have stayed in this shithole for a second and wouldn't have touched any of its contents without a Hazmat suit. But the Kate Joe knew wasn't the real Kate now, was she?

Realizing that turning the light on was a novice move that those scantily clad teenagers in the movies did, Joe quickly clicked it off and was plunged into gauzy darkness once again. He fumbled for his phone and pressed the flashlight button. His eyes began searching. For what, he wasn't sure. Some proof, some evidence that he was being set up. Ransacking the living room required nothing more than a quick scan, given the lack of anything capable of secreting anything. A more thorough search of the kitchen turned up plenty of out-of-date food and a rank stench that burrowed itself into every surface, but nothing of use.

The hallway housed four doors, two on the left and two on the right, all closed.

Let's make a deal, Joe Campbell! What'll it be, Door Number One? Or maybe Door Number Three? Behind one is the shiny new sports car, behind another is a sack of potatoes. And behind one is that price-

less evidence that just might save your ass! So, what'll it be, Joe Campbell?

Joe gripped the knob on the first door to his left. He hesitated, fear seizing him, squeezing and twisting the muscles in his arm, in his chest. How had he gotten to this point? He suddenly longed for the dull, uneventful life he'd despised before that fateful night in Griffin's. Now there was no turning back. He opened the door.

The air in here was thicker, with an odd smell Joe couldn't quite place. Unlike the living room, this room, though small, was a hoarder's dream. Cardboard boxes stacked to the ceiling, yellowed newspapers, torn magazines, dressers vomiting clothes from overstuffed drawers. Shit, it could take all day to sort through this disaster.

Monty, I think I'd like to try Door Number Two instead.

The hallway was more sinister now. Colder. Quieter. Joe was aware of his heartbeat, of the blood coursing through his body, pumping adrenaline at a dangerous rate. His temple throbbed. He pressed a finger to it gingerly, fearing too much pressure might burst the damn thing. *Get your shit together, Campbell.*

He moved further into the cavernous hallway, made his way into a bedroom with less clutter. A recently slept-in bed dominated the space, sheets and pillows discarded chaotically from an aggressive lovemaking session, Joe suspected. He imagined Rufus and his wife going at it like dogs, sweat glossing their sinewy muscles as they moved rhythmically, spasmodically. It left a hollowness he hadn't felt since Dolores Campbell patted him on the head and said, "Now you be a good boy for your daddy," and erased herself from his life.

Joe turned his attention to the closet staring at him. Random shirts and jackets hung limply from wire, mostly drab in color. Non-gender specific. Except for one. Joe's favorite football jersey, weather-worn and faded. Kate used to slip it on after making love to her husband, the oversized shirt not doing Kate's body the justice it deserved. And still, it was sexy as hell.

Joe had searched everywhere for his beloved Julian Edelman jersey, Kate shrugging with disinterest whenever questioned about it. While all this time it was here, in this hovel, her post-sex attire for a Neanderthal named Rufus.

He tore the jersey from the closet then, logic pushing aside anger, returned it to its spot, knowing its absence would throw up a red flag he didn't want waving. Something caught his eye. A photo album, something he hadn't seen in years, with today's technology favoring selfies and Instagram pictures over lasting memories preserved under plastic sleeves in books once proudly displayed on coffee tables.

The faux-leather book was tattered at the edges. Joe opened it. The spine let out a groan, as if it hadn't been opened in decades. The first several pages contained grainy images Joe guessed to be from the seventies, judging by the clothing and hairstyles. Two young girls, who appeared to be twins, mugged it up in the majority of the snapshots.

Joe flipped the pages. The twins again, older and prettier, having blossomed from those awkward adolescent years. Though not identical twins, the similarity was striking. Joe studied a photo of the girls, all eighties-chic with the hair piled high, the hoop earrings big enough to sink a basketball, and that off-the-shoulder look made famous by Madonna and Cyndi Lauper. The girl on the right, arguably the prettier of the two, looked familiar.

Is that Patty?

Joe moved in for a closer look. Yes! It was most definitely

Patty. In her prime. And she had a sister. Joe slipped the photo from its protective sleeve, slowly turned it over. He was very familiar with the handwriting.

Me & Charlene, Castle Island 6/3/85
The best sister a girl could wish for!

Charlene was Patty's sister. Then why had Patty lied and told Joe she was her best friend? Sure, sisters often are best friends. Joe doubted it had been an oversight. It had been a lie. Like everything else about Patty. Well, not everything. She clearly had been one of Guierriero's playthings. Joe suspected her sister had been, too.

He turned the page. His suspicions were correct. There was a young, vibrant Charlene, draped in the arms of a much younger, though still sinister looking, version of "The Skinner." More photos of Charlene, Patty, Guierriero, and various other tough guys.

This is your life, Patty Quigley, Joe thought as he flipped to the next phase of this enigma's life. More Patty, more Charlene. And two young girls, the older clinging to Charlene's side, the younger in her arms. Her daughters, maybe? The elder of the two girls appeared to be around three, while the other looked to be under a year old. Once again, Joe slid the snapshot out and turned it over.

His knees buckled. The photo dropped from his trembling hand.

Me, Charlene, Kimmy & Katie 2/17/88

Katie. Kate. His wife. Daughter of Charlene? Niece of

Patty? Sister of Kimmy? Confusion set in, then nausea. Joe stared at the photo. Or was Patty the mother and Charlene the aunt? Which would then make Patty Joe's mother-in-law. Joe's mind was processing this last thought when a loud *click* shook him from his stupor.

The door. Opening. Faint voices. They were back.

CHAPTER TWENTY-THREE

Dominic Guierriero, Jr. listened to the rhythmic breathing of the woman beside him, the smell of sex heavy in the air. His body demanded sleep, but his mind ignored the request. He knew he'd never sleep again until he exacted his revenge on the man who had killed his father.

He slipped from under the satiny sheets. A clammy chill ran up his naked spine. He padded to the bathroom and clicked on the light. The stranger staring back at him sent a mild shudder through his body. Though only thirty-eight, he suddenly looked twenty years older. Purplish crescents underscored sanguine eyes. His skin, usually healthy and glowing, was now a ghastly death mask. The saving grace was his still lean and taut body.

He downed more than the recommended dosage of aspirin, took a piss, and crept back into bed. The tangle of covers and silken hair shifted.

"You okay, baby?" his flavor of the week said.

Dom Jr. let out a puff of air. "Yeah. Go back to sleep."

The woman, beautiful even by his standards, caressed his sinewy arm, sending another chill through his body. "Baby, you look stressed. I know just the thing to fix that."

The cocaine did nothing except make him even more irritable, more determined to find whoever the fuck this Joe Campbell was and make him wish he'd never crossed paths with a Guierriero.

He needed to hide. Fast. But his options were limited. Either burrow himself deep inside the closet or squeeze under the bed. The bed seemed the safer bet.

Voices drifted from the hallway. Kate's one-part endearing, two-parts cloying, laugh cut through Joe's soul. The voices grew nearer. They were in the room.

The bed sagged under the weight of a body. Joe feared the unstable structure would give. A set of feet materialized inches from Joe's head. Large feet. Rufus.

"Get over here, you big hunk of man," Kate's willowy voice sang out.

Big hunk of man? Who was this woman? The same woman who turned to ice whenever her husband touched her. The woman he had trusted with his darkest secrets and deepest fears.

"Just a sec," Rufus said. His feet pivoted and moved away from the bed. "Just want to check."

"Again?" Kate said in that sing-song whine Joe knew all too well. "It hasn't gone anywhere since you last checked it."

Whatever it was that needed checking, Joe hoped it wasn't under the bed. The massive feet moved away, toward the closet. Shit. The closet. He'd forgotten to close the door. What if they noticed? And what if they investigated further, noticed the missing photo album, the photo album gripped tightly in Joe's hand? He was glad he'd had the good sense to leave the Edelman jersey, which stood out like a beacon among the drab blacks and grays bookending it.

But Rufus didn't go to the closet, nor did he comment on the open door. Instead, he moved to an old dresser, slid it from its spot. Heavy, judging by the grunts emitted by the walking steroid.

Rufus knelt, his skinned watermelon head and tattoos now in Joe's line of vision. Rufus produced a pocketknife, grunted some more, then pried up a floorboard.

"Let me guess," the sing-songy voice overhead said. "It's still there, like it was an hour ago when you last checked."

"Smart ass." Rufus laid the floorboard back in its place.

"Show me! Show me! I want to see it again!" Kate squealed.

Rufus grunted. "Baby, it looks the same as it did an hour ago."

"Show me," Kate said, "and I'll show you my appreciation." The familiar whine was now a deep, sexy voice. A voice foreign to Joe.

Another grunt. "Fine." Rufus pried up another board, his meaty paw disappearing into the crevice. When it emerged, it held a thick brick of money. Dominic "The Skinner" Guier-riero's money.

Kate squealed. The bed groaned. "Now get over here and screw me like there's no tomorrow."

Her brashness was stunning. Joe had never heard as much as a mild expletive from his wife. She'd played her role so well. And he supposed he'd played the role of doting, dutiful husband even better.

Rufus returned the brick to its cache, replaced the floorboards, and slid the massive dresser back in place. Less than a minute later, he granted Kate her wish, and screwed her like there was no tomorrow. The betrayal was now complete.

Every muscle in Joe's body screamed. His back spasmed. Lips parched. He'd been trapped all night, having endured the Kate and Rufus show three, count 'em three, times before they'd finally drifted off to sleep.

Daybreak split the blinds, slivers of light bouncing off the walls, the dresser, the Edelman jersey. His back spasmed again, and he knew he wouldn't be able to endure it much more. Then, when he thought he'd reached his breaking point, Patty Quigley saved the day. She barreled into the room, kicked the bed soundly.

"Get the hell up, you lazy lovebirds. We've got business to take care of."

There was the Patty Joe knew and loved.

The bed shifted, springs straining in anguish. Just like Joe's back. Mumbled curses, then two very large, very unmanicured feet plunked themselves down inches from Joe's head.

Rufus cleared the evening's congestion from his throat, spit it out onto the floor. "I don't know why we can't just take the dough and hop a plane today," he said. He spit again.

"We've been over this," Patty said. "The cops still need access to your bar, which, in case your pea brain has forgotten, is still an active crime scene. How would it look if the owner just up and disappeared?"

"Aunt Patty's right," Kate said. Another set of feet plunked to the floor. A much smaller and perfectly manicured set. The ones Joe used to massage in their early days.

So, there it was. Patty was the aunt. That made Charlene Kate's mother. Mystery solved.

"We've planned this for too long to fuck things up now," Patty barked. "Like I said, we stick to the plan. You continue to make yourself available to the cops. As soon as they give you the okay to open the joint back up, you go about business as usual. We lay low for a few more days, then we, and our four million little babies are off to paradise."

Rufus grunted and rose. The bed breathed a sigh of relief. "Yeah, yeah. Coffee on?"

"Brewed and ready," Patty said. "Now put that thing away," she said with disgust. Her hurried footsteps vanished down the hallway.

When, at long last, Kate and Rufus made their way to the kitchen, Joe slid from his cramped quarters. He knew it was risky, but his aching body begged for relief.

Clanking dishes and idle chatter resounded through the musty air. When he felt it was safe, Joe stood on shaky legs. He stretched his back, neck, arms, pain ricocheting through them with each movement. Through the window, his eye caught a fire escape. His escape. All he had to do was get the money and slip out the window.

Just one problem.

He'd first have to move the dresser, the dresser Rufus the Hulk had trouble budging. Then he had to pry up the floorboards with his bare hands. Piece of cake.

The best option right now was to get out of here with his life. The money would have to wait. He moved toward the window, the photo album clutched to his side. He stopped.

Footsteps. Heavy footsteps. Rufus.

Panic seized his still achy muscles. He slipped into the closet and closed the door, hoping Rufus would forget it had been open only minutes before. He thought about the gun, tucked away in his car, that he now wished he'd kept on his body.

Mensa child that he was not, Rufus didn't notice. Joe listened as the lummox once again slid aside the dresser, pried up the floorboards, and plunked what sounded like a sizeable amount of cash onto the floor.

"How much do you want?"

Patty's voice entered the room. "Give me two grand and put the rest back. It's all in hundred-dollar bills so even you shouldn't have trouble counting it out."

"I'm not stupid," Rufus said.

"Then how many hundreds makes two thousand?" Patty said condescendingly.

Silence. Joe imagined the dumb oaf taxing his brain, trying to do the math. At last, an exasperated Patty said, "Never mind. Just give me twenty bills."

Rufus grunted. "I knew that," he said, though Joe knew better.

Patty exited the room. Rufus cursed, then repeated his routine of replacing the floorboards and returning the dresser to its original state, mumbling and cursing all the way. When Joe was sure it was safe, he slipped out of the closet and moved to the window. He tugged on it. It didn't budge. Upon further investigation, he noticed it was painted shut, layer upon layer of chipped paint sealing it tightly, maybe sealing his fate.

There was only one way out. The door he'd come in through. And if memory served him right, he had to pass the kitchen to get to it.

He swiped sweat from his forehead, pushing soppy hair back. He crept down the hall, a hall that now seemed to go on for miles. The clatter grew louder as he neared the kitchen. His pulse quickened at an alarming rate, and he feared his heart would give up in surrender. He paused at the entry to the kitchen.

"You think he'll look for me?" Kate asked.

Patty laughed. "Honey, he'll be either dead or behind bars before the week is over."

"Poor schmuck," Rufus said. "I was actually starting to like him."

"Well," Kate said, "I'd like to think he'd look for me. He's in love with me, after all."

I was, my dear. I was.

Patty laughed again. "You did what you had to do. Your mom would be proud."

Kate sobbed. An emotion Joe hadn't witnessed before. "To Mom."

"To Mom," the others chimed in.

Joe took this as his cue. He rushed past the doorway, expecting Rufus's meaty paw to be on his shoulder by the time he reached the door. But there was no paw, only the continuous chatter slamming him in the back.

He slipped out the door. It was only when he reached the street that he realized he'd pissed himself. He rushed up the desolate street, spent and shivering. He needed to get that money. And there was only one person who could help him get it. He quickened his pace, the early morning breeze gently caressing his face.

PART TWO

Brothers in Arms

CHAPTER TWENTY-FOUR

M ick-Mac stared at the contents of the envelope strewn across his kitchen table. A variety of photographs, all with one common theme. Dominic "The Skinner" Guierriero.

Sorting through the snapshots, he noticed the same woman appeared in the majority of them. He turned one of the photos over. *Dom and me.* He flipped a few more over and found other notations, all in the same neat handwriting. *Charlene, Me & Vixen —Summer 2002 Castle Island. Me, Dom & Charlene—Sal's 50th.*

The question was, who was this *Me* in all these photos? And how were she and the recently departed Dominic Guierriero connected to Pretty-Boy Mitch Wasserman and this Campbell guy who found the need to secret these photos away under his desk?

Maybe this was the break Mick-Mac had been waiting for. To prove to Eddie, to the whole fucking force, that he was The Man. The Man who solved the biggest case Boston had seen in decades. The hit on one of the most notorious gangsters in modern times.

There were a lot of unanswered questions, but Mick-Mac's gut told him that the key to connecting all these people was the enigmatic Joe Campbell, keeper of secrets.

I'm coming to get you, Joe Campbell.

CHAPTER TWENTY-FIVE

J oe headed north on I-93. He made a quick detour to Target, changed out of his soiled clothes, and got behind the wheel, fueled by Red Bull and a healthy array of junk food. Joe had left nearly a dozen messages on his brother's cell and email. When he'd just about given up hope, his brother finally responded via email, apologizing for being off the grid.

Glen Campbell, up until a few years ago a successful commodities broker, one day decided that Corporate America was for "fucking automatons," and chucked it all for a simple life far from civilization in the middle of nowhere. Deep in the woods of New Hampshire.

Glen had been everything Joe was not. Handsome, charming, off-the-charts intelligent. Luckily for Joe, the five-year age gap meant not having to suffer through high school in the shadow of the starting-quarterback-homecoming-king-chick-magnet who, by the way, also happened to be class valedictorian. The only blowback Joe received was in the form of teachers and coaches who expected Glen's baby brother to follow in those shoes that were just too damn big to fill.

Yet, despite his brother's overachievements, Joe never felt resentment toward Glen. Maybe it was because Glen had pretty much taken on the role of big brother, mother, and father, all wrapped into one. It was Glen who'd cheered him on at his track meets. It was Glen who was there for both his high school and college graduations. Hell, he'd even let Joe borrow his vintage Camaro on the rare occasion Joe could score a date.

Or maybe it was because Glen was the only person who had ever truly loved him.

Joe thought back to the last time he had seen his brother. His wedding day. Kate and Glen had never hit it off, and on that particular day things came to a head. The hurtful accusations were hurled like a Cy Young recipient's fastball. Barbs like *gold digger* and *elitist* from Glen, *shallow* and *womanizer* from Kate. Joe couldn't even remember what had precipitated the attack. What he did remember was Kate vowing to never step foot in a room with his brother again. Which was just fine with Glen.

Since that fateful day, the brothers had spoken on occasion via phone (Glen had sworn off social media), but the conversations had been strained, the wounds from that day still festering, unhealed, leaving scars Joe wasn't sure would fade with time.

Joe shoveled a fistful of Doritos into his mouth and washed the cheesy mess down with a Red Bull. His second within the last hour, sleep deprivation finally kicking in. He cranked up the radio and cracked the window, a blast of fresh air revitalizing his senses. The majestic views of the White Mountains were a pleasant respite from the Boston skyline. The winding pass cut a breathtaking swath through the mountains, dipping and rising, lush greenery gliding by his periphery, yawning open to the imposing peaks beyond.

Joe had once heard this was the only single-lane interstate highway in the country. Probably from Glen, the king of useless trivia. Particularly when it came to geography. Joe recalled the carefree and reckless days hiking these mountains with his big brother. Before Kate, before Patty, before his life had become one big cluster-fuck. Simpler days. Better days.

Franconia Notch had been a favorite spot of Glen's, and Joe could see why. Stunning waterfalls, treacherous gorges, and endless hiking trails were a nature lover's dream. It had also once been home to the Old Man of the Mountain, a series of granite ledges on Cannon Mountain that resembled the jagged face of a man.

Due to constant freezing and thawing throughout the decades, fissures in the rocks were patched and mended each summer. Despite the painstaking efforts, in May of 2003, the formation finally threw in the proverbial towel, collapsing to the ground. Though the famous face had been erased, it remained permanently etched in Joe's memory.

Just like the image of Kate kissing Rufus would be forever etched in his mind. How had he been so blind? Glen had once cautioned him that there was "just something I don't like about that girl," which led to Joe pushing his brother further away. He still loved his brother, and he was certain Glen still loved him, but the cracks in their relationship, like the cracks in the Old Man of the Mountain, were warning signs of imminent disaster.

Joe only hoped it wasn't too late to keep things from collapsing this time.

He was so deep in his thoughts that he nearly missed the turnoff. Though even the most alert of Boy Scouts may have missed it. The road was unpaved and unmarked. In fact, it was so inconspicuous it seemed to meld into its woodsy backdrop.

The narrow path was soggy and rutted. Listless branches reached out on both sides, gently *scritch-scratching* the Rover's glossy paint job. The Rover jostled and groaned as it made its way deeper into the forest, deeper from civilization. The path wove and pitched aimlessly, appearing to narrow as it plunged further into the darkening wilderness.

Finally, when Joe thought the overgrowth would swallow the Rover up completely, the road yawned open, exposing a sun-dripped field of wild grass and dandelions. Beyond the field, which swelled like a balloon, a roofline emerged.

Joe climbed the final leg of the route, at last reaching his destination. The cabin was compact and efficient, yet well maintained and neatly landscaped. Beyond the structure was a lake, its gentle ripples dotted by the sun. Beyond the lake, stately peaks that disappeared into feathery clouds loomed with equal parts serenity and menace.

Joe's concerns that Glen would not be home were quickly allayed. Before the Rover was in Park, the front door opened, and a black Labrador Retriever galloped toward him. Blaze or Blazer, Joe couldn't remember which.

Then the imposing figure of his brother emerged, beefier looking than Joe recalled. He threw Joe a friendly wave. Then his expression changed. To one of grave concern.

Joe imagined the familiar face of the Old Man of the Mountain, sighing in defeat, tumbling down the mountainside.

CHAPTER TWENTY-SIX

"You look like shit, bro."

"Thanks," Joe said. He sunk into a well-worn leather couch. "Good to see you, too."

"Want something to drink? Water? Coffee?"

"I think something stronger may be in order."

Glen laughed. A laugh Joe hadn't heard in a while. A laugh Joe sorely missed. "I think that can be arranged." Glen ruffled the tangled mess on Joe's head and moved to the kitchen.

Joe scanned the place. The space was neat and functional, decorated in signature bachelor style. Rich leathers, distressed wood, sleek shades of greys, browns, and blacks. It was as though Glen had recreated the lush penthouse apartment he'd once loved, then grown to despise, now repackaged inside a rustic log cabin.

"Beer okay, Joey?" his brother yelled from the industrial, high-tech kitchen. Funny, for someone who was "living off the land," Glen wasn't exactly roughing it.

"Sure, whatever you got."

The black lab—*is his name Blaze or Blazer?*—sidled up to Joe, briefly sniffed him, and proceeded to hump his leg.

Glen returned with two cold ones gripped tightly in his meaty paws. "Blazer! Down!"

Right, Blazer, as in Trail Blazer. Should have remembered that.

Glen pulled the libidinous mutt off and sent him cowering to his corner. "Sorry about that. I guess he really likes you." He waggled the beer in front of Joe. "And sorry, I don't have anything stronger. If you'd given me more notice, I would've restocked the bar."

Joe took the beer being thrust at him. "This is fine. It's not like you have a shopping mart just up the road. Or within fifty miles."

Glen laughed. "Yeah, don't really have to worry about keeping up with the Joneses out here." He laughed again. "Cheers, brother. Good to see you."

"Cheers," Joe said. They tapped bottles together, a ritual that Joe suspected went all the way back to the days of the caveman. His parched throat tightened as he washed down the cold liquid. Damn, it felt good.

Joe studied the man seated before him. His once closest friend now seemed like a stranger. Although Glen had always been powerfully built, he looked more ripped than ever. The black AC-DC t-shirt strained against impossibly perfect muscle. His once long, lustrous hair was cropped high and tight, military-style, which made his chiseled jawline more pronounced and his tree-trunk neck all the more intimidating. Intricate tattoos enhanced the bulging veins on arms that looked as if they'd been inflated by one or two pumps too many. He could be the poster boy for the U.S. Marine Corps. *Semper Fucking Fi.*

Glen grimaced. "Bro, what the fuck did you get yourself mixed up in? Your face is all over the news."

Joe sat bolt upright. Had they found the photos hidden beneath his desk? Now, on top of the mafia looking for him, he had the feds too. "Glen, I am so screwed."

Glen took a healthy drag off his beer and said, "They're saying you're wanted for questioning in the murder of your co-worker. Who happened to be found dead in your office. And who your boss said you had an axe to grind with."

Shea. First, she fucks him over on the promotion and then throws him under the bus. "What about Guierriero? Did they mention him?"

Glen looked shell-shocked. "What are you talking about? Dominic Guierriero? Whoa! Why would they mention him?"

Joe sighed heavily. So, they hadn't found the envelope. "Nothing," he mumbled. "Never mind."

Glen slammed down his beer and got up in Joe's face. "What the fuck, Joey? Did you have something to do with that hit on Guierriero? Are you mixed up with the mob?"

Joe laughed at the absurdity of it all. "Do I look like mob material? Never mind, don't answer that." He paused. Let out a dramatic sigh. "It's a long story."

Glen plunked down on the couch next to Joe and said, "I've got nothing but time, Joey. Lay it on me."

Three beers later, Joe had filled his brother in on the whole story, from his initial meeting with Patty, right up to the narrow escape from the apartment.

"Well, that's about it," he said.

Glen stared at Joe for a very long time, speechless. At last, he said, "Wow, I had no idea my baby brother was such a badass." He grinned, exposing a perfect set of pearly whites.

"Glen, this isn't funny. It's my life at stake here."

The smile dissolved. "Sorry, of course it's not funny." Then he added, "I hate to say I told you so, but Kate has been nothing but bad news from day one."

Joe slammed down his beer and shot from the couch. "The last thing I need right now is a lecture about women, especially from someone who lives like a fucking hermit out in the middle of nowhere with his dog!"

He moved to the window and gazed out at the lake. Specks of light tap-danced across its glassy surface. A majestic bird, an eagle perhaps, glided across the open water, dipping and weaving, at last soaring high above the tree line and out of eyeshot. Joe longed to fly away, too, from this crazy new reality that was his life.

A hand rested on his shoulder. He flinched. Glen engulfed Joe in his impressive arms and hugged him tight. The weight of his situation hit Joe with the force of a hurricane. His body collapsed into itself, held up only by his brother. He sobbed and buried his face into Glen's chest, which felt carved out of granite.

"Whoa, Joey," Glen said. "Take it easy. Everything's going to be fine."

Joe pulled back. He locked eyes with his brother. "Really, Glen? Everything's going to be fine?" He swiped a hand across his face. "How the hell is everything going to be fine?"

Glen shrugged, then flashed that killer smile again and said, "Haven't I always been there for you, baby brother, when push came to shove?" Joe shrugged. Then nodded.

Blazer maneuvered himself between the brothers. For the second time, he began humping Joe's leg. Glen grinned. Joe laughed and said, "It looks like someone else is here for me, too."

His brother roared and hugged Joe, the tension eased by an oversexed mutt.

Glen released Joe from his bear hug. Joe noticed a faraway look in his brother's eyes. "Glen, what is it?"

Glen gripped his brother's shoulders and said matter-of-factly, "I've got a plan."

CHAPTER TWENTY-SEVEN

Mick-Mac staked out the house, watching for any sign of movement. Fifteen minutes went by. Nothing. "Fuck it," he said to his reflection in the rearview. He exited the car, glanced around for any nosy neighbors, then bee-lined it for the backyard.

It was quiet, private. Just an ordinary suburban home. But Mick-Mac suspected no ordinary suburban family resided here. He made his way across the deck, badly in need of refinishing and barren, aside from a beat-up grill and two cheap lawn chairs. Not exactly Party Central.

Mick-Mac approached a set of sliders. Stopped dead in his tracks. The slider was ajar. He slid his piece from its holster and peered inside. The décor was neat and tasteful, most likely done with a female's touch. No indication that any children had ever stepped foot in the place.

He listened for movement. When he was confident that he

was alone, he slid quietly inside. Upon closer inspection, he noticed the neat décor was not so neat after all. Wall hangings slightly askew. Drawers opened, their contents spilling across the floor. A shattered lamp.

So, Mick-Mac wasn't the only one interested in this Joe Campbell. Maybe the woman in those photos? Or maybe Guier-riero's henchmen? A glint of shattered glass caught his eye. One of those photo collage frames with the multiple windows, torn from its perch on a wall, now tossed carelessly on the floor. Several of the slots were now vacant, their photos having been hastily removed. But a few remained.

Mick-Mac stared at the remaining images. An attractive woman mugged for the camera in a few. In another, she embraced a rather ordinary man, not quite handsome but with an amiable face.

Is that you, Joe Campbell? What has a nice suburban guy like you gotten yourself mixed up in?

A sound. From above. Mick-Mac crouched, crab-walked toward the hallway. The sound again, subtle yet distinct. At the top of the staircase. Not the sounds of a house settling. No, someone or something was moving. He leveled his gun at the base of the staircase. A shadow.

"Show yourself," he said. He noticed a slight tremor in his voice. Silence. "I said show yourself now or I'll shoot!" No tremor in his voice this time.

A blurred figure shot down the staircase. He fired.

The cat, larger than a small dog, scuttled past him and disappeared down the hallway. *Fucking cat!* He exited the house, praying the row of hedges bordering the property was enough to conceal him. He took cover in the car. Waited for the sound of sirens. Of people running amok across their pristine lawns. None of that happened. Only the sounds of suburban life. Birds singing a shrill harmony. A dog barking in the distance. The steady hum of a lawnmower. A child's gleeful laugh.

Life continued as usual on this predictably boring street. A thirty-something guy jogged by, oblivious to everything except whatever motivational music was pumping through his earbuds. Children played blissfully, still immune to the disappointment life would one day dole out.

After a solid thirty minutes, Mick-Mac decided it was safe. He had to get back in that house before Eddie and the team swarmed the place, which could be at any minute. As he exited the vehicle, another thought occurred to him. His car, foreign to any residents, had been sitting in this spot for quite a while. And though none of them had been keen enough to distinguish the sound of a gunshot, a mysterious car parked on their street might just raise the eyebrows of a few. He hopped back in and started it up.

Once the car was tucked safely away on a nearby side road, he hightailed it back to the house. No sign of his good buddy Eddie Diaz. He sprinted around back and reentered the house, stepped over shimmery slivers of glass, and moved deeper into the house.

He made his way down a narrow hallway, stopping outside what appeared to be a home office. At the risk of exposing himself, he clicked on a light. A Red Sox jersey, emblazoned with ORTIZ 34 and signed by the legendary player, was framed and displayed on a wall behind a hefty antique desk. Papers and sketches lay scattered around a noticeably empty space in the center of the desk. Where a laptop most likely used to sit.

Mick-Mac scanned the room. A well-worn leather sofa to the left, a wall of bookcases to the right. An eclectic mix of genres stood at attention on the shelves. Crime fiction. Romance. Historical fiction and nonfiction. Guides and manuals on art direction, writing, and marketing. Self help. Home decorating and design.

He rummaged through the desk, finding the usual contents one would expect to find. A *ping* pierced the eerie silence. Mick-Mac recoiled, slicing his finger on a sharper-than-a-scalpel piece of paper. *Shit!* Why was it that a paper cut felt more painful than having your finger chopped off with a meat cleaver? Not that he'd ever experienced the latter, though he guessed it to be lower on the pain scale.

He sucked on the throbbing wound, looked at his phone, the cause of the injury. A text from his boss: *Where THE FUCK are you?*

Mick-Mac laughed, tried to remember the last time Eddie had sent a text that didn't include a curse word, all caps, or, in this case, both. He clicked off the phone and continued his search.

Just when he thought he'd come up with a big goose egg, he spotted a folded-up piece of paper tucked in the recesses of one of the drawers. It contained an address for someone named Glen. Funny, why wasn't this in the Rolodex right in front of him on the desk with all the other addresses? Even funnier was the fact that someone still used a Rolodex in today's high-tech world. Could this be the lead he was looking for? Besides, what else did he have to do other than road-trip it to New Hampshire?

He tucked the paper into his pocket. His cell lit up. Another text from Eddie.

Where the fuck you at Mick-Mac? Get YOUR ASS over to 6 Morningside Drive ASAP. Team on way.

6 Morningside Drive. Where he was now. He heard the crunch of gravel.

The team was here.

CHAPTER TWENTY-EIGHT

"You think it'll work?"

"You got a better idea?"

Joe shook his head. Though leery of his brother's plan, he had nothing else to offer up. In fact, he felt utterly hopeless. "Run it by me again."

Joe would call Patty. Assuming she answered, he would demand his wife back in exchange for the photos and Patty's notes on Guierriero. "As far as Patty knows, you still think Kate is an innocent victim and you'll do anything to get her back," Glen said. "She refuses and you say you're going to see that the stuff gets in the hands of Guierriero's son."

"I don't have the stuff," Joe said. "It's still in my office. Or with the cops."

"But they don't know that, do they?"

Joe shrugged halfheartedly. "I still don't get why we have to lure them here. Why not just go directly to them?"

Glen sighed. "Listen, Joey, we can't go into this guns-a-blazing like some Clint Eastwood movie. We need to take the upper hand here. On our own turf."

"And what if they don't come? Who's to say they won't just take the money and run?"

"You think they're going to risk having to deal with Guier-riero and his henchmen?" Glen smirked, then laughed.

"What the hell is so funny, Glen?"

Glen shook his head, still chuckling. "Just never thought I'd ever use the word *henchmen* in an actual conversation."

He laughed again, this time Joe joining in. At the pure absurdity of it all. "Welcome to my new normal," Joe said.

Glen got serious again. "They'll think they hold all the cards. As far as they know, you just want Kate back. And they won't be counting on your secret weapon."

"Which is?"

Glen laughed again. "Me." He furrowed his brow. "You're sure you never mentioned to Kate where I'm living these days?"

"You're the last thing that ever came up in conversation."

"That's good. They'll think they're meeting you at some remote location. Three of them, one of you. In their minds, they'll have you over a barrel. They get the evidence, take you out of the equation, and make their getaway."

Joe rubbed at the back of his neck, the vise tightening in his spine. "That's the part that worries me," he said. "Being taken out of the equation."

Glen put two meaty paws on Joe's unsteady shoulders. "That, my friend, is not going to happen."

Joe pulled away, fell into a chair. "Yeah, we've got that vicious attack dog of yours to fend them off. Maybe he can hump them to death." He fumbled in his coat pocket, produced the gun he'd almost forgotten he was still carrying. "Oh, and this."

Glen's eyes narrowed. "Wow, my baby brother really is a badass. Where did that come from?"

"Let's just say it was a gift." Joe placed it on the table with a loud thud.

Glen picked it up, caressing it gently, as if it were a baby bird. "A gift? From who, your mafia friends?" He winked.

"Come on, Glen," Joe said, "no more jokes, please." Then he added, "I don't even know how to use the damn thing."

"Then it's a good thing I do."

Joe sighed loud enough to stir Blazer from his slumber. "Great. A man and his gun and his dog. We've got nothing to worry about."

Glen sighed this time. "Joey, you've got to have faith." He leaned in, tugged on his brother's arm. "Come with me. There's something I need to show you."

CHAPTER TWENTY-NINE

Luckily for Mick-Mac, he'd been on the first floor when Eddie Diaz and his flunkies arrived. He was halfway out the window when he heard Diaz barking orders like a sous-chef on a busy Saturday night. His pant leg snagged on the windowsill. He heard a tearing sound, then a sharp pain ripped through his calf. He fell to the ground and rolled onto his belly. Voices. Outside. Heading toward the backyard where he lay sprawled out, blood oozing out of the two-inch gash in his leg.

He could just hear Diaz now, mocking him in Ricky Ricardo fashion. *You got some splainin' to do!* He pulled himself up, ditched it around to the side of the house. He pressed himself into the siding, listening to the voices that sounded only inches away.

"Hey, check this out," a voice he recognized as Dave Littlefield's said. "This window's open." Littlefield, an obese, perpetual smoker who reeked of nicotine and sweat, released a concerning cough in dire need of a doctor's attention.

The other voice, dripping with confidence, belonged to

Gina Gustafson, an ambitious rookie who knew just whose ass to kiss to slowly climb the rungs of the proverbial corporate ladder. Gina was undoubtedly the smartest member of the team. All she needed was a little more street time to show off her strengths, and she'd be knocking Eddie off his coveted throne. With astute focus and a keen eye for detail, she didn't miss a trick. "And there's blood on the sill," she said. *Good eye, Gina!*

Mick-Mac weighed his options. The backyard was out of the question, for obvious reasons. He'd be a sitting duck out front. That left the woods he was staring at. Woods that looked thick and riddled with thorns and all kinds of rash-inducing undergrowth. But what other option did he have? In a few moments, Gina would probably pop her head around the corner with her Sherlock Holmes Starter Kit.

"Let's get some samples," he heard Gina say. Littlefield coughed up a lung. Mick-Mac bolted for the tree line.

As he suspected, the brush was dense. Razor-sharp appendages poked and prodded him. He felt a twinge on his cheek and raised his hands to his face in defense. At last, he saw the light at the end of the tunnel. He pushed away the last of the treacherous branches and moved like a soldier toward his car.

Once safely in the car, he assessed the damage. Luckily, aside from the nick on his left cheek, his face remained unscathed. Tired and wan, but intact. His body was a different story. In addition to the bloody tear on the leg, small spots of red also spotted his shirt where the fabric had been punctured.

Another text. *Where are you Macavoy?* He pressed a Dunkin' Donuts napkin to his cheek to stop the flow, ran his fingers through his hair, and grabbed the sport coat balled up in the backseat. He figured he could brush off the mark on his cheek as a shaving mishap. The jacket hid the soiled shirt beneath it. The pants were a different story. Though he'd stanched the flow of blood from his calf, the red blossom staining his khakis couldn't be disguised.

Too late to go home and change. He'd have to wing it. He started the car and pulled up to 6 Morningside Drive. Maybe no one would notice the blood. He stepped out and moved up the walkway.

Officer Shawn Dixon, all puffed chest and on high alert, stood watch over the scene. As Mick-Mac approached, Dixon's toothy grin dissolved into a deep crease. "What the fuck happened to you, Mick-Mac?" His eyes motioned toward the leg. "Have a run-in with a lion?"

Think, Mick, think. "Actually, it was a dog," he said.

"A dog?" Dixon said incredulously. "What kind of dog?"

Mick-Mac owned the lie. "He was a small little shit, but he clamped on tighter than spandex at an all-you-can-eat buffet."

The toothy grin reappeared. Dixon laughed and said, "Diaz is pissed at you beyond belief. Better get your ass in there."

Mick-Mac saluted him and said, "On my way." He passed by a couple of other officers, who looked quizzically at his leg, then returned to their mindless banter. Upon entering, he was greeted by his superior. Diaz looked so incensed Mick-Mac thought he saw the guy's crew cut bristle.

"Well, well, if it isn't Boston's finest," Diaz said. Sarcasm dripped off the last word. He glanced down at the sanguineous spot marring Mick-Mac's pant leg, which appeared to have doubled in size. "What's that? Get into another bar brawl?"

Mick-Mac stuck to the lie. "It was a dog."

Diaz studied his face, then smirked. "Your grandmother been beating up on you again?"

Mick-Mac thought to one-up Eddie with a joke about his mother, then thought better of it. Instead, he said, "What can I say, Eddie? She's one tough old lady."

The lack of retaliation on Mick-Mac's part cut deeply. Diaz's face turned a rich shade of crimson. The bones on his clenched fists nearly popped through the blanched skin. "Just get to work," he said, a tremor in his voice. "And wipe that smirk off your ugly face."

Mick-Mac nodded and brushed past his superior, feeling the heat rising from the man's body. His smirk opened up into a full-fledged smile.

CHAPTER THIRTY

"What is this?"

"Were you expecting a wine cellar?"

Joe gazed around the room, slack-jawed and mesmerized. "Who are you?" he said incredulously. "*What* are you?"

Glen smiled. "I guess I should explain."

Joe's eyes scanned the room. The walls were painted in a drab shade of gunmetal. The concrete floor lent a cold, efficient air to the space. "Yeah, I think maybe you should."

"I never actually worked in finance."

"What do you mean? You were on Wall Street, you worked for—"

"No, Joey, I didn't. It was all for show. A cover."

"A cover for what?"

Glen glued his eyes to the floor, shuffled his feet on the coarse concrete, looking like a post-pubescent boy asking a girl on a first date. "Well, I—"

"Are you a spy?" Joe asked. He examined the assortment of guns and rifles, ammo, tasers, and one ominous crossbow.

Glen laughed. "Yeah, right, Joey. The name's Campbell. Glen Campbell." His eyes met Joe's. "If you mean, am I James Bond? The answer is no. Although I have been told I look like Daniel Craig on occasion."

"Then what? Your average law-abiding citizen doesn't have a bunker in his basement with enough firepower to take on a small country!"

Glen rested a meaty paw on his brother's trembling shoulder. "Easy, Joey. I was going to tell you. Eventually."

Joe brushed the hand away. The walls closed in around him. He stumbled toward the doorway, needing air. "So, what are you? A bounty hunter? An assassin? An arms dealer?"

Glen shuffled some more. "I'm not an arms dealer. I kind of work for the government."

Joe laughed. "Kind of? What are you? CIA? Special Ops?"

"I work alone," Glen said. "It's classified."

Joe laughed again, danced around his brother. "So, you are an assassin!" His voice cracked. "Well, brother, you always were a lone wolf. Hope you're at least killing bad guys."

Glen nodded, his usually tough exterior crumbling. "Of course. I'm not a bad person, Joe." Glen's face was painted in three shades of guilt, shame, and anguish. The first time Joe had ever seen a crack in the man's façade. He appeared deeply wounded by Joe's barb.

Joe moved toward the door, a heavy-duty steel number, then walked back and hugged his brother. For the first time, he felt like the big brother, the protector.

"Of course, you're not a bad person," Joe said. He pulled

back, locked gazes with his brother. "You're my hero. You always have been."

"Thanks, bro," Glen said. "Funny you should say that. I've always thought of you as my hero."

Joe frowned. "Bullshit, Glen. I'm no hero. Never have been."

Glen smacked him in the face. Harder than he probably meant to. "That's where you're wrong, Joey. You've always underestimated yourself, but you're the one who's always had his shit together."

Now it was Joe's turn to do the concrete shuffle. "Yeah, right." He massaged his still stinging cheek.

Glen gripped Joe's arms, the pressure of the big guy's strength reminding Joe he really should get back to the gym. "Listen, Joey, you think I had it all, right? The guts, the glory, the girls. Well, you'd be wrong."

"So, I guess I imagined all that shit about you being star quarterback, valedictorian, and the guy who got laid anytime he was within a mile of a girl."

"That was high school, bro. Things change."

"Then why don't you tell me all about it."

Glen sighed and said, "Alright, but first, let's get out of this musty old hole and grab a beer. Besides, I haven't shown you the whole place yet."

"Any more surprises I should prepare myself for?" Joe asked.

Glen smiled, shrugged, and started up the stairs.

CHAPTER THIRTY-ONE

Dom Jr. stared at the photo. So, this was the guy. How did a poor schlub like this take out his Padre, one of the most feared men in the country, maybe even the whole fucking world? And all he had was this picture of the smirking idiot with a woman who was way out of his league.

His goons had let the schmuck get away once and now a search of the guy's house had produced nothing but a few pictures. Maybe if he could find the beauty in the photo, he could use her as leverage to draw the fucker out.

A soft knock at the door. A knock he knew well. Desiree, his assistant and onetime lover. One of the few women he'd ever felt more than lust for. And one of the only people he truly trusted.

He signaled the okay, and the door yawned open. Desiree, looking as stunning as ever, nodded and sauntered into the room followed by a nerdish young man with disheveled, unwashed hair that fell haphazardly across a wan face that had probably never been touched by a speck of sunlight. Chunky black glasses added stark contrast to the man's pasty, feminine features. His jeans appeared to have been painted onto reed-like stalks. A beat-up messenger bag draped across an olive drab military-style jacket completed the hipster ensemble. Kids these days.

"This is Miles," Desiree said in a voice that always seemed to be out of breath. A voice that was sexy as hell.

After the useless goons surrounding him had failed him once again, Dom Jr. decided to try a new approach. And this bag of bones was his last hope. He summoned the young man forward.

"So, Miles, I'm told you're the best hacker on the East Coast," Dom Jr. said, reaching out to grip the man's waifish hand. If he squeezed a little bit tighter, he was sure he could crack every bone. The young man winced. Dom Jr. released his iron grip.

The young man massaged his tender fingers and said, "Yes, sir. But I could probably kick the West Coast's ass too."

Confidence. Dom Jr. liked that. Maybe this dork could get the job done after all. Dom Jr. turned to the delectable Desiree. "Love, would you see if the boy wants anything before we get started?"

"I'd love a Red Bull," he said eagerly. "The kiwi flavor is my favorite."

Desiree sighed. "Let me see what I can dig up." She shot Dom Jr. a subtle smile and left a smoldering trail of desire in her wake.

Miles shuffled his feet, nervousness creeping in around the edges of his smile. "She's nice," he said. "And pretty." Dom Jr.'s stern gaze held his, and the smile dissolved.

"Have a seat, Miles," Dom Jr. said, motioning to a slick,

minimalistic leather chair.

The man sat, squirmed a bit, and then said, "Nice chair. Comfy." Blood flooded his ashen complexion, turning an unhealthy shade of crimson. He pushed a soggy strand of hair back, exposing a moistened forehead. So much for the confidence.

Dom Jr. leaned against his desk, an imported hunk of wood his Padre had cherished, and looked at the quivering young man. "Relax, kid. I'm not going to bite you. I just need your help. And with what I'm offering to pay you, you can buy a life-time supply of that Red Bull kiwi shit."

Miles managed a slight smile, still unnerved by being face-to-face with the son of Dominic "The Skinner" Guierriero.

Desiree reentered, toting a can of Coke and a MacBook. "Sorry, kid, the guys must've polished off the last kiwi Red Bull." She threw Dom Jr. a quick wink. "Will a Coke do?"

Miles nodded dumbly, accepted the iconic can with a shaky hand. He raised the Coke to trembling lips, missing the target by a mile. The brownish liquid dripped from his chin, dotting his jacket and messenger bag.

Desiree stifled a laugh, shook her head and said, "He's all yours." She placed the MacBook on the desk before Dom Jr. "Will there be anything else?"

Dom Jr. shook his head and watched her beautiful exit once again. Then he turned his attention to Miles, who was surveying the mess on his clothing. "Listen up, kid," Dom Jr. said. The kid swiped at his chin and gazed intently at him. Dom Jr. pointed at the laptop. "Can you gain access to this?" Miles nodded, exhibiting that same cockiness he'd displayed earlier. Dom Jr. then held up the photo of Joe Campbell. "See this guy?" Miles nodded again. "I need you to find him."

CHAPTER THIRTY-TWO

The sun hung low, waiting impatiently for its coworker to take over the night shift. The wind had picked up since they'd walked down to the lake. The boathouse's weathered door swung lazily in the breeze. Glen reached for the door and they entered. Slivers of light trickled through the ancient structure's rotting façade.

I wanted to show you this before it gets dark," Glen said. Joe squinted. The scattering of light through the cracks in the walls created a dizzying effect, the rogue light rays ricocheting around them like a psychedelic laser show.

The structure housed two boats, one a weary Boston Whaler that Joe guessed to be around fifteen feet in length, the other a slightly larger Mastercraft racing boat. Joe caressed the Mastercraft's bow, a sleek fire-engine red polished to perfection. "She's a beauty," he said.

"Sure is," Glen replied. "She's my baby." He reached into a small wooden box nailed to the wall and pulled out a key on a leather fob. He tossed the key to Joe. "You want to take her out for a quick spin, brother?"

Joe snatched the key out of the air and said, "You leave the keys out here?"

Glen laughed and looked around. "Well, my friend, when your nearest neighbor lives over a mile away, the threat of theft isn't exactly a big concern."

Joe shrugged. "I guess. Anyway, it's getting a little late to take it out now." He tossed the key back at his brother. "Personally, I wouldn't risk the chance of someone making off with it."

"Probably right," Glen said and slipped the key in his pocket. "Maybe tomorrow I'll take you for a spin in her. If we're still alive," he said with a wink.

Joe pointed to the dull, weather-worn Boston Whaler. "You mean that's not your baby?"

"Hey, don't knock Old Molly," Glen said. "She may look a little worse for wear, but she gets the job done."

"Molly?" Joe said. "One of your many conquests? Must've been special if you named a boat after her."

Glen laughed. "No, numbnuts. She's named after Molly Brown. You know, the Unsinkable Molly Brown?"

Joe nodded. "Yeah, I get it." Joe knew the whole history of the Boston Whaler, thanks to Dear Old Dad. Back when life was simple and their family was intact, Tom Campbell used to take his boys on annual fishing trips in a Boston Whaler, not unlike the one before him now. During the family's last summer as a whole, the elder Campbell had distilled the entire history of the Boston Whaler as they lazed on the picturesque Lake Winnipesaukee, its history of which the elder Campbell had enlightened his boys on during a previous summer. Joe could still hear the raspy voice. *Look around, boys. Ain't she just beautiful? You know why they call her Winnipesaukee? Cuz it means 'smile of the Great Spirit.'*

On that postcard-perfect day, as Joe struggled to catch one lousy fish (of course, Glen had already reeled in half a dozen whoppers), Tom regaled them with his endless knowledge of the Boston Whaler. Designed of a buoyant foam material, the Whaler was virtually unsinkable. According to Dear Old Dad, the boat could be completely swamped and still remain afloat.

Halfway into his second six-pack of Miller Lite, Tom Campbell went on to say that you could saw the boat in half, and it wouldn't sink. That's when the perfect day turned ugly.

Though Joe doubted this story was true (only years later, he found out it was), he had enough sense not to cross the old man when the beer was flowing. Unfortunately, his fifteen-year-old brother did not. When Glen, already bigger and stronger than the old man, mouthed off and called his dad a liar, all hell broke loose. Fists were thrown, blood spilled, and the boat was swamped. And though the boat didn't sink, the already strained relationship between Glen and Tom Campbell did. It was the last time Joe had been to Lake Winnipesaukee. And the last time his brother and father had spoken.

"Earth to Joe!" Glen's booming voice shook him from his reverie. "It's getting dark. We should get back to the house."

Joe shook off the old demons and nodded. They climbed the steep hill back to the house, the cool breeze gently nipping at Joe's face. "Hey, Glen?"

"Yeah?"

"You ever get back to Winnipesaukee?"

Glen laughed and punched his brother in the arm. "Now, why the hell would I want to go back there?"

Joe shrugged. "Just thought. It's not that far. Maybe going back would give you, I mean us, some closure."

Glen stopped dead in his tracks. "Really, Joey?" he said incredulously. "Do you really believe that?"

Joe shrugged again. "Never mind. Bad idea. Forget I mentioned it."

Glen punched him in the arm again, only softer and more heartfelt. "No, maybe you're right. Maybe it would do us some good."

"You serious?"

Glen smiled that toothy grin Joe envied. "Yeah, let's do it. Just you and me. And good old Miss Molly back there." Glen's smile dissolved as quickly as the sun on the horizon. "But first things first. You have a call to make."

CHAPTER THIRTY-THREE

The evening rush hour congestion through Boston was the usual shitshow. Work-weary commuters cursed, beeped, and texted as they jockeyed for position, in a hurry but going nowhere fast. A red-faced businessman, gripping his steering wheel with unyielding determination, pulled up alongside Mick-Mac. Their eyes locked, and the guy assaulted him with a string of silent expletives. Mick-Mac kissed the air, which kicked the man's tirade into overdrive. Just what Mick-Mac had intended. The guy threw his sporty BMW into high gear and tried to nudge in front of Mick-Mac.

Up for a little spirited competition, Mick-Mac accelerated. *Bring it, bitch.* The man over-corrected, then braked. The sound of crunching metal interrupted Metallica's *Enter Sandman.* Mick-Mac glanced in the rearview in time to see the man, his shiny sports car a crumpled mess, thrust a middle finger his way. Mick-Mac smiled, cranked up the radio, and joined James Hetfield for some head-banging action.

As the Boston skyline dissolved on the horizon, the traffic on I-93 thinned out. A light mist dotted the windshield, just enough to be an annoyance. Mick-Mac eased the seat back and settled in for the two-hour-or-so drive to his destination.

What would he do when he got there? How did he even know the elusive Joe Campbell would be there? It was just a hunch. But hunches were what sometimes solved the most head-scratching of cases. A hastily written address secreted away in the back of a junk drawer wasn't much, but something about it smelled right. He'd check it out, see who this *Glen* was. If it turned up nothing, all he'd have wasted was a tank of gas and a night of sitting in front of the tube eating whatever left-overs he could scrape up. Alone.

Things hadn't always been that way. He'd been happy once. Over the moon in love. They'd met at a cousin's wedding a decade ago. A lifetime ago. Mick-Mac hadn't planned on attending. He'd been going through another of his loathsome self-pity parties. After relentless urging from his cousin, he'd reluctantly agreed.

The plan was to stay for the toast, then slip out the back. Dodging dear old Aunt Eunice, he made a break for it. Then he saw her.

She was breathtaking, but not in a movie-star-glamour way. The exit sign beckoned him. Aunt Eunice spotted him, signaled for him to join her and her cronies. He smiled and bee-lined it to the bar. She was even more stunning up close. Natural looks without the pretension. An elegant black dress accentuated her creamy, flawless complexion. Thin, delicate lips were pursed, not in anger but in deep thought, Mick-Mac decided. Her almond-shaped, bottomless blue eyes were mystical, casting a hypnotic, dizzying spell on anything in their sights.

Mick-Mac held his breath, intoxicated by her subtle yet potent scent. He was well beyond the boundaries of her personal space, but she hadn't noticed him. He could leave now. No harm, no foul, as his father used to say. Although he considered himself attractive in a boyish way, or so he'd been told, he was nowhere close to the chiseled Adonises this woman probably had breaking down her door. *Nice try, Mick. Time to cut your losses.* He turned to go, accidentally brushed her shoulder.

She faced him, those eyes sucking him into the vortex. "I'm sorry," she said in a sultry voice that completed the package.

Mick-Mac felt the heat rising in his neck, spilling into his cheeks. A phenomenon he experienced whenever he ate spicy food, drank red wine, or was at a loss for words. His brain signaled his mouth to get its shit together. "Sorry, my fault," he stammered.

Her face softened. "I'm Marnie." She extended a firm hand. Despite its gracefulness, her grip exuded confidence. Mick-Mac swallowed his voice. Marnie laughed. "Do you have a name?"

"Mickey," he mumbled. "Or Mick. My friends call me Mickey."

"Then Mickey it is," she said. "Can I buy you a drink, Mickey?"

The love affair lasted nearly two years. Despite all the naysayers and come-ons from dozens of men Mickey thought more worthy of this woman, the relationship flourished. They'd settled comfortably into a modest apartment in Cambridge. Mickey graduated from the Boston Police Academy, Marnie beaming with pride.

A talented writer, Marnie enrolled in a master's program in screenwriting at Emerson College. A fitness enthusiast, she biked to class weather permitting, which it was that cloudless, postcard-perfect day in May.

Mickey had been off after working a double shift. He'd slept in late, then Marnie had called saying classes were canceled due to a water main break on campus and did Mickey want to meet her for lunch at her favorite nearby French bistro. Mickey was tired but between him picking up extra shifts and Marnie busy with end-of-semester projects, their quality time together had been scarce as of late.

Mickey grabbed a quick shower and texted Marnie that if it was okay with her, he preferred a burger and a beer. Marnie, always the team player, agreed. On his way over to the pub on Boylston, Marnie texted, saying she'd run into a classmate and was running a few minutes late.

As Mickey strolled up to the pub, his instincts told him something wasn't right. Maybe it was the look of terror displayed by the elderly couple standing stock-still just up ahead. Or the young woman moving toward him more quickly than someone in heels typically did. The woman approached, fear etched into her soft features. She brushed by Mickey and yelled, "There's a man with a gun in the 7-Eleven!"

Mickey reached for his gun and ordered everyone to take cover. Passersby within earshot went into panic mode, scattering like cockroaches. Mickey approached the 7-Eleven with caution. Just feet away from the entrance, the door burst open and a tall, masked man barreled onto the now vacant sidewalk.

"FREEZE!" Mickey yelled.

The man fired. Mickey dove for cover behind a trash receptacle. Peeking from behind the bin, he spotted the gunman, now pressed against the convenience store's façade, appearing agitated and desperate. Then he saw something else. His muscles seized. His heart tensed. A one-two punch to the gut stole his breath.

Marnie. Pedaling up the empty sidewalk, oblivious to the danger ahead. Mickey rose, not caring that he was exposed, not caring if the gunman took him down. As long as Marnie was safe. Marnie spotted him and tossed him a wave. Mickey waved his arms in desperation. Marnie's smiling face turned to one of confusion and then comprehension. Her smile dissolved into a mask of dread.

The gunman emerged, taking aim at Mickey. The approaching bicycle, slowing yet still coming at a good clip, startled the man. He opened fire. Mickey bolted forward, unloading a barrage on the gunman.

Even as he cradled her still beautiful yet lifeless face in his arms, he insisted it was someone who resembled his one and only love. Even as her body was lowered into the ground on a dreary, rain-swept day, he convinced himself that was not her in that shiny steel box.

Even years later, he'd catch a glimpse of her on a street corner or in a store window. He'd take pursuit, only to be gazed at in horror by nameless, faceless women as he screamed her name.

A blaring horn shook Mick-Mac from his reverie. He'd drifted into the lane of an oncoming SUV, nearly sideswiping the much-larger vehicle. The previous drizzle was now a downpour. Through blurred eyes and monotonous sweeps of the wipers, he spotted a neon light indicating food, gas, and lodging. He exited the highway, ready to call it a night and sink his head into a cheap, germ-infested motel pillow. He put the car in park and killed the engine. He saw Marnie again. He squeezed his eyes shut, wishing away the image. That only brought things more into focus. The relentless torrent pummeled the car, obliterating his piercing wails.

CHAPTER THIRTY-FOUR

"She's not going to answer."

"You won't know unless you try," Glen said to his baby brother. "And if she's as bat-shit crazy as you say she is, she won't be able to resist."

Joe sighed and stared at the cheap burner phone Glen had pulled from a drawer Joe guessed contained a dozen more. "You're probably right. Funny, as fucked up as this situation is, there's a weird chemistry between us."

Glen slapped him upside the head. "Hey Loverboy, did you forget you're the numero uno suspect in the biggest mob hit in recent memory thanks to that bitch?"

Joe swatted at his brother's hand and said, "Yeah, bro, thanks for reminding me. I'd forgotten that she totally fucked up my life."

Glen ruffled Joe's mop. Joe pulled away in annoyance. He was growing tired of the slaps, the punches, and the ruffles. "The reason I said that is because we had kind of a Hannibal

Lecter-Clarice thing going on. So, I think you're right. She'll feel compelled to pick up."

Glen put a finger to his lips. "Remind me, which one are you? Lecter or Clarice?"

Joe shrugged. "These days, your guess is as good as mine." He began dialing, her number oddly committed to memory. "Well, here goes nothing."

"Remember," Glen said, "you think Kate's an innocent victim and all you want is to get her back."

Joe grimaced and waved off his brother. One ring. Then another. He expected an automated voice telling him the number he had dialed was no longer in service. Instead, he heard the familiar "Hello?" He froze. Glen shrugged, his face awash in confusion.

The raspy voice cut through him. "Hello? Who the fuck is this?" Her words were a bit slurred, as if she'd had a stroke or tossed off a few too many Jamesons. He'd bet his life on the latter. She muttered something incomprehensible. He sensed she was about to disconnect.

"Patty. It's me. Joe."

More garbled mumbling. Then she said, "That you, Cowboy? Well, I'll be damned. How the hell are you?"

"I've had better days, Patty."

The laughter on the other end turned to that signature cough Joe knew too well. "I'll bet you have, Cowboy," she said between coughs. "Thought Little Dom or the boys in blue would have caught up with you by now."

Glen nudged him to get on with it. Once again, Joe brushed him away. Glen was really starting to bug the shit out of him. "Well, Patty," he said, "I guess I'm a little more resilient than I thought." Then he added, "Oh, sorry, I forgot you don't like it

when I use the big grown-up words. *Resilient* means tough."
That ought to get her going.

He was right. Angry Patty spit venom through the phone
with such force it startled Joe. "I know what the fuck it means,
you arrogant piece of shit!" Ah, there was the Patty he knew
and loathed. "I only wish I could be there when Little Dom
peels the skin right off your fuckin' face!"

The plan to get her pissed off had worked. Time to move in
for the kill. "If he doesn't get you first."

Silence. Then mumbling, as if she were whispering to someone. Finally, she said, "And why would he do that? It's you he's
after. It's your ugly face all over the TV. You're a regular old
celebrity these days. Gangster Joe. Maybe that's what I'll start
calling you."

Though Joe was trembling, his steady voice exuded coolness.
"You so sure about that, Patty? Maybe you've forgotten about all
the photos you gave me. The handwritten notes. Something
about wanting to kill that bastard. It's all right in my hands,
wrapped in a big red bow, ready to hand over to Little Dom, as
you call him."

Again, more indecipherable muttering. The anger in her
voice was still there. Only now, it was coated in fear. "You
wouldn't do that," she demanded. "You go to him and you're as
good as dead."

"The way I look at it, I'm fucked either way. This way, I get
to fuck us both."

"I could disappear tonight," Patty said. "Hop a plane and
never be seen or heard from again."

Joe had counted on her playing that card. But his hand was
better. "You could do that, Patty. You could take your chances
that Little Dom will just let it slide. After all, it's only his dear

old dead daddy and how many millions of dollars probably soaked with daddy's blood."

"You fucker! I'll rip your face off myself!"

"Your call, Patty. Maybe you can run and hide. But for how long? My guess is that Little Dom will make it his one and only mission to hunt you down, however long, at whatever cost. But you probably know him better than I do. Word of advice?"

He could hear her labored breathing, could almost see the heat coming through the phone. "What's that?" she said, worry in her voice.

"I'd grow a set of eyes in the back of that crazy head of yours, because you're going to be looking over your shoulder until the day your sorry ass dies."

Glen gave a thumbs-up as the brothers listened to breaking glass and incoherent shrieks echo through the bare-bones Samsung flip phone. A deeper voice mixed in with Patty's shrill one, the screaming and smashing reaching a crescendo.

Joe waited, wondering if he'd pushed her too far, fearing she'd disconnect. But that was just not in Patty's nature. "Okay, Cowboy, what do you want?"

Joe breathed heavily, relieved the hook was still in place. "I want Kate back."

That shut her up. Joe imagined the stunned look on her face as she was struck by the realization that Joe didn't know. Which gave her the upper hand. Or so she thought.

"You want...all you want is..."

Joe had to stifle a laugh, picturing the confusion buzzing around in her head. "That's right. You took my wife. I want her back. Unharmed. You do that, I hand everything over to you and you go rot on some tropical island. Deal?'

"That's it?" she said. "Tit for tat?"

"Whatever you want to call it, Patty. One more thing."

Patty groaned. "What?"

"I want to talk to Kate."

"You what?"

"You heard me. How do I know she isn't already dead?"

"The girl is fine and dandy," Patty said.

"Then prove it. Otherwise, we have no deal and I hang up." Joe regretted saying that last part, hoping she wouldn't call his bluff.

She didn't. "Hold on."

Glen high-fived him. The plan seemed to be working. They waited.

"Hello?" The timid, distraught voice was barely audible. She'd always played the victim a little too well.

Joe could act, too. *And now, playing the role of the grieving husband, Joe Campbell.* "Kate, darling?" he said. "Are you okay? Did they hurt you?"

Kate's sobs were almost convincing, bordering slightly on camp. "Oh, sweetie, please just do whatever they say." Her voice cracked. *Nice touch, honey.* "I miss you and I love you." Okay, maybe a little too far with that last bit.

"Love you too," he said, gnashing his teeth. "See you soon."

Patty was back. "Okay, Cowboy, here's what we're gonna do. You meet me tomorrow at the—"

"NO! Listen up. From here on out, we do things my way. Stay close to your phone. I'll call you back with the plan." With that, he disconnected the call.

"Joey," Glen said. "I'm impressed. Didn't know you had it in you."

Joe swiped at the beads of sweat popping through his pores.

His body trembled. Heart clawed at his chest. He looked at his brother. "I'm not so sure I do," he said.

Blazer trotted into the room, tennis ball in mouth, ready for his daily game of catch. He nudged Glen. "Not now, Blazer," he said, pointing to Blazer's bed. Blazer, disappointment glinting in those always-alert black eyes, turned his attention to Joe as if to say, *What about you?* Joe reached for the ball. Glen's voice boomed. "I said not now. Go to your bed, boy." Blazer shot Joe one last hopeful look, then skulked off to his bed with a loud sigh.

The weight of the day finally crash-landed on Joe's shoulders. His head throbbed. "What if Patty changes her mind between now and tomorrow and does her disappearing act?"

Glen shook his head. "You said yourself, she's running scared. Remember, she thinks she's got the upper hand. Three of them against lonely old you. The rest of the world might think you're some mob-killing, workplace-killing maniac. But she knows the truth. And, no offense, Joey, but you're not very badass."

"None taken," Joe said. "Still the same pushover I've always been."

"No, Joey, that's not what I meant."

Joe shrugged. "I know you didn't," he said. "But it's true. That's why Kate saw me as the perfect scapegoat for their little plan. They played me beautifully."

"And now we're going to play them right back," Glen said, his voice rising enough to stir Blazer from his slumber. Then he added, "You look like shit. Why don't you go get some sleep? I'll make sure everything is prepped for tomorrow."

Joe yawned, his brother's remark reminding him of how

exhausted he was. "Okay, you're right. Maybe just a couple of hours."

Glen pointed. "Second room down the hall on the right. Towels and whatever shit you need are in the closet. And please, take a shower. You reek."

"Thanks, Glen," Joe said. "Really, man. I mean it. Without you, I don't know who I could've turned to."

"Hey, that's what family is for, right?"

Joe nodded sleepily. He trudged down the hall, Blazer eyeing his every move. He stopped and turned to his brother. "Hey, Glen?"

"Yeah, Joey?"

"When all this is behind us, let's do that Winnipesaukee thing. Just you and me. For old times' sake."

Glen smiled. "Sounds good. But I think you're forgetting someone." He motioned to Blazer, now fully alert, tail in motion.

CHAPTER THIRTY-FIVE

"Mr. Guierriero!"

Dom Jr. nearly fell off his chair as the lanky hipster charged into his office, followed by a fuming Desiree. "What the fuck?"

Desiree threw up her arms. "I told him nobody comes in here without my say-so, but the little prick ran right by me." She shot Miles a killer glance. Dom Jr. always thought she was at her most stunning when she was angry. Right now, she looked ravenous.

Miles, seemingly on a Red Bull high, shifted nervously from foot to foot. "I'm sorry, Mr. Guierriero." He held up the laptop. "There was nothing of use on it."

Dom Jr. stood and emerged from behind the colossal desk. "It's okay, Desiree," he said, motioning for the young man to sit. "You can leave us." Desiree nodded curtly and slipped out without a sound.

Dom Jr. leaned on the desk, crossed his arms, and studied the man. "What do you mean, nothing?"

Miles started to rise, then sank back into the chair on Dom Jr.'s command. "Well, it turns out your guy has a pretty boring life." Miles chuckled. "Even more boring than mine. Mostly just work stuff. And some writing stuff—just a bunch of short stories and I think the start of a novel, maybe."

Dom Jr. sighed. "You're absolutely sure? What about anything he may have deleted?"

Miles shook his head. "Oh, yeah. Well, most people think when they permanently delete emails, they're gone forever. But they're always still out there." Miles motioned dramatically to the heavens.

"So, you found something then?"

Miles shook his head again. "I checked everything he deleted, even the deleted things he deleted. Nada."

Dom Jr. moved to the window, gazed out at the dusky sky. "Shit!" A giggle. A schoolgirl's giggle. "Are you laughing at me, you little twit?" He lunged at Miles.

Miles recoiled, throwing his gangly arms up, nearly dropping the laptop. As Dom Jr. went for the throat, Miles yelled, "I found him!"

Dom Jr. grabbed him by the collar of his jacket, which felt as grungy as it looked. "Are you fucking with me, kid?" He released his grip.

"No, sir," Miles said, his voice tinged with fear.

"But you said there was nothing on the—"

"But there was on his phone," Miles interrupted. He placed the laptop down and reached into his pocket. "I was able to hack into his phone." He pulled out his phone, and the screen lit up.

"You can do that?" Dom Jr. said incredulously.

Miles nodded. "You can if you're me." Fear was a distant memory now, replaced by arrogance. "Check out these text messages."

Dom Jr. snatched the phone from Miles, his eyes locking in on the illuminated screen.

Joe

Need your help. Urgent. Respond asap

Glen

Joey? Just saw you on TV. WTF? Tried calling you. Keeps going to voicemail. What have you gotten yourself into?

Joe

I'm being set up. Need to get out of here. Can you help?

Glen

Get your ass here bro!!!!

Joe

Still in Franconia?

Glen

Where else would I be? Remember how to get here?

Joe

No. Only been once. Can't find address.

Glen

You want exit 38 off 93. I can send directions from there

Joe

give me address & I'll gps it

Glen

5 Mountain Pass Lane

Joe

Thanks bro on my way
Glen

be careful. Luv you bro
Joe

Luv you too Glen

Dom Jr. smiled. Miles smiled right back. "Nice work, kid."

The kid's smile dissolved. He furrowed his brow, his pasty face a portrait of apprehension. "So, is it okay if I go now, sir?"

Dom Jr. gripped the kid's brittle shoulders. "Of course you can go." He patted the kid's stubbly face. "Of course."

Miles cracked an unconvincing smile. He nodded and high-tailed it for the door.

"Miles?" The kid stopped in his tracks. "Aren't you forgetting something?" The kid turned. "You do want your money, don't you, kid?"

Miles did his shuffling act and said, "That's okay, Mr. Guierriero. I'm good." He turned toward the door.

"Nonsense, son," Dom Jr. said. "You did what was asked, didn't you?"

"I guess so," Miles stammered.

"Then you earned your keep." Dom Jr. moved toward the desk. "Kid, you'll never amount to anything if you go around giving free handouts to everyone. Take what's rightfully yours. That's what my father always told me."

"Ok-k-ay," Miles spit out. "Thank you, sir."

The desk drawer slid open. Dom Jr. reached in, pulled something out. Miles flinched. "Well, kid, are you going to take what's rightfully yours or not?"

Miles moved forward like a death row inmate taking that long last walk. He reached for the outstretched hand and gingerly took the brick of cash.

"Now go on and buy yourself some stock in that Red Bull shit you love, kid," Dom Jr. said.

The kid relaxed, the tautness in his body exhaling. He grinned and tucked the brick into that oh-so-trendy messenger bag. "Thanks again," he said and moved toward the exit.

Dom imagined the kid was dreaming of that Red Bull shit as the bullet exploded in his brain. Miles hit the floor without a sound.

"Sorry about that, kid," he said, wishing he'd had the sense to avoid the mess blossoming out on that carpet Padre had loved so much.

CHAPTER THIRTY-SIX

"We should leave now."

Patty Quigley stubbed out her cigarette, twisting her toe with increasing anger. "We leave when I say we leave." Rufus opened his big fat mouth to speak again, but she put up a defiant hand. "That little pissant ain't going to threaten me and live to tell about it."

"But, Aunt Patty," Katie argued, "what if he's setting us up? I agree with Rufus. We should get the hell out of here tonight."

Patty lit up another cigarette and gazed at her niece. "You know him better than any of us, sweetie. Do you really think that twit has it in him to do anything?" Katie looked to her feet for answers. "No, I didn't think so," Patty added.

Rufus threw up his gorilla arms in defeat and fumed out of the room. His puppy dog skittered out behind him.

Patty let out a puff of smoke and gazed out at the street-lit night. A light mist blurred her vision. Maybe the kids were right. They could just pack up and hop the next flight to Fiji or wherever they wanted.

No. They couldn't.

They didn't know Little Dom the way she did. As impossible as it was to believe, he was more ruthless than his father. There was nothing but ice in that heart. Patty knew all too well. She'd seen what Little Dom was capable of. She'd watch from the shadows as he forced himself on the new girls, brutalizing them without mercy. She still hated herself for standing by in silence. But what could she do?

And the tortures. Sure, most of those lowlifes deserved what they got. But the viciousness with which Little Dom exacted his revenge was beyond reprehensible. Sometimes he made the girls watch. Took pleasure in watching them squirm.

She was not going to spend the rest of her life looking over her shoulder. If it meant delaying their departure by a day or two, so be it. Besides, she had the power. Cowboy was naïve to think Katie loved him, or ever had. Which is why they'd chosen him from the get-go. He was the perfect patsy. Just a puppet on a string.

And Patty was the master puppeteer. Had been from the start. Sweet Katie had done her part, played her role well. Lured in the pathetic nice guy, charmed him with her beauty, inserted the hook. Rufus, dumber than a box of rocks, was the muscle. Nothing more, nothing less.

She'd been wanting Dominic dead long before Charlene's death. The beatings, the sordid sex rituals, the constant state of fear he'd imposed on her. And to think this was the man she'd fallen in love with. Her protector. Her soulmate. But those things only happened in the movies.

Charlene's death had been the breaking point. She'd been in

the wrong place at the wrong time. In fact, it was Patty who should've been there, would've been there if not for a bad case of food poisoning.

Dominic had a so-called high-profile meeting and needed Patty to come along to smoothly seal the deal. In other words, fuck this high-profile client into submission. In the beginning, Patty was flattered. Flattered that Dominic held her body in such regard. But that feeling quickly dissolved and resentment took hold. And so, the food poisoning, painful as it was, came as a blessing.

Charlene, always Dominic's number two girl, reluctantly agreed to the gig. Patty could still see the fear in her eyes as she waved goodbye and told her to get better soon.

Later that night, Patty was roused from a deep sleep by a distraught Charlene. The high-profile meeting turned out to be with a sleazy government official whose sexual fetishes were sleazier than his politics. Things got out of hand, and Charlene, never the wallflower, fought back. She escaped with a dislocated shoulder and a bloodied face.

"You shoulda seen the other guy," she said through choked tears.

During the struggle, a broken wine glass found its way lodged deep in the sleazebag's throat. Dominic told Charlene everything would be okay. And there she was, spilling her guts to Patty, fear coating every word. Patty reassured her everything would be just fine, that she'd never allow anything to happen to her.

Two days later, Charlene was dead. A heroin overdose, according to Dominic. Which Patty knew was a lie. Unlike Patty, Charlene never touched the stuff, vehemently chastised Patty for partaking in it. Patty knew questioning Dominic would only lead to another overdose, or something much worse.

Instead, she hatched a plan. A plan that took patience. Patience she had. What she needed was a scapegoat. Katie was easy to rope in. Devastated by her mother's murder, she wanted revenge. Her natural beauty and charm only made the fishing that much easier.

The fall guy had to be a writer. So, Katie enrolled in writing classes at the local college and blended in with the creative crowd. One guy in particular caught her eye. Not for his looks. Not for his dynamic personality. No, this guy had to be vulnerable, easily cajoled, easily molded.

Joe Campbell checked off all those boxes.

All she needed next was opportunity. Dominic had been meeting at a shithole called Griffin's for most of his private meetings and transactions. Why he'd chosen a place like that Patty could never understand. Although, in hindsight, it made perfect sense. Discreet. Forgettable.

She occasionally accompanied Dominic to these meetings. That was when Rufus entered the plot. The guy was a tank, just stupid enough to coerce yet smart enough to keep his shit together. Once again, Katie worked her wiles and roped the big lunk in more easily than she'd been able to do with Cowboy.

And the plan was set in motion.

Cowboy could be bluffing. After all, he'd have to be insane to willingly be in the same room with Little Dom. Then again, like he said, he was fucked either way. She couldn't risk it. Besides, it would be like taking candy from a baby.

He still believed his dear little Katie was the helpless victim tied to the railroad tracks waiting for her Dudley Do-Right to ride in and rescue her in the eleventh hour. The guy was so easily manipulated, so trusting. So dead.

She'd watch as Rufus made him suffer, just as she'd watched so much suffering over the years. Only this time, she'd watch with glee. Maybe she'd even let Katie take his final breath. She stared at her phone, willing it to ring. *What are you waiting for, Cowboy? I'm ready to play. Bring it on.* The phone stared silently back at her. Maybe she should try getting some shut eye. Only she knew there'd be no sleeping tonight, or any night, until she watched one Joe Campbell take his last breath, her smiling face his final memory.

CHAPTER THIRTY-SEVEN

Threatening clouds loomed heavy in the distance, casting an ominous pall over the restless lake. The waves lapped thirstily at the dock, spilling across its weather-weary surface. A lone bird perched itself on the dock's railing, gazing skyward, stock-still, as if unaware of the approaching menace.

The early morning air was heavy and damp, sending a shiver through Joe's body. What if Patty called his bluff and skipped town, leaving him to face the wrath of Guierriero? What if Kate sensed he knew the truth about her? What if...

"Joey!" His brother's booming voice snapped him back to reality. "Where are you?"

Joe moved toward the kitchen, the busy sounds and smells of breakfast leading the way. Glen stood shirtless, coffee pot in hand, a perfect specimen that would make Michelangelo's David blush. "There you are." He hoisted the coffee pot. "You look like you could use some of this."

Joe nodded and slid into a chair. He'd hardly slept, and his head throbbed.

"How do you take your eggs?"

"Not hungry."

"You okay, bro?" Glen said. "Look shittier than you did last night." He plunked a hefty mug in front of Joe. The steamy contents beckoned him. He lifted the mug. It was like lifting a dumbbell.

"Didn't get much sleep," he replied. "Guess I've got a little on my mind."

Glen laughed. "Well, drink up. We've got work to do."

"What kind of work?"

Glen grinned that shit-eating, Cheshire Cat grin. "It's a surprise."

Joe sighed and took a swig of coffee. "I don't think I can handle any more surprises."

His brother hoisted him up. "C'mon, little brother. It'll be fun."

"If you're going to own a gun, you need to know how to shoot one."

"I don't own a gun."

"Well, you waltzed in here toting one."

"It isn't mine. And I don't intend on using it."

Glen's eyes narrowed. "Joey, let's get real. Do you think those lowlifes are coming with tea and scones? You need to be prepared."

"I thought that's what you were here for," Joe said. "Besides,

I'd rather give that thing a go." He pointed and smiled like a schoolboy getting his first look at porn.

The glossy gunmetal crossbow glimmered from its perch on the wall. Its draw was alluring. It looked part medieval, yet equal parts futuristic—like something you'd see in a mash-up of *Braveheart Meets The Terminator*.

"Uh-uh," Glen said. "Too dangerous."

Joe laughed. "And a gun's not?"

"A gun is easier to handle and there's less chance of you accidentally killing yourself. Or me."

Joe scoffed. "I'm not going to kill anyone. I just want to try it." He moved toward the sensual weapon like a moth to a flame.

Glen deflected him. "Down, boy. Okay, I'll show you. But it's not a toy. Grab that box and meet me out on the back lawn."

Joe lifted a box containing assorted guns and ammo. It was heavier than expected and his efforts to hide his struggle were in vain. Glen shook his head, rolled his eyes, and said, "Let's go take on the world, badass."

CHAPTER THIRTY-EIGHT

The dream is always the same. He and Marnie are making love as a steady rain hammers the skylight above. Their bodies move in rhythm with the perpetual drumming. They reach climax as a shot of lightning lights up the room. The room is familiar, though he doesn't know why. The angry sky ignites the room again. Marnie is now standing at the foot of the bed, fully clothed, backpack slung loosely over her shoulder, hair slightly mussed.

The darkness swallows her up. Her voice is barely audible over the rain, now a relentless torrent. "Gotta run, Mick."

"Where?" he asks.

The room lights up again. Marnie is grinning. "I've got class to get to, silly."

"But the weather," he says. "Come back to bed."

In the darkness she calls, louder this time, "A little rain never killed anyone."

He waits in the black silence. A crack of lightning strikes the skylight above, shattering the glass. As the slivers of glass rain down on *him, the spot where Marnie stood is now occupied by Eddie Diaz. "You'd better go after her, Mick," he says. "She'll catch her death of cold out there." Diaz's baleful laugh is more terrifying than the thunderous booming around him.*

Mick races out the door, down the stairs, into the violent night, the rain like daggers slicing at his naked body. He sees her up ahead, pedaling her shiny Schwinn with the speed and grace of an Olympian. His feet slap the raw pavement, but she pedals faster, moving further away. A mesmeric orb of light ahead.

"Marnie!" he screams but his voice is swept up in the gale. An intersection ahead. Green turns to yellow turns to red. She'll stop. Instead, she pedals faster, further distancing herself from him. He pumps his muscles faster, pain seizing his body. The light brightens as it bears down on her. An ear-splitting crack of thunder. Then a loud flash of lightning consumes her.

"Housekeeping!"

Mick-Mac sat bolt upright, dizzied by the disorienting blackness. He groped desperately in the dark, panic seizing him. Blindness had always been his greatest fear. He clawed at his face, tugging at his eyes. His greatest terror now a stark reality. He let out a guttural cry and thrashed violently in his pitch-dark world.

Then he saw it. A sliver of light. From beneath a doorway. The fog lifted, and he remembered he was in some shithole motel in some shithole town. He untangled himself from the sheets and planted his feet on a carpet nearly as damp as his t-shirt.

The person on the other side of the door knocked gently, as

if they feared they were waking a beast. Which is what he felt like at the moment. Another *rap-rap-rap*, louder this time.

"Come back, later!" he yelled, suddenly aware of how hoarse he sounded.

"Okay, sir," a timid voice squealed. He listened as the mouse and her cart rumbled away.

Mick-Mac stumbled to the bathroom, groped for the light switch. The flickering fluorescent light was a beautiful sight. He steadied himself against the grimy sink and let his heart nestle itself back into his chest. He slowed his breathing, let the shockwaves coursing through his body dissipate. He pushed a soggy clump of hair from a clammy forehead. The reflection gazing back at him in disgust looked foreign. Was that really him inside that mottled husk with eyes collapsing into it as if they were being sucked into an endless chasm?

He drew back the shower curtain, half expecting Norman Bates to be waiting on the other side. No Norman. Just a mold-encrusted enclosure and a half-used bar of soap. He showered quickly, feeling no cleaner than he had a minute ago. But the frigid water had gotten the blood pumping and the juices flowing.

Marnie, if you could see me now.

Mick-Mac stepped out into the early morning air, a chill wind and still-damp hair sending shockwaves up his spine. He looked skyward. Angry clouds loomed above, resembling giant water balloons ready to burst and unleash their fury.

Gazing across the fractured pavement, he spotted a diner, its dim glower beckoning to him through the dusky air. Like something out of an old movie. With coffee and eggs just as old, no doubt. But with seemingly limited options, it would do just fine.

He picked up his pace, a surge of excitement overtaking him. His hunch felt right this time. He was onto something. Something big. And this time, Eddie wasn't going to pull the rug out from under him. No, this one was going to be all his.

CHAPTER THIRTY-NINE

"**E**asy! It's not a toy!"

Joe shrugged and hefted the crossbow.

His brother tore the weapon away, fury etching his face. "That's not the way I told you to cock it." Glen heaved a loud sigh. "Pay attention this time." Joe watched as his brother cocked the weapon. "Now, do you remember what I told you about the arrow?"

Joe rolled his eyes, peeved at his brother's lack of patience. "The feather at the end—"

"It's called a vane," his brother interrupted.

Joe felt a torrent of blood flood his face. He resisted the urge to tell his brother to go fuck himself and said, "The vane at the end that's a different color from the other two goes into the groove."

"Good boy," Glen said. Then he added, "And it's called a rail."

Just can't help yourself, can you, Glen?

Glen loaded an arrow. "Remember, if you like having ten fingers, keep them out of the path of the string." He hefted the weapon to his shoulder and took his stance. "Align your sight, release the safety, take a deep breath, let half the breath out, and squeeze the trigger."

The arrow hit its target dead on. As Joe knew it would. After all, nothing Glen did was ever short of perfection. And right now, Joe hated him for it.

"Okay, Robin Hood, your turn."

Joe cocked the crossbow correctly on the first try, to the delight of his brother, then loaded the arrow into the slot—the *rail*. He took his stance, hefted the weapon onto his shoulder, and took aim.

"Stop!" Glen screamed. "You grip it like that, and the string is going to seriously fuck up your fingers." He tugged on Joe's hand. "You've got to keep it below the flight deck."

"I got it," Joe said, brushing his brother's hand aside. Secretly, though, he was grateful that Glen had kept all his digits intact. But he sure as hell wasn't going to admit to that. He took aim again, breathed as his brother had taught him, and pulled the trigger.

Not only did it miss the target by a country mile, but it nearly impaled Blazer, who came trotting out of the woods at the wrong moment. Blazer winced and ran to Glen, cowered behind him.

"Shit, Joey," Glen said, "you almost shish-kabobbed my dog. I think we'd better find you a new weapon of choice. I think I've got an old Louisville Slugger lying around somewhere."

"Funny, bro," Joe said with a smile, a smile that masked his wounded ego. An ego that had been crushed a long time ago, like one of Patty's cigarette butts. "Let me give it another try. I'm just warming up."

Glen shook his head, snatched the weapon from his grip. "It's time to give old Patty a call and get this show on the road." He looked up to the inky sky, menacing clouds rolling over one another in a dizzying dance. "Looks like we're in for a bad one. Which just might work to our advantage."

Joe's body tremored, the intensifying wind thrashing his bones. "How do you figure that?"

Glen winked, seemingly unfazed by the growing tempest. "Because if it storms like I think it's going to, they're going to be disoriented and off their guard. I, on the other hand, could find my way around this place blindfolded." He picked up the box of weapons. "Now, let's go call your friend and let the show begin."

CHAPTER FORTY

Patty stubbed out her sixth—*or is it seventh?*—cigarette and took a drag off the already lit one waiting on deck. *What are you waiting for, Cowboy?* She hadn't slept a wink last night but had the pleasure of being serenaded by the big lunk's incessant snoring. Enough sleep in him to go around.

Maybe Katie was right. They should just pack up and start their new life. Their rich new life. By tomorrow, she could be sitting on a warm beach with a cold one and a suntan. But Katie didn't know Little Dom the way she did. He made Daddy Dearest look like a choirboy. She thought about what Cowboy had said when they last spoke.

Maybe you can run and hide. But for how long?

He was a fucker all right, but there was truth in those words. Little Dom would exhaust all efforts in his power to hunt her down. He certainly had the manpower and the money. Well, maybe a few million short now. But Patty knew it wasn't about the money. Like his father, Little Dom was no more than a walking ego dressed up to the nines. She'd seen the hatred pulsing through his body on more than one occasion over issues most people would brush off their shoulder like a piece of lint.

She imagined the rage festering inside him, tearing away at his insides, clawing its way to the surface. And when it reared its ugly head, she didn't want to be in the same time zone. No, she wouldn't run. Not yet. Not until Cowboy was fed to the wolves.

"Aunt Patty."

Though Katie's voice was soft and unthreatening, it startled Patty. Her body and heart tensed all the same.

"I'm sorry," Katie said, resting a warm hand on Patty's ice cold one. "I didn't mean to scare you."

Patty squeezed her niece's delicate hand and said, "It's okay, I'm all right."

"Did you get any sleep? You look exhausted."

Patty shook her head and took a long drag off the butt she'd forgotten she was holding. "Not a wink." Her eyes wandered to the door that rumbled from the cacophony behind it. "And I don't know how the hell you did either, with that buzz saw going all night."

Katie laughed and shrugged like a little girl. "You get used to it."

"I'll bet Cowboy didn't snore like that. Doesn't seem like he'd have it in him."

Katie laughed again. "I guess I never really noticed. He was there, but not really there. You know what I mean?"

This time Patty shrugged. "Yeah, I think so. Story of my life."

Katie suddenly looked sad. "Can I ask you something, Aunt Patty?"

"Shoot."

"Have you ever been in love? I mean really in love?"

Patty shook her head, stubbed out another butt. "Naw. Well, there was this one guy..."

Katie raised a hand to her mouth, chewed at her manicured nails, looking like a pre-pubescent girl just rewarded with a front row seat, complete with backstage pass, to that sold-out-forever Justin Bieber concert. "Tell me," she begged.

Patty lit up another smoke and said, "Not much to tell. Boy meets girl. Girl falls head over heels in love. Boy dies."

Katie's gleeful expression washed away, replaced by a mask of horror. "Died? How?"

Patty closed her eyes, willing his rugged face back to memory. "His name was Vincent. Vincent Giraldi. Vinnie."

Katie's expression went from shock to curiosity. "What was he like? Was he nice? Handsome?"

"Oh, yes, that he was. Tall, dark, and beautiful. Inside and out. Treated me like a queen." Patty grunted and tapped her cigarette, sending a poof of ash into the air. "Only man who ever did."

"How did you and Vinnie meet?"

Patty expelled a weary sigh. "Through Dominic."

The mask of horror slapped itself back onto Katie's face. "Did he work for Dominic?"

Patty nodded solemnly. Dredging up the best-turned-to-worst time in her life hurt more than she could have imagined. "He was Dominic's go-to guy at the time. And Vinnie knew he was playing with fire, getting mixed up with the likes of me, but he said you can't choose who you fall for."

"But you were Dominic's girl, weren't you?"

"One of many, your mother included. But I guess I was the

one who was off limits. We kept it hidden for a while, nervous but at the same time excited by the thrill of pulling one over on the big guy. But one night..." Her voice trailed off.

Katie rested a tender hand on Patty's shoulder. "Are you okay? I'm sorry, Aunt Patty, I didn't mean to upset you. You don't have to go on if it's too much."

Patty sniffed and said, "No, I want to. I've never told anyone about Vinnie, and it feels good to finally get it out." She released a heavy sigh and continued. "Anyway, Vinnie decides he's tired of hiding in the shadows, so we make a plan to get out. To just up and skip town. It doesn't even matter where we go, he says. As long as we're together."

"Sounds like Vinnie was a romantic," Katie said.

"And then some. So, he makes the arrangements. Buys a couple of tickets to some island I'd never even heard of. Tells me to pack my things and wait by my window that night. He'll be by at midnight and flash his lights once. So, I wait. And I wait. But he never shows."

Tears dotted Katie's eyes. "What happened?"

Patty took a long drag and released a puff of smoke. "Someone ratted on Vinnie. I never found out who, but I had my suspicion that it was this smarmy little weasel named Petey or Patsy or whatever the fuck his name was who was jealous of Vinnie. Maybe Vinnie told him about us or maybe he saw us together, but somehow word got back to Dominic."

"And he killed Vinnie?" Katie was trembling now.

"Hell no. Dominic never got his perfectly manicured hands dirty. He had someone else do his dirty work. But just for fun, he showed up the next morning with a beautifully wrapped gift, which he told me was because I was his special girl. I opened it and..." Patty let out a sob loud enough to rival Rufus's background music.

Katie gasped. "Was it his—"

"Heart. It was Vinnie's heart, neatly wrapped in festive tissue paper. Dominic looked at me and said, 'You ripped my heart out, so I did the same to him.' Then he took the heart out of the box and threw it on the bed and said, "Be careful who you share your bed with, love." And that was that. I've never loved anyone since. Except you, of course."

Katie reached out to hug Patty. Patty's cell lit up. "Looks like it's showtime," she said. She put it on speaker mode and said, "Well, it's about time, Cowboy. Was wondering if you'd changed your mind."

The voice on the other end was all business. "Write down this address. And I'd better not see anyone other than you and Kate or the deal's off."

Patty scribbled down the address, pushed it toward Katie. Katie shook her head and shrugged. "Okay, Cowboy, is that it?"

"That's it," he said. "Oh, one more thing. Bring an umbrella. I hear we're supposed to get a little rain." Then a *click* and he was gone.

"You don't know this place?" she said, eyes bouncing from the paper to Katie.

"No. I don't think we've ever been to New Hampshire."

"No relations there? A family cottage? High school chum?"

Katie shook her head again. "The only family he has is a brother in New York and a piece-of-shit father down in Florida. He doesn't even talk to either of them anymore."

Patty pursed her lips and shook her head. "Something just doesn't seem right. Why New Hampshire? Why not right here?" Then she added, "Better have Sleeping Beauty in there bring extra firepower, just in case."

Katie giggled. "Aunt Patty, did you forget who we're talking about here? I lived with this guy. I ate dinner with him every night. Watched all his stupid sports and crime shows pretending to be interested. And speaking about pretending, I did that every night in bed. Trust me, Joe would be afraid to pull the trigger on a squirt gun, never mind a real one."

Patty smiled and nodded, remembering Cowboy's initial reaction to the gun she'd given him. "You're probably right, sweetie. But it doesn't hurt to be extra cautious. Now, go see if you can wake the beast so we can get this done."

CHAPTER FORTY-ONE

A light mist dotted the windshield as Mick-Mac reached his destination. He hadn't seen a car for miles. A great spot if you were hiding from the world. Which is exactly what this Campbell guy seemed to be doing.

Though his GPS confirmed he had arrived at 5 Mountain Pass Lane, all he saw was a nondescript dirt path with no sign or mailbox. Upon closer inspection, he noticed ruts prominently stamped in the thick mud. Tire tracks. Likely from a pickup or SUV. And they appeared to be fairly fresh. His pulse quickened.

Not wanting to risk being spotted, or getting stuck in that mess, he continued down the road for a few hundred yards until he found a shoulder in the road that appeared to be a scenic viewing area, although the only view was a dense wall of trees. He tucked the car into the tight spot. A wind gust slammed him as he exited the vehicle. He was nearly knocked on his ass but regained his footing in the heavy muck.

His shoes made a *suck-suck* sound as he plucked them from

the inches-deep mud. He cursed and looked to the heavens. Though it was still morning, the ceiling of grizzled grey clouds obliterated any indication that it was any earlier than early evening.

The thought of getting back into his car, crusted feet and all, crossed his mind. Then he thought of his pal Eddie Diaz and erased the thought. He grabbed a flashlight and an extra round of ammo from the trunk, pulled on an extra layer of fleece that had been balled up in the far reaches of the compartment, and backtracked toward 5 Mountain Pass Lane.

The sky had darkened a shade or two by the time Mick-Mac reached the dirt road. He sidestepped the muddy ruts, wallowing instead through the heavy thicket that was equally treacherous to navigate. Briars bit angrily at his shins. Cold, liquidy muck seeped deeper into his shoes with each step.

The dense woods shielded him from the raw wind, which grew fainter as the forest swallowed him up, swaddling him in a cocoon of silence. A sense of claustrophobic panic gripped him, the trees stacking closer upon one another, like a wall of soldiers preparing for a siege. He kept the dirt road in his sights to avoid becoming hopelessly lost, muddy footprints his modified trail of breadcrumbs.

He thought again about ditching the plan and heading home, but then he saw it. An opening in this maze of vegetation. He stepped into a small clearing dotted with dandelions, felt air move back into his lungs. Up ahead, a roofline. He slogged forward and there it was. A tidy, well-maintained cabin.

Fresh paint and manicured grounds indicated somebody was playing house here.

A silver Range Rover, its sleek body spattered with mud, sat front and center. In the distance, Mick-Mac spotted a bright red pickup, the model of which he couldn't make out. Behind it was some sort of structure, a barn or garage.

What really struck him was the view, a picturesque lake with looming mountains breaking its surface. The water was the color of an old washtub, its restless surface churning beneath a blackish sky that now resembled a hastily sketched charcoal drawing. The agitated water lapped angrily at a weathered boat dock. An orangey glow painted the cabin's windows.

Is that you in there, Glen Whoever-You-Are? Or is it you, the enigmatic Joe Campbell, who seems to be eluding everyone? Everyone except for me.

Mick-Mac stayed low and crept along the fringes of the forest. A shadow cut through one of the fiery, orangey squares. Mick-Mac suddenly remembered the old pair of binoculars tucked away in a box somewhere in his apartment, a gift from Marnie (*in case you're on a stakeout and need to remain invisible*, she'd said). A smarter man would have had the sense to bring those along. Then again, a smarter man wouldn't be kneeling in a soggy carpet of weeds and thorns and muck with a storm of epic proportions boiling overhead.

Comfort no longer an option, he propped himself on one elbow, the cold, spongy earth breaching the thin layers of cloth, sending a shock of electricity through his arm. All he could do now was wait.

CHAPTER FORTY-TWO

"So, any special ladies in Glen Campbell's revolving door?"

Glen frowned. "Joey, I gave up those days long ago." Then he smiled sheepishly and added, "But, yeah, there is someone special."

"I'm impressed," Joe said. "And surprised."

"Why? You don't think I can be a one-woman kind of guy?"

Joe laughed. "Sure. One woman a night."

"I'm a changed man, baby brother." Glen gathered up the dishes, Joe's half-eaten omelet cold and rubbery. He moved toward the kitchen. Loud *clank-clank* sounds disrupted Blazer's slumber. Glen reentered, toting a steaming pot of coffee. Blazer eyed him in annoyance, sighed, and resumed his siesta.

Joe hefted his mug and noticed a tremor in his hand as Glen refilled him. Probably too much coffee. Or not enough sleep. Or the fact that today could be his last day on Earth. Or all of the above. "So, tell me about this lady who caused my playboy brother to do a one-eighty."

Glen plunked down with a thud. Blazer sighed again. "Her name is Rebecca. She works for a marketing firm in Boston. Smart as a whip. And funny as hell."

The fact that he'd made no mention of a killer body indicated that maybe Glen had changed after all. "Wow," Joe said. "I'd love to meet her."

"And you will," Glen said. "After this shitstorm is over."

"Does she—" Joe paused.

Glen eyed him. "What? Know I'm a gun for hire? No."

"What I was going to ask is if she knew about me."

Glen chuckled. "Oh, right. Yeah, she does."

Joe smiled. "Good." He hesitated, then said, "So, does she—"

"I knew it would get back to that," Glen said. "As a matter of fact, I've been meaning to tell her."

"Just haven't gotten around to it yet, is that it?" Joe said.

Glen dissolved into his coffee cup.

"The answer isn't in that cup."

Glen half-smiled, then frowned. The pain Joe had seen earlier in his eyes resurfaced. More intensely this time. "I've never felt like this about anyone before, Joey. I'm afraid if she found out, she'd leave. Like everyone else in my life who I ever cared about."

"Ouch," Joe said.

"Sorry, Joey, I didn't mean you."

"Sure you did," Joe said. "But I think we both know who left who."

Glen nodded solemnly and said, "That may be true, but I'm here for you now."

Joe shrugged and smiled weakly. "Brothers in arms, right?"

"Absolutely."

"Now tell me, Mr. Bond, how did a clean-cut Ivy League boy destined for the fast track wind up here?"

Glen rose and said, "We're gonna need another pot of coffee for that story, my friend."

CHAPTER FORTY-THREE

Rufus tossed the last of the bags into the SUV's caboose. "Okay, ladies, let's get the lead out."

Patty flipped him the bird and climbed in shotgun. She glanced up at the mottled sky. The bloated, graphite clouds looked ready to burst. "I hope the weather's a little better up north."

"In a couple of days, we'll be sitting on a sunny beach in our bikinis, Aunt Patty," Katie squealed from the backseat.

"Sweetie, I think my bikini-wearing days are long gone." Rufus glanced over, his eyes saying it all. "And not a peep out of you, you big buffoon," Patty said, waving a fist his way.

Rufus threw up his arms. "I'm not saying a word."

"Just drive," Patty said, her eyes growing heavy. "You know where you're going?"

"Got it right in the GPS, ma'am," Rufus said. "Now why don't you try to get a little shut eye?"

Patty closed her eyes. Cowboy's face filled the blackness.

She tried to wash the image away, but it had defiantly planted both feet in the ground, refusing to move from her line of vision. How had she let him get so buried inside her head? She was the ringleader here calling the shots, not that pathetic milquetoast—one of those fancy words she'd learned from him —so, why did it feel like he'd suddenly gotten the upper hand?

No! He's a scared little child, Patty, probably shitting himself right now. And so naïve to actually think Katie still loves him and wants to be back in those scrawny arms. I'll let him think it's all hunky-dory and then once I get what I want I'll let Rufus go to town on him. No, I'll do it myself. Yeah, this one is all mine.

And still, apprehension clouded her thoughts. What if there was more to Joe Campbell than meets the eye? After all, he'd managed to evade the cops and Little Dom so far. What if he was capable of more than she or Katie ever imagined? What if—

She was jolted from her daydream. She bolted upright and said, "What the *hell?*"

"Sorry," Rufus said. "Must have hit a pothole or something. You okay? Your head hit that window pretty hard."

Patty massaged her temple. "I'm fine. I'm fine. Just keep your eyes on the goddamn road," she said with venom. "That money sitting back there ain't gonna do any of us a bit of good if we end up dead in a ditch."

Rufus apologized again, but Patty was already drifting back into her reverie. Only this time, instead of Cowboy's face, she saw Dominic's. The man she thought she'd once loved. The man who had brought so much pain upon her. The man who, even in death, was still bringing that pain.

That final night replayed in her head like a song stuck on repeat. The last time she would see Dominic "The Skinner"

Guierriero. It had been a day much like today, raw and stormy. The day she knew she had to make her escape or end up like Charlene.

Dominic had said he'd had enough with the waterworks, and it was time for her to move on and forget about Charlene. Forget about her? He'd just taken away the person she loved most in the world, and she was now supposed to just sweep it under the rug? And yet, afraid of what may come, she moved on —well, let Dominic think she'd moved on.

She played the role of the devoted woman, lover, companion. Endured the sexual fetishes, the verbal and physical abuse, all the while plotting her escape. It wouldn't be easy. Even when Dominic wasn't around, he seemed to know her every move. If she wanted to leave the house, Dominic insisted on a driver accompanying her. She was denied access to a cell phone or computer. She was free to move around the expansive grounds, and showered with expensive clothing and jewelry, the more elaborate gifts coming immediately after a brutal beating usually set off by something trivial. And yet, for all the lavish amenities, she was a caged rat.

Then, one stormy fall afternoon, she saw her window of opportunity. Dominic had to head to Florida on business, and he was taking along two of his most astute, and ruthless, lackies. He insisted Patty join him, but she feigned illness.

Dominic cupped her face in his sandpapery paw. His touch made her skin crawl, had for a long time. A fat, calloused thumb gently caressed her cheek, still swollen and throbbing from the prior evening's festivities. "I'm sorry, love," he'd said in a tone so gentle, so convincing, she'd almost believed him. Until reality slapped her as hard as he had. "You just get me crazy sometimes. I'll make it up to you, I promise."

That meant she could expect a gawdy, ridiculously over-priced trinket upon his return. Maybe rubies, better yet, diamonds. Being a punching bag did have its perks, after all. But this was one perk she wouldn't be cashing in. She'd be long gone by then.

Patty watched through tear-streaked glass as the Lincoln disappeared down the serpentine driveway and was washed away in a blur. She moved quickly, having already packed a bag, her escape route planned to a tee. She knew the rough where-abouts of everyone in the estate. Sergio and Lefty were likely stoned, and Stevie was probably off yanking it somewhere.

She took the back staircase, a winding masterpiece of marble, and entered the darkened kitchen. The staff wouldn't be rolling in for another hour or so. A narrow hallway off the kitchen led to a delivery alcove. She nearly tripped over a crate of fresh greens. A weathered barn door, shipped from an old Sicilian vineyard, led to the outside. To her freedom. She moved toward the door.

"Where you going, little lady?" It was Stevie.

Think, Patty, think. She turned and smiled. "I was feeling better, so I thought I'd take Dominic up on the offer to join him."

Stevie, not the brightest bulb, stared in confusion. "But Boss left already."

"I called an Uber to come pick me up," she lied. "Figured I'd surprise him at the airport."

Stevie appeared to be buying the story. Then he frowned and said, "It's raining like a motherfucker out there. Cancel the Uber. I'll drive you."

Patty's pulse quickened. Was he on to her? "I wouldn't want to trouble you, Stevie."

"No trouble at all," he said. He moved toward her. "It's what Boss pays me to do. In fact, if he found out I let you go off in this weather with a fuckin' stranger, my ass would be grass."

"Not if he doesn't find out," Patty said. "I'll tell him it was you who drove me. No one has to be any the wiser."

Stevie moved closer. "I'm sorry, but I can't let you do that." He grinned. A sinister grin. "Unless..." He unzipped his fly, fumbled around inside, grasping for purchase. With his hands busy, Patty made her move. She grabbed a hefty cast iron pan from a wall rack and swung like Derek Jeter. The pan connected with a dull *clank*. Stevie's eyes went wide, then rolled up into their sockets like a turtle retreating into its shell.

He went down hard, his manhood gripped loosely in his hand. Patty eyed a butcher knife, looked back at the limp appendage, and considered pulling a Lorena Bobbitt. Then she looked at the pathetic face with a quickly growing goose egg protruding from the massive forehead. She tossed the heavy cookware to the cement floor where it landed with a deafening crash. She cringed, hoping it didn't send Sergio and Lefty running.

But nobody came. Patty yanked the hood of her jacket over her head and slipped out into the pelting rain.

She stayed holed up for weeks, terrified that Dom would hunt her down. It was during this lonely stretch that she plotted her revenge. Katie, devastated by the loss of her mother, jumped on board with fervor. Then the seduction of one Joe Campbell. The perfect patsy. Rufus, the last puzzle piece, didn't take much persuading. Dangling the prospect of money and a chance to get out of the shithole dive that was slowly sucking the life out of him was all he had to hear.

So, she waited. Katie lured in her prey. And Patty waited. Patiently, methodically, setting the wheels in motion. Until at last, Joe Campbell was primed and ready. She continued the dance, played the part of crazy yet lovable storyteller. And waited for the opportunity to present itself.

Then the call came from Rufus. Dominic was arriving at Griffin's in a few days for a private meeting. Rufus would be paid handsomely to close the place early, as was typical on such occasions. And Patty's plan had come full circle.

Rufus slipped her in the back door. Dominic's voice boomed through the cavernous bar. He sounded angry about something. She moved with stealth through the darkened tavern and caught a glimpse of him in the faint glower of light overhead. Dominic's shadowy face looked more grotesque than usual. Like one of those gargoyles perched on top of an old gothic church.

Dominic continued his tirade and stopped abruptly when he saw her. His jaw fell open and hung motionless, as if on a hinge. Patty smiled and said, "Hello, Dominic."

The slack jaw found its purpose again and said, "What the fuck?"

The man sitting beside him, whom Patty vaguely remembered meeting on another occasion, looked on in bewilderment. "Who's this?" he said at last.

Rufus appeared next to Patty. Dominic glanced from one to the other, then fixed his gaze on Rufus. "What the fuck is she doing here?" He made a sudden move toward his coat, which was neatly draped over the booth.

Rufus leveled a gun at him. "I wouldn't do that if I were you, Mr. Guierriero."

The other guy, who Patty now remembered as Salvatore Cappucci, started to rise. The bullet pierced him dead center between the eyes. A line of red streamed down his startled face. He fell forward, his face slamming the table with a sickening jolt.

"Whoa! Easy big guy," Dominic said, his voice calm but his expression a mask of fear. "Patty, what are you doing, love?"

"Love? You have the audacity to call me that after all you've put me through?"

Dominic sat stock-still, his eyes shifting momentarily to the liquidy puddle slowly fanning out around Sal's fat freckled head. "Whatever I've done to upset you, we can talk about it."

Patty laughed. "Well, that would take more time than I care to give you, you lowlife piece of shit." Saying that on any other day would have gotten her a trip to the emergency room or the bottom of the Charles. But today she was in charge. Today she was the boss.

"Is this about Charlene?" Sympathy tinged that last word. But it cut deep.

"Why'd you do it, Dominic?" Tears welled up, something she vowed she'd never do in his presence again. "Charlene was harmless. She was good. Probably the only good thing to ever touch your sorry, pathetic life. A life, which, by the way, ends here. In this rundown shithole."

Rufus leveled the gun. Dominic cowered, his lip trembling. For the first time, Patty saw genuine fear etched into the gargoyle's stony face. "Please," he pleaded. His panic-stricken eyes shifted to Rufus. "Hey, big guy, how much to make all this go away?"

Patty raised her hand, and Rufus lowered the gun. Dominic let out a relieved puff of air.

Patty snatched the gun from Rufus and raised it to Dominic's head. "Don't worry about him, Dominic. He's on my payroll now." She cocked the gun. "This one's for you, Charlene." Dominic's scream was lost in a blur of red.

Patty gazed in silence at the lifeless body of the man who had once saved her, whom she'd once loved, and now hated with all that she was. Knowing he could no longer hurt her brought her less solace than she thought it would.

She pointed the gun at Rufus. "Tell me you weren't thinking about taking him up on his offer," she said.

Rufus, hands in holdup position, laughed nervously and said, "Of course not, boss."

Patty contemplated for a moment, really just to put the fear of God into the usually stoic lummox, then lowered the gun. "Okay, big guy, you ready for Act Two?"

CHAPTER FORTY-FOUR

"So, you never went to NYU?"

Glen nodded. "I did. I just didn't finish like I told you I did."

"Why not? What happened?"

Glen sighed. "In my third year, I fell into a funk," he said. "I was in a bad relationship, partying a little too hard, and my grades were in the shitter." Glen rose, moved to the window, gazed out at the agitated lake through tear-streaked glass. His gaze swept upward to the equally unsettled sky. "It's going to be one hell of a storm."

"Nice try," Joe said. "But you're not skirting the issue like you usually do. What happened next?"

Glen, his back to Joe, continued. "So, I was trying to figure out what I was going to do. Do I drop out? Change majors? Join the army? I hopped in my car and just started driving around, planning my next move. And then fate stepped in."

"Fate?"

Glen turned to face his brother. "Yeah, I guess you could call it that. Here I am just driving aimlessly down some road with no clue as to where I was. Tom Petty was playing on the radio. *Free Fallin'* I think. Anyway, it was getting dark, and I had no idea how to get back to campus. Then, out of nowhere, this deer runs out in front of me. You know that expression about deer in headlights? Well, I get where it comes from, because that big mother didn't budge. Just stood there wide-eyed, waiting to be plowed down."

"Did you hit it?" Joe asked.

Glen shook his head. "No. Lucky for that son of a bitch, your dear old brother has lightning-fast reflexes. I missed him by inches. And still he never budged. Unfortunately, my reflexes weren't quite as good as I thought, and I ended up clipping a tree and wound up in a ditch."

"Were you okay?"

"Yeah. Only thing bruised was my ego. And the front end of the car. The car was pretty jammed up, so I had to call a tow truck." He looked at Joe. "Am I boring you yet, Joey?"

"Just get to the fate part," Joe said.

"Well, it turns out the car isn't drivable, so I wind up at a body shop, which luckily is still open. The mechanic's heading out for the night, but I make up some sob story about how I'm going to see my sick grandmother to say my last goodbyes."

Joe laughed. "And he bought that story?"

Glen smirked. "I've always had a talent for getting people to buy whatever shit I was shoveling."

Joe nodded. "That you have."

"So, after I slipped the guy a few extra bucks, he says he'll take care of the car, but it's going to probably be a couple of hours. Tells me there's this bar just up the road with decent grubs."

"Let me guess," Joe said. "This is where fate steps in."

"Hold your piss, Joey. I'm getting to it. So, I walk in and it's pretty busy for a Tuesday night. And, you want to know something funny? Tom Petty was playing just like when I went off the road."

"So that's the fate part, Glen? Seriously, with all the buildup, I was expecting a little more."

Glen laughed. "No, that's not the fate part. I just thought it was kind of ironic. Anyway, I pull up a stool at the bar and order a beer and some chicken wings, which came highly recommended by the mechanic. Then someone sits down beside me and says hello."

"A hot chick, I hope," Joe said. "Because so far this story doesn't exactly have me on the edge of my seat."

Glen shook his head. "No, it was this older dude in a suit. Real polished and professional looking."

"Ooh, plot twist," Joe said. "Was he your type?"

"Funny, Joey. Anyway, we get talking and he asks me where I'm from and what I do. Honestly, I didn't know this guy from Adam, so I wasn't about to give him any information about myself. I made up a fake name and other shit. Then he pulls out a business card. It's classy looking but plain. Just a guy's name, a phone number, and an obscure logo. He asks me if I've ever seen any military action or combat. I tell him no, but he keeps pressing me."

"Probably because you look like someone nobody is going to mess with."

Glen shrugged. "Maybe. Anyway, I tell him I've got to go, and I pull out my wallet. He tells me the bill's already been settled. Then he pushes the business card in front of me and says, 'You look like you're a bit lost, my friend. If you decide you need a change in your life, give me a call. I think you could be just what we're looking for. And we'll make it very worth your while.' Then he ups and walks out. Just like that."

"So, you called him," Joe said.

"Not at first. In fact, I pushed the business card aside and walked out of the bar. But as I was walking back to the auto shop, something stopped me in my tracks. Made me go back. Lucky for me, the card was still sitting there right where I'd left it. I snatched it up and stuffed it in my pocket." Glen moved back to the window. Rain hammered the glass.

"So, when did you call him back?" Joe said eagerly. Finally, the story was picking up.

"Not for a few weeks," Glen said. "I went back to class, tried to wrap my head back around my studies. But all I could think about was what that guy with the slicked-back hair and thousand-dollar suit had said to me. That's when I decided something needed to change in my life."

"Why didn't you tell me?" Joe said. "All that time, telling me you were a stockbroker living large."

"Well, that part wasn't a lie," Glen said. "I definitely was living large."

"Yeah, that I know," Joe said. "Remember, I saw that insane apartment in Manhattan, which had me wondering why I didn't go into the field of finance."

"I'm sorry I lied to you all those years, Joey," Glen said. "But what I was doing was top secret. What was I supposed to say, that I—"

"—Kill people?" Joe interrupted.

These words cut deep. Glen, visibly taken aback, said, "Whoa, that's not fair."

Joe shot up and moved toward his brother, anger propelling him forward. "Not fair? You want to know what's not fair, Glen? That you were the only family I had, and you pushed me away and just vanished from my life. And on those rare occasions when you were around, you weren't really around. I needed you. So many rough patches I went through, and you were never there."

"I'm here right now, right in front of you," Glen said.

Joe fought back the tears he knew were clawing their way to the surface. "But is it too little too late?" he said.

"You don't really believe that, Joey."

"I don't know what I believe anymo—"

Glen's outstretched hand stopped him. "What the fuck?" he said, his voice rising several octaves.

Joe, still boiling with emotion, said, "What?"

Glen pressed his face against the glass, peered through the ripple of water cascading before him. "There's someone out there in the woods."

Joe's anger morphed to alarm. "Wha—where?"

"Right off beyond the boathouse."

The torrent made it nearly impossible to see anything. "I don't see squat," Joe said.

"I'm telling you, there's a guy out there." Glen brushed by Joe.

"Where are you going?"

"To see who that fucker is," Glen said. "You stay put." Glen moved to a closet, grabbed a raincoat. Then he went to a cabinet and pulled out a shiny object. "Take this."

Joe gazed at the pistol resting in his palm. "Glen, I don't even know how to use this thing."

"Just remember what I taught you earlier." He produced another gun, this one larger and more sinister looking.

"Glen, I don't think I'm ready for this," Joe said.

Glen looked at him with adamant eyes. "Brother, you don't have a fucking choice." He moved toward the door and stopped. "One more thing."

"What?" Joe said.

Glen pointed at Blazer, who looked at the men quizzically, tail wagging hesitantly. "He may look like the friendliest, most harmless mutt, but he's also trained to protect to the death." He leaned in close and whispered, "If things get ugly, just say *qué pasa.*"

"Glen, are you serious?"

Glen pulled the hood over his head, mouthed the phrase, and disappeared into the storm.

CHAPTER FORTY-FIVE

The rain had intensified since Mick-Mac set up camp trying to devise a plan. He realized he didn't have one. He'd just hopped in the car and driven all the way out into the middle of nowhere, and now he was sitting in a pile of muck soaked through to the bone. A shiver spidered its way up his spine. He hugged his knees, rocked back and forth. No movement from the house. Maybe it was time to pack it in.

"Don't move."

The deep voice was calm yet urgent. And he knew what the hard object pressing into his back was. Instinctively, he raised his hands in surrender.

"I said don't move!" The menacing voice was underscored by a clap of thunder in the distance. The man moved quickly in front of Mick-Mac. Big man with a big gun.

Mick-Mac remained rigid, nodded slowly. The rain spit at his face, blurring his sight. He resisted the instinct to swipe at his eyes.

"Okay," the man said, "Slowly clasp your hands behind your head and stand up."

Mick-Mac obeyed, nearly slipping in the thickening mud. "Listen, man, I don't want any trouble."

The man shoved him hard, gun at the ready. "Shut up and move."

Fifteen excruciating minutes had passed since Glen had disappeared into the storm. Visibility was next to nothing. Blazer brushed up against Joe's leg and emitted a soft groan.

"Where's your daddy, boy?" Joe said. Blazer tilted his head, his face a mask of worry. Dogs supposedly had higher sensory outputs than humans, enabling them to sense imminent danger. "What is it, boy?" Blazer groaned again, then growled.

Joe moved to the window, squinting to catch a snapshot through the angry rivulets running down the glass. Then he spotted a flash of color. Glen's raincoat. He pressed his nose against the cold glass, his rapid breath fogging his vision. He swiped the glass and saw it again. Glen. And another man. The man stumbled forward, prodded on by the hulking man and his gun.

They disappeared from view, then the door burst open. A spray of rain introduced the two men. Blazer growled but remained rigid. Glen shoved the drenched man to the floor and shut the storm out.

"Joey, get some rope," Glen demanded. "You'll find some in the metal cabinet in the garage." Joe stood as stiff as Blazer, gazing at the shivering, terrified man at his feet. "Joe! Do it now!"

Joe nodded and moved quickly. By the time he returned, Glen already had the man propped up on a wooden chair. "Tie his hands behind him," Glen barked like a drill sergeant. "Make it tight." Joe obeyed.

Once Glen looked confident that his captive was properly secured, he lowered the gun and his taut body loosened. "Well, well," he said, "looks like we have a Peeping Tom here, Joey. Is that right, Tom?"

The man, hair plastered to his forehead, shook his head. "No, it's not like that," he said.

Glen produced a billfold from his pocket and tossed it to Joe. "Looks like our Peeping Tom here is a Peeping Mickey. Mickey MacAvoy." Glen paused. "Detective Mickey MacAvoy."

Joe stared at the official badge, and his heart raced. The cops had found him. But how? Joe rushed at the man, grabbed his shoulders, and shook him violently. "How did you find me? And what do you want?" Glen made a move as if to intervene, then stepped back.

"Answer the man," Glen said.

The disheveled cop looked at Glen, then his gaze zeroed in on Joe. "I was investigating the homicide of your colleague," he said. The fear seemed to have drained from his face. It now took on the color of arrogance. "A homicide for which you are the prime suspect," he added.

"I didn't kill Mitch!" Joe screamed.

The detective smiled. "Well, now you can add kidnapping a police officer to your rap sheet, Mr. Campbell. Looks like you're in deep shit from where I'm sitting."

Glen moved toward them. "My brother hasn't done anything. And you want to pin a kidnapping charge on anyone, that's on me."

"Listen," MacAvoy said. "Why don't you boys untie me, and we can sort this whole mess out."

"We untie you, and you're just going to arrest me, aren't you?" Joe said, his voice cracking.

MacAvoy appeared calm, almost relaxed. As if he felt he had the upper hand, even in his restraints. "No, Mr. Campbell. I'd just like to bring you in for questioning is all."

Joe thought about Mitch sprawled out in his office, not a hair out of place, bleeding all over the worn carpeting. "Like I said, I didn't kill Mitch," he said. "I was there, but it wasn't me. It was—it wasn't me."

"Then who was it?"

"I don't know. Two men. They almost killed me too, but I got away."

MacAvoy winced. Apparently, the restraints were getting tighter. "These men—they wouldn't happen to be associates of Dominic Guierriero, would they?"

Hearing the name shook Joe to the core. How did this guy know about Guerriero? "Wha—how do—?"

"I found the photos, Joe," MacAvoy said. "So, how's about you untie me and tell me what a nice guy like you is doing hanging around the likes of The Skinner?"

CHAPTER FORTY-SIX

D om Jr. took a drag from the Cohiba Esplendido, a tradition passed on by his Padre. The expelled smoke swirled in a chaotic dance before him in the confines of the sedan's cabin. He typically preferred to have a window cracked when enjoying a cigar, but the unrelenting rain dashed those plans.

He pressed the intercom button. "Diego, how much longer do you anticipate?" Diego, a muscular man with cocoa-colored skin and an amiable face, nodded from beyond the privacy panel and indicated they'd reach their destination in roughly forty minutes, give or take with the torrent. Dom Jr. gave a slight nod, stubbed out the Cohiba and sank into the imported Poltrona Frau leather, another indulgence stolen from Padre.

The luxuries that surrounded him were a constant reminder of the man who made him who he was, the man he strived to be. The man who lay naked and exposed on a cold slab, likely being poked and prodded by an apathetic coroner who relished in the notion of having the upper hand on a man of such immense power.

He'd selected his six most competent men for this mission of vengeance. And though these men were capable of inflicting the utmost pain and cruelty upon the hapless Joe Campbell, it would be he who sent this man to his maker, slowly, agonizingly, and without mercy.

The throbbing in his head was almost unbearable. He squeezed his eyes shut, the sound of the rain like a fat juicy steak sizzling on a grill. A memory crept through the pain. A memory from his seventh birthday.

The party had been a lavish affair, as were all his birthdays. A circus of performers roamed the stately grounds, executing mind-boggling tricks and impossible acrobatics to the glee of the rambunctious children—the spawn of Padre's business associates rather than playmates of Little Nicky, as he was dubbed by his mother, a woman of consummate beauty and grace.

For all its extravagance, the affair proved far too showy for a seven-year-old boy, and Little Nicky despised it. From the phony wannabe friends to the dizzying display of chocolates and cakes to the touchy-feely clown with bad breath and a sinister grin that terrified Nicky, it was all too much.

He found solace in an elaborate solarium, probably larger than the houses his so-called friends lived in. Beyond the glass wall was a swimming pool that frightened him more than the evil clown. It was here that Little Nicky had watched his Padre emerge, carrying his baby sister's lifeless, dripping body. It was the first time Nicky had seen his Padre cry. As he watched the man's convulsing body cradle his dead sister, her sunflower-dotted bathing suit brilliant in the morning sun, he vowed to never go near water again—a vow he'd stuck to.

"Were you thinking about Felicia?" Padre's voice was soft, comforting. Little Nicky nodded. "Are you enjoying your party, son?"

Nicky gazed up at the larger-than-life man before him. "Yes, sir," he whispered.

Padre knelt and laid his massive hands tenderly on Nicky's slight shoulders. He hoped Padre hadn't noticed he was shivering. Padre smiled. "You haven't opened your gift yet, Nicky." He motioned to the door. "It's just outside. Come." Padre lifted Nicky up and enveloped him in crushing arms.

He gazed at the object before him, wrapped in shimmery paper with a bright blue bow on top bigger than his own head. "Well, go on, open it." Padre nudged him forward gently.

He tore gingerly at the paper at first, then ripped feverishly, exposing a shiny bicycle the color of the fire engine he recalled seeing outside his classroom window one day. Fear had crept into his bones at the sight of the massive truck with sirens blaring, until Miss Davenport assured her students that all was well, that it was simply a fire drill.

"Well, ace, do you like it?" Padre looked pleased with himself. Nicky liked when Padre was happy. He usually seemed sad or angry. But Nicky never felt afraid, even when Padre was yelling at the phone or throwing things across the room. With Nicky he was never angry. Nicky felt safest when Padre was holding his hand or enveloping him in those giant arms.

Nicky bobbed his head up and down and threw his scrawny

body against his father's unyielding legs. "I love it, sir," he said. "It's the best gift ever." And it was.

"How about we learn to ride it?" Nicky bobbed his head again.

Thirty minutes and a couple of scraped elbows and knees later, Nicky was pedaling on his own, Padre beaming with pride. It was indeed the best gift ever. And the one memory he would recall above all others.

He was jarred back to reality by a violent jolt. The sedan swerved right, then left, at last steadying itself. Dom Jr. leaned forward, his heart in overdrive. "Diego, what happened?"

Diego's furrowed brow appeared in the rearview mirror. "Everything's okay, Mr. Guierriero," he said, though the tremor in his voice expressed otherwise. "There was a large moose in the road, but luckily we missed it."

"A moose?" Dom Jr. said incredulously.

Diego laughed. "Well, boss, we are in New Hampshire, after all."

Dom Jr. smiled and nodded. Then he thought about how a moose could have been what saved Joe Campbell from a brutal and untimely end. This made him smile again. Then he laughed. A laugh robust enough to raise curiosity in Diego's eyes.

Padre's beaming pride as Little Nicky disappeared in a cloud of dust on that shiny fire-engine red bicycle entered his thoughts again, blurring out everything else.

No, Mr. Joe Campbell, you won't get off that easily.

CHAPTER FORTY-SEVEN

"So, that's how I'm connected to Dominic Guierriero. I never even met the guy—alive, that is." Joe sighed. He was growing weary of telling this story. And the look in MacAvoy's eyes told him the detective didn't buy a bit of it.

MacAvoy took in the story, nodding occasionally, though Joe could see right through the ruse. "Okay, Mr. Campbell, I believe what you're telling me is the truth."

Like hell you do.

MacAvoy shifted and winced. The restraints had grown taut and discomfort was etched in the man's weary, weathered face. "What say you untie me so I can help you straighten this out?"

Glen scoffed. "Right, so you can slap the cuffs on us?"

MacAvoy grunted. "I'm sorry, Glen is it? In case you've forgotten, you stripped me of my weapon and my badge. I don't think I'm much of a threat." He sized Glen up. "Especially looking at the likes of you."

"He has a point," Joe said. "Maybe it's time I turn myself in and hope for the best."

"Hope for the best?" Glen said incredulously. "Joey, a body was found in your office. The body of a guy everyone knows you despised. And who knows what evidence was found at the bar? Fingerprints? DNA?"

"I wiped it down pretty well."

"You sure about that, Mr. Campbell?" MacAvoy seemed to be enjoying himself.

"Shut the fuck up, Mickey!" Glen's face was a picture of rage. He turned back to Joe. "And what about that tape recorder?"

"Tape recorder?" MacAvoy said.

"I said to stow it!" Glen looked ready to pounce.

"Take it easy, Glen," Joe said. "Besides, Patty doesn't have the tape recorder."

Glen scoffed. "No, it's in even better hands. The Skinner's son."

MacAvoy sat up, groaned against the binding ties. "Joe, if you clue me in, maybe I can help you out."

Joe shook his weary head. It felt like one of those Bobbleheads you see on dashboards or nodding from back windows at you as you idle in dead traffic. Joe's neighbor, an avid collector of kitsch, had a trio of them on her dash—Elvis, the Queen of England, and Pennywise the Clown. Joe had always found this bizarre tableau to be unsettling. While Elvis crooned, Pennywise leaned in to the ever-smiling, ever-waving Queen, offering her a red balloon.

He looked at Glen, defeated. "Untie him, Glen."

"Are you insane?" his brother said.

"I'm in so much shit already," Joe said. He sighed loud

enough for Blazer to bolt upright. "I don't need kidnapping a cop thrown into the mix too."

"Think about this, Joey," Glen said. "Is this really what you want to do?"

Joe threw up his arms. Blazer perked up again. "What other choice do I have? We can't just leave the guy tied to a kitchen chair."

Glen shook his head. "I say we take things one step at a time. We deal with the situation ahead of us, then we can decide what to do with our Peeping Tom."

"No," Joe said, anger tingeing the edges of his voice. "This has gone too far. Besides, maybe he can be of help." MacAvoy smiled and nodded.

"Help?" Glen said incredulously. "Why would he help?"

"I'm not the enemy," MacAvoy said calmly. "You can trust me."

Glen scoffed and handed Joe a gun. "He makes any sudden moves, shoot him," Glen said matter-of-factly. Joe nodded, though he knew when push came to shove, he wouldn't be able to pull the trigger. Glen moved toward the bound man. MacAvoy grunted and wriggled as Glen worked the rope. "Hey, shitbag, this'll go a lot easier if you stay the fuck still," Glen said.

The rope dropped silently to the floor. MacAvoy rose slowly, twisting and stretching, pumping blood back into his sinewy frame. Glen took the gun back, keeping it trained on the cop. "Move to that chair over there." MacAvoy complied.

"Now what?" the cop said.

"Now we wait for our friends to show up," Glen replied.

"Detective, can I get you anything? Water? A beer?" Joe said.

"Joey, are you kidding?" Glen said. Joe shrugged.

MacAvoy smiled. "A glass of water would be great. Thank you."

Joe ignored his brother's grumblings behind him as he made his way to the kitchen. He ran the faucet, watched the eddy circle the drain before sliding down into the abyss. He felt as though he were caught in a whirlpool, his body spinning haphazardly, clawing for purchase at anything that could save him from being pulled under. With no safety net to grab hold of, he felt the pressure of the vortex sucking him down into an inky chasm. Over the deafening roar of the maelstrom, he could hear Patty's raspy voice laughing, taunting. *Hey Cowboy, need a hand? Grab tight, I'll pull you back in.*

He reentered the room where his brother stood on high alert and handed the water to the cop. MacAvoy nodded thanks and downed the contents in one motion. Joe gazed out at the listless grey sky, as bleak as his future. The rain had let up some, the lake and boathouse now visible through the blur.

"What the hell?"

Joe's head shot in the direction of his brother's alarmed voice, focused his eyes on the roadway leading into the property. Blazer's ears stood at attention. A dark SUV approached slowly, stealthily. They were here.

"It's them," Joe said. "What should we—" A flash of color on the edges of his vision strangled his voice. MacAvoy. Lunging toward Glen, his brother's attention focused on the vehicle rolling into view. It happened quickly, yet seemingly in slow motion. The hefty glass crashed down on his brother's head. Glen stumbled, tried to regain his footing. MacAvoy slammed his weight into the much larger man, sending him crashing forward. Glen's head connected with the thick granite top of a coffee table and he went down with a sickening thud. The gun flew through the air in a slow-motion spiral.

Blazer raced around, whining and pouncing. Yet he didn't attack. Joe remembered his brother mentioning an attack word. Something in Spanish or French, maybe? Blazer whimpered and sat stock-still. Some watchdog.

MacAvoy grabbed the gun midair and pointed it at Joe. "Don't be stupid," he said.

Joe raised his arms in surrender. Glen struggled to sit up, an alarming amount of blood seeping from the gash on his head. Joe had once read that head wounds were usually not as bad as they appeared. That the scalp has a high number of blood vessels close to the skin's surface, causing heavier bleeding. *But that's a lot of blood.* He hoped for Glen's sake, this was true.

MacAvoy danced around the men like an adrenaline-fueled rookie boxer facing his first contender. His eyes ping-ponged from Joe to Glen to the car looming outside. They refocused and locked in on Joe. "How many are there?"

"Three. My wife, Patty, and Rufus." Then Joe added, "Rufus is a big motherfucker."

MacAvoy's face was painted in two coats—excitement and fear. "Okay, so only one real threat," he said.

Joe laughed. "Don't underestimate Patty, my friend. She's even tougher than that Neanderthal."

Glen let out a loud groan. Blood slid down his ashen face. Joe looked at MacAvoy, seeking approval. The cop nodded and Joe rushed to his brother's side. He slid Glen's t-shirt over his injured head and pressed it into the gaping wound. "Glen." His dazed brother didn't make eye contact. "Glen." This time he did. "I need you to keep pressure on this for me. Can you do that?" His brother nodded weakly. He turned to MacAvoy. "I'm going to get some ice." MacAvoy complied once more with a slow nod.

Blazer slinked over to his master with trepidation. He sniffed and began licking the seeping wound.

"Blazer! Get away!" Joe screamed as he reentered with an ice pack. Blazer eyed him with what looked like a mixture of fear and loathing but backed off. Joe replaced the blood-soaked tee with the ice pack. Glen flinched but held it tight. Like the rain *tap-tapping* the window, the bleeding appeared to be receding.

"What the—who the hell is that?" MacAvoy said.

Joe moved to the window. A bright red umbrella bobbed up and down on the crest of the driveway, shielding a striking young woman with auburn hair. She moved with purpose, head down to shelter her face from the slowing-yet-still-soaking rain. The woman approached the SUV containing the triple threat. Joe looked at MacAvoy. "I have no idea." Then it struck him like a ton of bricks as he realized who it was.

CHAPTER FORTY-EIGHT

"Where the hell are we?" Patty said. "This doesn't feel right."

Rufus grimaced. "I told you it was probably a setup," he said. "And now we're gonna end up stuck in this friggin' mud bath."

Patty swiveled her head. "Katie, do you know this place?"

Katie leaned forward, straining to take in the distorted view beyond the droning sweeps of the wipers. "Uh-uh. Never seen it." Her eyes narrowed. "But that's my dearly beloved's car."

Patty scanned the landscape. Cowboy's vehicle was the only one in sight, though the erratic flourishes of rain washed out much of the panorama, creating the illusion of a giant watercolor. "I don't know. It feels wrong. Why here? Why not somewhere more public?"

Rufus shrugged. Katie, concern etched into her lovely face, said, "I agree, Aunt Patty. Wouldn't it make more sense for him to do the handoff somewhere safer, where he could make a quick exit?"

"Maybe he isn't planning on a quick exit," Rufus said.

Patty furrowed her brow. "Well, we ain't come this far to just turn around. I want what's mine. And I want my pound of flesh."

"Then let's do it," Rufus said. "Let's get the fucker and be done with it." He reached for the door handle. Stopped. Shot Patty an alarmed look.

"What's wrong?"

Rufus was peering through the rearview. "Looks like we've got company."

Patty glanced through the side mirror and a splash of red came into view. An umbrella. A young woman perched beneath it. The woman caught Patty's reflection in the mirror. Smiled. Threw a casual wave. Pretty little thing. For the moment, anyway.

The woman looked up at the churning, malevolent clouds overhead, tugged a shiny hood over her pretty little head and reached the car door. A red blossom exploded before Patty. The umbrella rose, exposing the woman's fresh-scrubbed features.

Patty rolled the window down a few inches, beads of rain ricocheting off the glass, splashing her face with the exhilarating cold. "Hello," she shouted in the sweetest voice she could muster.

The woman clutched the red umbrella with determination, as though it might lift her off the ground and shoot her straight to the heavens. "Hi," she said. "Lovely weather we're having, isn't it?"

Patty dabbed at her moistened face. "Sure is, honey."

The woman looked toward the house, then back to Patty. "Are you friends of Glen?" she asked.

Glen. Cowboy's brother. Patty beamed. "Why, yes. As a

matter of fact, we are." Katie shot a friendly wave from the backseat. Rufus was stoic, steely-eyed.

"I'm Rebecca," she said. "Glen's girlfriend. I've been so busy with work lately, so I thought I'd surprise him."

Oh, you're in for a surprise alright.

"Had I known the weather would be this bad, I'd have reconsidered," she said. "In fact, my car got stuck in the mud when I tried to climb the slope." She looked down at her muddied boots. "I tried to put it in reverse, but it won't budge. I guess I need four-wheel drive like you."

Patty rolled the window down a bit more. "Well, honey, you're gonna catch your death out there. Hop in and get warm."

Rebecca smiled and shook her head. "Oh, thanks for your kindness, but I'll just run on up to the house."

Patty's face turned to stone. "I said get in the car."

The woman, her face awash in mist and confusion, said, "Excuse me? I'm sorry, but—"

She was silenced by the gun pointed directly at her face.

Joe instinctively knew it was Rebecca, that *someone special* Glen had referred to. He watched her approach the massive vehicle, speak briefly to the passenger in the SUV—*Patty, maybe?*—then her expression changed. First to one of confusion, then to sheer terror. The rear door opened, and she disappeared into the backseat.

"Glen?" His brother was returning to the land of the living, though he was clearly still in a state of confusion. "Glen."

Glen looked up from his perch on the floor. "Joey, what happened?"

"Never mind that. Does Rebecca have red hair?"

The sea of confusion washed over Glen again. "What? Yeah, she—why?"

"Were you expecting her?"

Glen sat bolt upright, reality sinking into his throbbing brain. "No. Why?"

Joe needed to tell Glen but knew it wasn't going to sit well with him. Not well at all. And until they got that bleeding under control, he wasn't going to be of use to Rebecca or anyone else. "I think she just showed up."

As Joe suspected, Glen was alive and kicking. He tossed the ice pack aside, ready to take on the world. A line of red slid down his beefy head. He wobbled, tried to steady himself.

"Easy, bro," Joe said, catching him before he toppled. "Before we do anything, we need to close up that wound." MacAvoy nodded in agreement.

Glen grabbed Joe by the shoulders. Though dazed, his strength was still palpable. "Go to my desk."

"What? Why?"

"There's a stapler in the left drawer."

"Are you kidding me?" MacAvoy said.

Glen ignored the cop. "Joey, we don't have time for a clean and stitch job. Do it. Now."

Joe looked at MacAvoy, who shook his head in disbelief. He brushed by the cop and hightailed it to the desk.

Armed with his makeshift surgical weapon, he moved toward Glen, who was now pressed to the glass. "Where is she?" he said. "I don't see her or her car."

"Glen, all I know is she was standing outside the SUV and then got inside." Glen staggered, his sturdy legs looking as fragile as toothpicks. "You need to sit," Joe said. His brother complied. "Mickey, can you give me a hand here?"

MacAvoy hesitated, then tucked the gun in his back and stepped forward. "What do you need me to do?"

"Just hold his head steady." Joe looked at his brother. "You ready, tough guy?"

Glen smiled weakly. "Work your magic, doc."

MacAvoy gripped Glen's head like it was a basketball. Joe dabbed at the three-inch long gash and pushed the tattered pieces of flesh together. Blood bubbled from the slit, washing over Joe's fingers. Glen winced but held still. Blazer sighed and rested his head on his owner's leg.

The curve in the crown of Glen's head made it difficult to connect the flaps of ragged skin and the first couple of attempts failed. Though the pain was clearly excruciating, Glen didn't flinch. On the third attempt—*third time's a charm*—Joe slammed down hard with the stapler. Glen released a guttural cry, which was mimicked by his four-legged friend. But the staple held. With each new seal, the gap grew narrower, the blood flow diminishing.

Pleased with his do-it-yourself handiwork, Joe said, "Okay Frankenstein, you're as good as new."

With that, Glen pushed the cop away and jumped into action. MacAvoy raised his gun. "Seriously, man?" Glen said.

MacAvoy stood his ground. "Where do you think you're going?"

Glen's anger came to a boil, then receded. "Listen, Mickey," he said, feigning compliance, "I get it. You need to do your job. But right now, my girl is in danger and I'm going after her. Either shoot me or step the fuck aside."

MacAvoy studied the large man, let out a sigh, and moved to

his right. Glen moved like an Olympic athlete, oblivious to the staples in his head or the blood streaking his face, congealing in the stubble.

Joe watched this dance in silence as Glen pulled an impressive gun from a cupboard one would expect to house a set of dinnerware or a Crock-Pot. As Glen brushed by, Joe gripped his brother's meaty arm. "Glen, do you have a plan?"

Glen pushed him away, irritation settling into the blood-caked lines in his face. "Yeah. The plan is to go out there and save my girl."

Joe laughed. "Gonna go all Liam Neeson on them, is that the plan?"

"Damn straight," Glen said. "Now step aside, baby brother."

MacAvoy, whom Joe had briefly forgotten was at arm's length, said, "Your brother's right, Glen. We need a plan."

"*We?* We need a plan? This has nothing to do with you, so stay the fuck out of my face." Glen's eyes were feral, the veins bookending his forehead pulsating at an alarming rate. Joe half-expected to see his surgical expertise go to ruin, staples popping like firecrackers.

"Glen," Joe said, "Think for a second. You don't know what kind of firepower they have. You run out there willy-nilly and you're a sitting duck."

Glen's face relaxed. Then his lips curled up into a ghoulish smile. He laughed. "Willy-nilly? Did you actually just say that?"

Now Joe laughed. It was a term their mother used when they were boys, before the booze, the affairs, the dysfunction. During that brief period when they had the semblance of a normal family.

Joseph, don't do your homework all willy-nilly! Don't you want to get into college?

Boys, your room is a pigsty. Go clean it—and don't be all willy-nilly about it!

This simple memory, before all the bad ones, before the Campbell household went all willy-nilly, struck a nerve in Glen. His shoulders sagged, the pulsing temples took a breather, his steely gaze softened. He stood silently for a moment and then said, "You're right, Joey. So, what's our plan?"

PART THREE

Collateral Damage

CHAPTER FORTY-NINE

The lugubrious sky softened, the mottled grey clouds taking on a silvery glow, dotting the restless ridges in the lake. The rain had at last relented, downgrading to a light mist. Joe wasn't sure if this sudden shift in weather was going to benefit them or impede them.

Though the SUV had only been staked outside for twenty minutes, it felt like they'd been held hostage for hours. No movement from inside the vehicle. Joe suspected Patty was going to wait for him to make the first move. He was the pawn, feeling things out for the troops, setting in motion a series of tactics, with the intention of capturing the Queen. The Queen in this life-or-death game being the stealthy and totally unpredictable Patty Quigley.

"I think I should go out there," he said at last.

Glen scoffed. "Are you crazy, Joey? Like you said before, we don't know what they're armed with."

MacAvoy nodded. "I have to agree with your brother."

Joe paused, waiting for Glen to tell the cop to go fuck himself. When he didn't, Joe continued. "Listen. They still think I just want Kate back. I go out there and tell them to release Rebecca and Kate and I'll give them what they want."

"And you think they're just going to take it and go on their merry way?" Glen said. Joe didn't appreciate the mocking tone in his brother's voice.

"No, Glen, I don't," he responded in an equally sardonic tone. "That's where you two come in."

Glen looked at the cop, then at Joe. "Two? Do you really think you can trust this guy?"

MacAvoy opened his mouth to speak, but Joe deflected him. "Do we have a choice?"

Glen grumbled and fingered his makeshift surgical job. MacAvoy looked alert and eager to go, like a child waiting in line to ride a high-speed rollercoaster—a mix of excitement, adrenaline, and sheer terror coursing through his veins—at once anticipating and fearing the ride.

"I'm in," MacAvoy said. He looked at Glen. "And like your brother said, do any of us really have a choice?"

Glen stroked Blazer's lustrous coat, which seemed to have a calming effect on the big man. "Okay, bro, so you said that's where we come in. What's on your mind?"

"If I can distract them long enough, you and Mick can flank them on both sides."

"That's assuming they haven't already blown a hole in your midsection," Glen said. A slight smile crept into his rugged features, made all the more rugged by the dried blood, now a muddled brownish-burgundy.

Joe smiled back. "Yeah, well, how about you guys make sure

that doesn't happen. I kind of like my midsection right where it is."

MacAvoy moved toward Glen, who flinched, then relaxed. "Glen, truce?" The cop extended a hand.

Glen studied the man's hand as though it were a foreign specimen. Then he said, "What the hell," and took the man's hand in his crushing, vein-swelled baseball mitt. MacAvoy winced but held firm.

Glen released his iron-clad grip. MacAvoy massaged his hand, a feeling Joe knew well. Then the cop said, "So, what kind of firepower do we have?"

Joe and Glen locked gazes and simultaneously smiled.

MacAvoy shrugged. "Am I missing something here?"

The brothers laughed in unison and Glen gave MacAvoy a follow-me.

As they moved toward the basement, Glen said, "You like candy, Mick?"

MacAvoy, his face a mask of confusion, said, "Um, candy? I guess so. Why?"

Glen quickened his pace and bounded down the narrow basement steps. "Because you're about to be a kid in a candy store, my friend."

CHAPTER FIFTY

M ick-Mac stared in awe at the display before him. The arsenal was impressive, if a bit alarming for a man living alone in the middle of the woods. An army of munitions and hardware stood at attention on the drab walls. The overhead lighting bounced off the gleaming metal, creating an unconventional light show. Amid all the flash-and-glitter, one object cried out for attention, stealing the show from its distant cousins.

Mick-Mac reached for the imposing crossbow, eager to wrap his hands around its lethal beauty.

"Don't touch."

Mick-Mac froze, his fingers close enough to the object that he could feel its electricity. He recoiled.

"That's off limits," Glen said. "But there's plenty of other candy in the store."

Mick-Mac nodded, though none of the other *candy* looked quite as appetizing as that shimmering hulk of sculpted metal enticing him to give her a go. Mick-Mac had developed a fascination with crossbows since running across a much-forgotten eighties movie called *The Osterman Weekend* on cable during one of many sleepless nights following Marnie's death.

Though the film, based on a Robert Ludlum novel, was a bit convoluted, it featured a bloody, pulse-pounding climax in which Rutger Hauer's family falls under siege. His wife, played by Meg Foster, the actress with ice-blue eyes so hypnotic they couldn't possibly be real, wielded a crossbow with the precision of a skilled marksman, taking out an assassin with those unwavering eyes.

Mick-Mac window shopped, finally settling on a reliable Smith & Wesson semi-automatic pistol and a lightweight Glock 27 to strap to his ankle. But, damn, he still wanted that crossbow.

Glen tossed a Kevlar vest to Mick-Mac, and another to his brother. The vest was heavier than Mick-Mac anticipated. "You don't mess around, do you?" Mick said.

Glen winked and motioned them to the stairs. The stapled gash in his head didn't appear to impede him and he bounded up the stairs without hesitation. Joe, looking like a fish out of water toting his body armor and weaponry, followed with trepidation in each step. Mick-Mac pulled up the rear. His cell vibrated. A text from Eddie Diaz.

Where the fuck are you, MacAvoy?

If only Eddie could see him now. He thought to respond, then clicked off his phone and joined his new brothers in arms.

They sat in silence, the only sounds the faint drumming of the ebbing rain and the hushed sobs of the pretty little redhead. Patty was tempted to put a cap between those pretty little eyes to shut her up but decided she might make a good bargaining chip.

"Are we just going to sit here all day?" Rufus mumbled and shifted in his seat.

Patty's patience had been stretched way beyond its limit. Between the little Kewpie doll's weeping and the Neanderthal's increasingly annoying edginess creeping under her skin, her inclination was to toss them both out of the car, leaving her with her silent thoughts. *Calm yourself, Patty.*

Her gaze shifted to the cabin. At the blackened squares flanking each side of the doorway. Wondering what Cowboy and his brother were conspiring. With Cowboy, she knew exactly what she was up against. But with the enigmatic brother tossed into the salad, she felt an odd sensation she hadn't experienced since her last days with Dominic. Utter dread.

Patty turned to face the sobbing woman. "Turn the faucet off and listen up, Buttercup," she said. The woman, her pretty appearance smeared by a mix of rain and tears, sniffed and looked at Patty with pleading eyes.

"Do as I say, and nobody gets hurt. Got it?" The woman nodded and swiped at her cheek. "Do you know what they're up to?"

The woman was a sea of confusion. "I'm not sure what you mean," she said, a slight tremor accenting the last word. "Like I said, I haven't seen Glen in about a week."

"Do you know his brother?"

The woman shook her weary head. "No. Glen's mentioned him before, but we've never met."

Patty turned her attention to Katie, who had been peculiarly silent. "You've met this Glen guy before. What are we up against?"

Katie frowned. "Well, he's a motherfucking bastard, for one thing." She looked at the petite redhead. "No offense."

Patty sighed. "Katie, I'm not interested in your personal relationship with him. What I want to know is if he's as weak and useless as your husband." She smiled and added, "No offense."

"None taken, Auntie." She paused for a moment, as if she'd forgotten where she'd left her thoughts and was now gathering them up in her head. "It's been a while since I've seen him, but he's big."

"How big?"

Katie went back to her imaginary thought collecting. Then her eyes sparked. "Big like Chris Hemsworth, but not as hot." She looked to the woman and once again said, "No offense."

"None taken," the woman spat back. The weeping willow seemed to be growing a spine.

"I think he's some kind of banker or something. But he looks like a surfer dude on steroids. And I think he has a mean temper."

The woman, now brimming with venom, sprang forward and said, "Glen is the kindest person I know!"

Patty smirked. "Okay, so we've got Cowboy, who I could snap in two with one hand. And we have a finance nerd who's kind but has a temper. I think we're good." She punched Rufus in the arm. "What say you, big guy?"

Rufus grinned, a malevolent grin, like the one Dominic wore when something bad was about to happen. The thought made her shudder. Rufus said, "I say we go in there and rip them apart."

"Down, boy," Patty said. "All in due time." She gazed again at the silent house. This standoff was growing tedious. If Cowboy wasn't going to make the first move, she may have to alter her plans. She pulled out her cell and prepared to dial him up.

"Who are you calling?" Katie said.

"Your useless waste of space hubby," Patty said, her impatience hitting a peak, the sudden urge to end this thing screaming inside her. "If he's not going to—"

"He's right there," Katie interrupted.

Patty, finger set to hit *Cowboy*, followed Katie's pointing finger. Standing in the cabin's doorway, arms raised in surrender, was one Joe Campbell himself. "Well, I'll be damned," she said. "It looks like this party's about to get started."

CHAPTER FIFTY-ONE

"We're here, boss," Diego announced through the speaker. Dom Jr. lowered his window. The deluge had briefly waned, and the light spray felt good on his face. A lack of sleep since entering that shithole bar was taking its toll on him, mentally and physically. The relentless stiffness in his neck and clawing on his insides he could handle. It was the mental part that was unbearable, the image of Padre's lifeless face on an endless loop tormenting every waking moment.

Dom Jr. gazed at the muddied roadway. A small Toyota sat dead center, knee deep in the muck. It listed slightly to the right like a run-aground boat and appeared to be unoccupied. "You sure this is the place, Diego?"

Diego nodded. Dom Jr. slid the window up. A black SUV rolled up alongside the Lincoln. Frankie T, a dark-eyed lady killer and one of the best sharpshooters Dom Jr. had ever seen, yelled something incoherent. Dom Jr. slid the window back down. It suddenly occurred to him that he'd never asked what the T stood for. Maybe once they got this business settled, he'd ask him.

"Boss, what's the plan?" Frankie T said, those black-as-pitch eyes bright and alert.

"We can't gain entrance this way," he said, gesturing at the swamped Toyota.

Frankie T nodded. "We pulled the place up on Google Maps," he said. "Looks like there's nothing but forest and a lake surrounding the place. Not another house in sight."

Dom Jr. nodded, pleased by the news. No other houses meant no other people. Which meant no other witnesses. Which meant no collateral damage. Not that he was concerned about collateral damage. Sometimes it couldn't be helped, and he was just fine with that. Except—and he'd never speak this aloud to his troops—when the collateral damage involved children.

Though painted by the media as a *sadistic thug with a heart of stone* or his favorite bit of editorial drivel, *the bad apple didn't fall far from the rotted tree*, he drew the line at kids—and dogs, for that matter. Ever since the unfortunate incident in the Public Garden three years ago, he vowed he would never allow a repeat of that fiasco, one that still haunted his waking moments.

Boston Public Garden. The place that had haunted his dreams, often sliding into his waking hours. After much dispute, Dom Jr. had convinced Padre to let him take the lead on an operation. The take was big, the client prominent.

Though he'd already gotten his feet wet out in the field, Dom Jr. had never run an operation. Padre had a bad feeling about it, but after much persuasion, Dom Jr. had won the battle. A battle neither of them would dare breathe a word of to his mother. Dom Jr. was paired up with a short, rotund, pasty-faced guy he knew only as Wile E. Coyote. As the two men headed for their rendezvous, Dom Jr. asked the man how he earned the nickname.

"Like in the cartoon," Wile E. said. "You ever watch the Road Runner, Nicky?"

"The name's Dom," Dom Jr. spat out, anger scorching the edges of his voice. Ten minutes on the road with this jackass and he was ready to toss the guy into the Charles River.

Wile E., clearly sensing he'd ruffled his cohort's feathers, smiled and said, "Sorry about that. I just thought I heard Mr. Guierriero call you that the other day."

"You did," Dom Jr. said, "And nobody other than my parents calls me that. Nobody. Are we clear?"

Wile E. gripped the steering wheel tightly, his pale knuckles turning two shades paler. "Crystal," he said.

They drove in silence, Wile E. stoic, his pasty face now a burnished red. The guy had struck a nerve, calling him something reserved solely for the two most important people in his life. But, hell, this little Weeble didn't know any better. Time to let him off the hook.

"Sorry, man," he said at last. Wile E.'s body remained stiff, hands in the ten-and-two position, eyes locked on the endless highway. "Come on," Dom Jr. said. "Tell me how you got the nickname." The man's eyes remained locked in position, but his body relaxed a bit.

Wile E. shrugged. "You don't really care," he mumbled.

Truth be told, Dom Jr. really did want to know. "Sure, I do," Dom Jr. said, feigning sincerity.

Wile E. smiled, his doughy face morphing back to its original pallor. "Well, I'd tell you, but then I'd have to kill you," he said. Dom Jr. gazed icily at the man. The floodgates reopened on Wile E.'s face, crimson blotches exploding like it was Independence Day. His grip on the steering wheel loosened, and he nearly drifted over the pavement's center line. "I'm sorry, Mr. Guierriero, it was a joke—you know, industry humor." The man's chubby lip tremored.

If he had a dime for every time he heard someone use that tired line, he'd be a rich man. Then again, he was already richer than the Hollywood elite and the LeBrons and Tigers of the sports world. Dom Jr. toyed with the man, enjoying his unease. Finally, he said, "Ease up, man. I'm just fucking with you. Now how's about clueing me in on this name."

Wile E., though still visibly shaken, smiled and nodded. "Well, you know the Road Runner cartoon?"

Dom Jr. nodded and made a get-on-with-it gesture.

"Well, that coyote's always trying to catch him, but he never does. He always falls off a cliff or blows himself up or an anvil falls on his head."

Looking at the man's bald, flattish head, Dom Jr. was tempted to ask him if an anvil had, in fact, landed on his head. Fearing one more upset would send them into a ravine, he just smiled and nodded again.

"I never actually blew myself up or fell off a cliff," he said, "but I always end up in situations where I get hurt, sometimes bad enough where I've almost died." He shrugged and said, "And that's how I got the name."

They drove in awkward silence for the remainder of the trip, Dom Jr. hoping things went as smoothly as Padre assured him it would. It was a simple plan. Head to the Boy and Bird Fountain to the south of the Arlington Street entrance. Look for a man wearing a yellow and green Oakland A's baseball cap carrying a nondescript black backpack seated by the fountain. Switch their black backpack for his. Simple. Piece of cake. In and out. If only that had been the case.

Dom Jr. spotted the fountain up ahead. The famous park was teeming with tourists and locals on this perfect, cloudless day. Kids running about everywhere. Dom Jr. was suddenly gripped by apprehension.

"There he is," Wile E. said, pointing toward the bold cap.

"Be discreet, you dumb fuck," Dom Jr. said through gritted teeth. Wile E. recoiled, back in defense mode. "Let's just do this and get the fuck out of here."

They approached the man. Dom Jr. felt a tug on the back of his jacket. He turned. A young boy of about six or seven gazed up at him.

"Hey, Mister," the boy said. "Did you know that if you throw a coin in the fountain, you get to make a wish?"

Dom Jr. smiled and turned away. Another tug.

The boy held up a shiny penny. "If you throw a penny in, you only get one wish," he said. *Where the hell are your parents?* "But my sister said if you throw a quarter in, you get three wishes."

"That's very nice," Dom Jr. said, again trying to distance himself from the little shit. "Why don't you go make your wish?"

The boy stamped his feet. "But I wanna make three!" he said. "Gimme a quarter, Mister, or I'll scream."

"I don't have any quarters, buddy," Dom Jr. said, feeling the eyes of passersby burning through him, drawing exactly the kind of attention he had hoped to avoid. The boy opened his mouth to scream. "Okay, okay," Dom Jr. said. "I'll get you your quarter, kid." The boy beamed, obviously used to getting his own way. Dom Jr. turned to Wile E. "Got a quarter?"

Wile E.'s fat face scrunched up. "A quarter? Why?"

"Just give me a fucking quarter," Dom Jr. demanded. Wile E. dug into his baggy trousers and produced a dime, three nickels and a penny. Dom Jr. snatched the coins and spun around. The little shit was standing stock-still, his face cracked into a big smile. Dom Jr. put the coins into the boy's tiny, outstretched hand.

The boy frowned. "These aren't quarters," he said, looking ready to erupt.

Dom Jr., at his wit's end, said, "No, but these are worth more than a quarter, so you might even get four wishes. How about that?"

The boy furrowed his brow and studied the coins. He rolled his eyes. "Everyone knows that nobody gets four wishes, Mister. Duh!" With that, he stuck out his tongue, closed his tiny hand over the coins and ran off.

Dom Jr., relieved to be rid of the little pain in the ass, turned back to his partner. The guy in the Oakland A's cap was poking Wile E. in the chest, his face ablaze with fury. Dom Jr. rushed over. "Is there a problem here?"

"Yeah, there's a problem," Oakland A's said. He pointed at the black backpack dangling from Wile E.'s arm. "This shit you've got here," he spat. "It's shit."

Dom Jr. glanced around, noticed eyes gazing their way. "Listen, there must be some kind of misunderstanding. Let's take a breath."

Oakland A's, who looked as though he might be tripping on something, shook his head the way a dog does after it's had a bath. "No, I will not take a breath," he said. "When my boss finds out, you're fucked."

Wile E., who had remained silent, reached into his coat and removed something. Dom Jr. couldn't see what it was from his vantage point, but the wide-eyed panic painted on Oakland A's' face gave him a pretty good indication. "Whoa, man, take it easy," Oakland A's said.

Then Dom Jr. caught the glint of metal in the blazing sunlight. "Hey, man, what are you doing?" He gripped Wile E.'s arm. Wile E. shrugged him off and said to Oakland A's, "When my boss finds out, we're all fucked so hand over the money and walk away."

A shrill cry reverberated through the park. The fountain boy screamed, "Gun! That guy has a gun!"

That was when everything went to shit. Oakland A's reached for the gun. The two men struggled. Screaming families, couples, and joggers scattered. A gunshot. Wile E. fell with a heavy thud.

Oakland A's leveled the gun. Dom Jr. dove for cover. The gun exploded again. *I'm dying,* he thought. But, to his surprise, there was no pain in death. The world seemed to spin. At last, his brain processed the fact that he wasn't dying after all. He sat up. The crowd had dispersed. Oakland A's, with both backpacks in tow, faded away in a blur.

Dom Jr. gazed in horror at Wile E. His face was frozen in a ghastly death mask.

I guess the Road Runner finally got the best of you, pal.

An unearthly wail behind him. He spun around. The fountain boy. He rushed over to the dying boy. The boy whispered something inaudible. Dom Jr. put his ear closer. This time, he heard the boy clearly. "I made a wish, Mister."

Dom Jr. who hadn't shed a tear since the death of his baby sister, let out a guttural cry. "What did you wish for, buddy?"

The boy flicked his eyelids a few times. He opened his mouth to speak, his voice a watery whisper. Dom Jr. pressed his ear to the boy's mouth. The boy let out a hollow gasp and was silent.

Dom Jr. stared at the lifeless face. What was the boy's dying wish? Perhaps something grandiose like a trip to Disneyworld. Or maybe something as simple as a candy bar or that toy he'd been eyeing in Walmart. Whatever the wish, Dom Jr. had stolen it. And any future wishes.

"Mr. Guierriero. Boss!" Dom Jr. bolted upright. "Are you okay, boss?" Frankie T said.

Dom Jr. realized he was sweating profusely, his hands unsteady. He swiped at his brow, adjusted his tie, nodded slowly and snapped, "I'm fine. Let's move the team out."

CHAPTER FIFTY-TWO

J oe inched apprehensively toward the SUV, the rain still
steady enough to make any movement behind the tinted
glass indiscernible. The imposing vehicle taunted him in
its stillness, its sleek muscular physique ready to pounce,
menacing eyes studying him, as if anticipating his next move.

He inched forward, stalling enough to give Glen and Mick
time to get into position but quick enough to avoid raising
suspicion from the ever-perceptible Patty Quigley. The rain
pelted his eyeballs, tickled his nose. He swiped at his face
slowly, fearful any sudden movement may wake the sleeping
monster.

The driver's door swung open. He froze. For a long moment,
nothing happened. He stood motionless, even his breathing on
pause. Then Rufus's ugly mug emerged. Followed by a heavily
inked arm attached to a gun. Pointing directly at Joe's face.

Joe instinctively raised his hands. Rufus remained focused

on his target. "I'm unarmed," Joe yelled over the steady din and increasing wind.

"Do I look like I give a shit?" Rufus said. "Now, where's the stuff, Campbell?"

Joe relaxed his shoulders, started to lower his arms. Rufus stiffened and drew a tighter bead on his target. Joe raised his arms and said, "You'll get them when Kate and Rebecca are safe."

Rufus remained locked in on his target. "No, you'll get them when we get—"

Rufus's mouth stopped moving, and his body suddenly jerked forward. The gun slipped from his fingers, falling to the ground. The big man's face twisted up in pain. He clutched his left shoulder then lifted his hand out in front of him, a curious look on his face as he inspected it.

Is that blood?

Rufus spun his head to the left then to the right and back again, as if he were watching a high-speed tennis match. Then his gaze fell to the vehicle's interior. "I've been shot!" he yelled. He retreated into the safety of the SUV.

Shot? Glen would never randomly shoot. He was too methodical, too precise. Besides, if his aim was to take the guy out, Rufus would be face-planted in the muck. No, Glen wasn't that reckless. Could it have been Mick? Joe didn't know anything about the guy, but his gut had said to trust him. Now he wasn't so sure.

A loud cracking sound. Thunder? Then pain exploded on the right side of his face. Joe reached up, running his fingers along the slick surface of his face. The rain felt thick, liquidy. Then he remembered what Rufus had said and the way he'd looked at his hand. He mimicked the action. A mix of blood and rain streamed down his fingers. His hand shot back up to his face, fingers tracing the contours of his cheeks, his nose, his lips. All seemingly intact. So where was all this blood coming from?

His fingers walked across his cheek, reaching out for his earlobe. Where the hell was it? Panic seized him. He groped feverishly for his ear. His fingers connected with flesh. Tattered flesh. He realized with horror that part of his ear was gone. Like Rufus, he'd been shot. He turned to race back into the house. Another loud crack. From the tree line. Someone was out there. Not Glen. Not Mick.

He bolted for the house, planning to make it with one ear completely intact.

Mick-Mac was approaching the SUV when a crack exploded in the air. Years of training immediately told him it was a gunshot. He looked around. Ducked out of instinct. With his vision blurred by the unremitting deluge, he couldn't tell what direction the shot had come from.

He'd seen the big bald guy exit the vehicle, then saw Joe raise his arms. Their voices were indistinguishable over the sizzle of the rain. Then the big guy had jerked forward, clutched his shoulder and retreated into the SUV. Seconds later, he saw Joe make a similar move, only he clawed at his head. Joe then turned and sprinted for the cabin, arms over his head as if a piano were about to drop onto him.

Someone else was out here with them. He wasn't sure of Glen's exact location, but he was no doubt as exposed as Mick. Mick-Mac glanced around, studying the forest on either side.

Majestic trees soared high into the angry clouds, the blurred spaces between them looking as though they'd been hastily scribbled in with a black crayon. A brilliant flash disrupted the eerie blackness of the dense woods off to Mick-Mac's left.

He dove for cover, the cold mud seeping into his clothing, reminding him he was still alive. He crawled through the thick muck toward a sizeable pine tree and shimmied himself into a seated position. The heavily decayed bark pressed into his back. If there was only one shooter, he was safe for the time being. But if there were others out there, he was a sitting duck.

Did Patty have backup out there? Based on what Joe had told him about her, he doubted it. But, who else could it be? Then it hit him. And he realized he was in way over his head.

Dom Jr. sat in the dry warmth of the car, one of the perks of being in charge. He'd done his time in the field—by choice. That time, Padre had tried to dissuade him, saying it was not only dangerous, as he would eventually find out in the Boston Public Garden, but also beneath his status as a Guierriero.

"Nicky, my son, you're a Guierriero," Padre had said. "You must command respect from your men. By teaching them. Guiding them. And sending them off. Remember, they're expendable. You, my son, are not."

Dom Jr. had argued the point, stating that to earn respect, one must understand them, see things from their eyes. It was only then that you truly gained their respect and allegiance.

Despite Padre's disapproval, it was finally agreed that Nicky was to get his hands dirty. Nicky enjoyed the adrenaline rush and could sense the admiration of the team. And for a while, things were good. Until that fateful day when he watched that young boy die in his arms, much like his baby sister had died in Padre's arms. From that day on, he swore never to place himself in a situation like that again. Padre was right. He was a Guierriero. He deserved better.

And so, he sank into the warmth of the luxurious imported leather, listening to the incessant drumming of the rain. Diego, the ever-protective guard dog, sat stock-still in front, watchful for any signal of imminent danger. The crackle of Frankie T's voice startled him from his reverie.

"Boss, shots have been fired. Repeat, shots have been fired. Two confirmed hits. No known casualties at this time."

"Two confirmed hits?" Dom Jr. replied. "Was one of those Joe Campbell?"

Frankie T's voice, a bit distorted but decipherable, said, "Roger that. Confirm that Campbell was one of the targets. Appears to be a flesh wound, sir." Frankie T was militant in his delivery. Respectful and articulate, unlike most of his other flunkies. And loyal as hell. Might be time to move him up in the ranks.

"Remember what I said? No kill shots on Campbell. He's all mine."

Roger that, boss."

"Any idea who the other target was?"

Frankie T's voice crackled loudly this time, the reception on the line worsening. "No ID on Target B. Big guy, tough guy. It appears he also has a beef against Campbell."

Dom Jr. contemplated this thought. Who the fuck was this Joe Campbell and who else wanted him dead? "Frankie, any other sign of life out there?"

There was a pause, as if Frankie T were getting all his ducks in a row. At last, he said, "Still determining, boss. A third target has been spotted and we have reason to believe there are other subjects in the vehicle Target B is holed up in."

He'd anticipated two targets. Campbell and his brother. In and out. Who were these other people fucking up their mission?

"Boss?"

"Yeah, Frankie?"

"Permission to eradicate any other targets on site, aside from Campbell?"

Dom Jr. pondered the thought for a moment. He had no idea how many other players there were or who they were. But they were unwelcome intruders in his game. Call it bad luck. Call it wrong place, wrong time. Whatever their reasons for being here in this moment, that was their decision. And their own damned bad luck. Call it collateral damage.

"Boss, permission to—?"

"Anything so much as moves, take it out," he said, rage building up inside.

"Boss?"

"What is it, Frankie?" he spat at the receiver, anger at last getting the better of him.

There was a long pause, Frankie T probably shitting his pants at the infuriated voice of his boss. Maybe he'd rethink that promotion after all. Finally, Frankie T said, "I...I...just want to clarify."

"What the *fuck* do you want to clarify?" The rage came to a boil, spilling over.

"When you say anything that moves," Frankie T stammered, "does that include kids?"

Dom Jr. was right back in the park again, the kid tugging on him, demanding a quarter. If only he'd had a quarter on him from the start, the kid probably would've tossed it in the fountain, made his wish, and been on his merry way before the shooting had begun. The tiny face and tiny voice still haunted his restless dreams.

I made a wish, Mister.

What did you wish for, buddy?

Dom Jr. knew the logical response to Frankie T's question. But then he thought of Padre lying on a cold slab. He thought of his baby sister's body hanging limply from his father's arms, the man's tears washing over her. And the grief permanently etched in his mother's eyes, once luminous, now as dead as her baby and husband.

His response likely shocked Frankie T, as it did him. "Like I said, if anything moves—I don't care if it's a granny in a wheelchair or a kid in diapers—if it moves, eliminate it. And then bring Campbell to me on a silver platter with the biggest fucking carving knife you can find. Is that clarification enough for you?"

The silence on the other end of the line indicated it was.

CHAPTER FIFTY-THREE

Joe inspected the damage under the too-dim bathroom light. A chunk of earlobe hung listlessly, held on by a thread of skin. Well, at least it was all there. He pressed a towel to the open wound, pain spidering into his synapses. He removed the blood-soaked towel, lifted the dangling flesh as if to reconnect it.

Still clutching the ravaged earlobe, Joe exited the bathroom, his eyes searching. Blazer tipped his head, eying him curiously. He scanned the room. "Ah, there you are." He snatched up the stapler and hightailed it back to the bathroom.

He lifted the stapler. Hesitated. It had worked on Glen, so why not give it another go? Then again, it was a lot easier to jump right in when you weren't the one on the other end. "Just do it, Joe." He pressed the pieces of flesh together and raised the stapler. "Here goes nothing."

The pain was excruciating. After the first three makeshift sutures, Joe's vision felt fuzzy around the edges, his head playing a steady drumbeat. His chest heaved and his legs went weak. He squeezed his eyes shut, the blackness a welcoming respite. Then he remembered his brother. Out there, in the line of fire. His eyes clicked open.

"Suck it up, Campbell," he said to the ashen reflection studying him. He clutched his ear, gritted his teeth, and completed the surgery. The stapler *clank-clanked* into the sink. Joe inspected his handiwork. Not bad for an amateur.

The disfigured appendage looked like something out of a monster movie, but the bleeding had been staunched. And as grisly as it looked, it also looked kind of badass. Which is exactly how Joe was feeling. To minimize the throbbing in his head, he downed a handful of ibuprofen and a couple of swigs of whiskey. Blazer gazed up at him, a mix of concern and excitement in his eyes. Joe took another swig from the bottle and said, "Let's go get 'em, boy." Blazer's tail indicated he was ready to go.

He stared at the arsenal, adrenaline pumping through his body with an intensity he'd never felt before. He needed a weapon, but what? Without Glen to guide him, he was a fish out of water. Until recently, he'd never even seen a gun up close, much less loaded and shot one. Until that fateful day he met Patty Quigley.

It seemed like years, not days, since his life had become a shoot-em-up action movie. As dull as his previous life had been, he now longed for it. But that life was long gone in the rearview. He'd reached the point of no return. Even if he somehow survived this day, what would his tomorrow be? He couldn't simply go back to his old life as if it were business as usual. His former office, now a blood-soaked crime scene. *Mitch, you poor bastard.* His home, no doubt teeming with law enforcement, analyzing everything from his laptop to the cereal he ate, painting their profile of the elusive Joe Campbell.

Blazer brushed against his leg, tail wagging hesitantly. Joe ruffled his scruff and said, "What do you think, boy?" The dog sighed and plunked down on the cold concrete floor. He considered the sleek crossbow in all its sexiness, then remembered how he'd nearly mangled his fingers and skewered Blazer on his last go with the contraption.

Joe surveyed his options for another moment, then chose a small pistol that looked relatively easy to handle and a couple of larger, more intimidating handguns. He gathered up an assortment of magazines and clips, none of which he had any clue how to use, tossed them in a black duffel and bounded up the stairs, Blazer hot on his heels.

The rain had picked up significantly since he'd made his way to the basement, obscuring any view of the SUV. Thunder rumbled in the distance. Or was it another gunshot? A sharp pang reminded him of his mangled ear. He laid out the array of ammo on the countertop. Everything looked foreign to him. Though Glen had shown him how to lock and load, the throbbing in his ear made it difficult to focus. He pushed the pain aside and picked up a magazine, turning the device over in his hand.

The door tore open, bringing with it a torrent of rain and wind. Glen's massive body rocketed in with it. He slammed the door, bolted it, and turned to his brother. The mud caking his face couldn't hide the sheer mask of terror. "We're fucked, Joey."

"What do you—what happened?"

Glen, looking like he'd been to hell and back, plunked down on the couch, his chest heaving, his breaths short and laborious. "There's a freaking army out there," he said at last.

"Army?" Joe said. "What does that mean?"

Glen sat forward, paused until his breathing became steadier. "Like what I said. There's a team of guys out there. Heavily armed. And from what I can see, they're not here to play paintball." He locked eyes with Joe. "Any idea who they could be?"

Joe felt bile rising in his throat. He noticed he was still holding the gun magazine, his hand shaking uncontrollably. He nodded slowly and said, "Guierriero."

Glen's eyes widened. "You've got to be fucking kidding me. Joey, how the hell could he know you're here?"

Joe shrugged. "I don't know. Maybe he followed Patty." The pain in his head spiked. "How many are there?"

Glen pushed himself up. "Best guess, around six. Maybe ten. Saw three. Took one out. And—"

"Whoa!" Joe said. "Back up. What do you mean, you took one out?"

Glen, tough guy that he was, was trembling. He looked at the arsenal laid out on the counter and grinned. "Nice choices, bro. But I think you're going to need more than that."

"Glen, you said you took one out. What does that mean?"

Glen glanced around the room, as if looking for a lost set of car keys. "What do you think it means? It means we have one less threat to worry about."

"You killed him?" Joe said incredulously.

Glen smirked. "No, Joey, we sat down and exchanged recipes. Yes, I killed him. It was either him or me. I think I made the wise choice."

"Where?"

Glen, eyes still ricocheting around the room, said, "I was making my way toward you when the shots rang out. After I saw you bolt, I sensed a presence behind me. I heard a *click* and dropped. The bullet just missed me. But then I slipped trying to get up in the muck and the guy was standing over me, shotgun leveled right between my eyes."

Joe noticed blood streaming from his brother's hand. "Glen, your hand."

Glen looked down dumbly at his hand. A large gash yawned open. "Well, I'll be," he said. "Hadn't noticed that." He grabbed a dishcloth by the sink and wound it tightly around this hand to stop the hemorrhaging. "So, there I was, this handsome face of mine about to be blown to oblivion, and the damnedest thing happened."

"His gun jammed."

Glen shook his head and laughed. "No, that only happens in the movies, bro. Our old friend Mick saved the day. Shot the guy."

"But you said you took him out."

"Yeah, so after the guy went down, I told Mick to get to safety. We thought the goon was dead. He sure looked dead. Then, as I got up, the guy was on me. Turns out he was very much alive. A hole in his chest and he still wants to play. And now the guy's got this massive Bowie knife inches from my eye. This motherfucker was strong. He almost overtook me." Glen winked. "Almost." He held up his wounded hand, the towel now soaked through. "I was able to get my hand free."

Joe winced. "You mean, you grabbed the blade?"

"Well, Joey, it was that or lose a baby blue. So, yeah, I grabbed it. Hurt like hell. But it caught him off guard for a second. Which was all I needed." He looked at his hand and grimaced. "And here I am."

"Unbelievable," Joe said. "Not only do I have the mafia gunning for me, now I'm teamed up with Rambo."

Glen frowned and said, "Just remember who drew first blood." His eyes scanned the room. "Where's Mick?"

Joe shrugged. "How the hell should I know? He was with you."

"After he saved my ass, I told him to hightail it here."

"Well, he's not here."

Glen slammed a heavy fist on the table, stirring its lethal contents. He reassessed the ammo before them and said, "Come on, we don't have much time. We've got to find Mick and Rebecca."

The house shook violently, as though it had been struck by a locomotive. Blazer whined. Joe hadn't even noticed the faithful dog had been by his owner's side the whole time.

"What the hell was that?"

"Let's move," Glen said. Was that fear in his voice?

"Where to?" Joe said.

Glen winked and hightailed it toward the bunker.

CHAPTER FIFTY-FOUR

"We need to leave now!" Katie's shrill voice was jarring. Patty had witnessed her niece's hysteria on more than enough occasions and could usually talk her off the ledge. Or toss her a few pills. But with no meds readily handy and a claustrophobic sense of dread enveloping the vehicle, Katie was working her last nerve.

"Katie, you need to relax," Patty said, though she knew her words were futile.

"Calm down?" Katie's face twisted up into itself, morphing into something slightly demonic. She pointed at Rufus, blood coursing through the fat fingers clutching his shoulder. "Who else is out there?" Her glistening eyes exhaled. "You don't think—"

Patty slapped her hard across the face. Katie gazed in disbelief, frozen, as if she'd been put on pause. "You need to stop this nonsense! Your hysterics aren't doing us a damn bit of good." Her eyes moved to the pretty young thing beside her niece.

"And who do you think might be helping out your man and his useless brother?"

Rebecca simply shrugged, either unable or unwilling to speak. Patty's head pivoted back to Rufus. "What about you, ya big lug?"

"I say we get the fuck out of here," he said. "Did you not notice I was shot?"

Patty scoffed. "It's just a flesh wound, you big baby."

"It's Little Dom, isn't it, Auntie?" Katie's voice whispered to the back of Patty's head.

Patty laughed, though the same thought had crept into her brain. "Now, how would he even know about this place?"

"Then who the fuck is that?" Rufus spat out, pointing with his good arm.

Patty peered through the fogged windshield. Between sweeps of the wipers, she spotted two shadowy figures. Growing larger. Guns raised. Though she couldn't be certain through the blur, one appeared to be Enzo, one of Little Dom's closest confidantes, and one of his most ruthless. She'd seen some of the unspeakable things this man was capable of doing.

"Get down!" she screamed. The windshield exploded in a spectacular display, showering them in a mix of rain and glass.

Rufus slammed on the gas and the SUV jerked forward. Patty, still slumped, heard a dull thud and the vehicle stopped with a crushing jolt. Slowly, she slid herself up, ignoring the screams of the two women behind her.

"Oh, shit," Rufus said. It was Enzo alright, now crushed between the massive hunk of metal and the cabin's façade. He gazed blankly at Patty, eyes agape, blood gushing from his orifices.

"Watch out!" Rebecca screamed. Patty sensed movement to her right. The other shooter leveled his weapon at the car.

"Move! Now!"

Rufus threw the vehicle into reverse. It lurched backward as another shot connected with Patty's window, spraying her with more crystalized shards. "Go! Go! Go!" she screamed.

Rufus spun the vehicle, searching for purchase in the thick mud. The truck slalomed a few times, then righted itself. He slammed on the gas and bee-lined it for the exit.

"Stop!" The demand came from the petite woman in back.

Rufus slammed a heavy foot on the brake. The increasing deluge pummeled the car, the rain ricocheting off the hood, spraying its occupants with a sludgy mix of water and mud. Patty swiped at her face and turned to the woman. "What?"

Rebecca pointed toward the hilly drive. "You won't get through that way. My car is stuck in the middle of the road. There's no way around it." Patty thought to tell Rufus to give it a go, then remembered how narrow the path was, with heavy undergrowth on either side.

"She's right. We'll never get through." Patty pointed toward the lake in the distance. "Head down that way."

Rufus again spun the vehicle around, spewing muck all around, sending the other shooter diving for safety. The cabin slid by them on the left as they maneuvered a semi-steep decline that led to an old barn and beyond that, the restless lake. Rufus pulled up beside an impressive fire-engine red Dodge Ram and killed the engine. "We need to get to cover," he said. "We're sitting ducks out here."

Patty gazed out at the massive barn before them. Unlike the well-maintained house, the ramshackle barn looked like it could be felled with a strong wind. Or a swift kick. "In there," Patty directed. "Katie, keep your eye on the princess. We don't want her sneaking off on us."

Rebecca shot her an icy gaze. "Where would I go? Out there to get shot like this big oaf?"

Rufus moved as though he were about to lunge, but Patty's down-boy motion put him at ease. "Well, little miss," he said, "maybe your big, bad boyfriend will come to the rescue."

Rebecca, all full of piss and vinegar now, lurched forward, clawing at Rufus. Katie yanked her back. Rebecca brushed Katie away and said, "When he does, he'll rip your ugly head clean off."

Patty was starting to like the little firecracker. Appearances can be deceiving. Which appeared to be the case with Cowboy. He seemed to be more resourceful than she'd anticipated. Unless it was his brother pulling all the strings. No. There was definitely more to the meek, mild-mannered Joe Campbell than met the eye. Which would make killing him all the more satisfying.

She suddenly felt vulnerable, as exposed as she did on stage at The Landing Strip so many years ago. She brushed shards of glass from her lap and pushed open the door. "Let's get inside before we end up as target practice."

Rufus motioned them to go inside. "I'll grab the money and some more ammo from the back." Patty nodded and swiftly ushered the two younger women toward the barn. Without warning, a barrage of bullets *ping-pinged* the SUV. The remaining intact windows exploded in a shimmery display. The tires buckled. The sleek body shuddered violently.

Patty recalled the final scene of one of her all-time favorite movies, *Bonnie and Clyde,* which she'd watched a dozen or so times with Dominic. As the doomed couple drives leisurely down a peaceful country road chomping blissfully on a pear, an old man ahead signals them to stop. Clyde exits the car and approaches the man. As the old man dives for cover under his truck, Bonne and Clyde lock eyes, the realization hitting them that they've been ambushed.

In real life, the couple were both seated in the car when the shooting began. But Hollywood, as it tends to do, took liberties with history, placing Clyde outside the vehicle. This modification upset some historians, but Patty found the alteration all the more impactful. As Clyde realizes the horrific truth, he moves as if to run to Bonnie's aid. Their quick exchange of glances, from confusion to terror and finally to acceptance, was more powerful to Patty than the sight of watching Warren Beatty and Faye Dunaway being peppered with dozens of bullets in a bloody massacre. She'd never seen a more romantic moment in a film since.

Not wanting to end up a bloody mess like Dunaway, she hightailed it to the barn, the heavy steps of Rufus right behind her. Arms free of any ammo. Or any money.

CHAPTER FIFTY-FIVE

After Mick-Mac took out the guy standing over Glen, Glen had motioned for him to head for the cabin. He slogged through the gluey muck, his feet like cement blocks. He yelled to his newfound friend, assuming Glen was right on his heels.

"Hey Glen, you trust me now that I'm on your side?"

No response.

He turned. Glen was nowhere in sight. He called out to Glen, his voice dissipating in the swirling wind. *Where the hell did you go?* He spotted the cabin up ahead. Having broken free of the heavy mud, he trotted toward the structure. Then stopped dead in his tracks.

A silhouette ahead, between him and the safety of the house. The silhouette wasn't Joe and it most definitely wasn't Glen. He dropped to the ground, hoping he hadn't been spotted. The cabin no longer a viable option, he changed direction and headed toward a ramshackle building by the lake.

The tumble-down barn loomed large before him. A red pickup truck, probably Glen's, sat yards away. As he considered his options, a loud roar overtook the steady din of the rain.

The SUV barreled toward him, jostling violently as it descended the hill. Mick-Mac took cover behind a pile of soggy firewood, hoping he hadn't been spotted. A weather-worn axe stood at attention nearby, resting idly against its chopping block. He considered grabbing it, then decided the cold metal in his pocket made a more reliable partner.

He watched the SUV careen by, its windows shattered, its once sleek body a muddied mess. He caught a glimpse of a woman in the front passenger seat. Too old and tired looking to be Rebecca or Kate. Must be the infamous Patty Quigley. She appeared to be yelling something to her pilot. The vehicle pulled up beside Glen's truck. No movement from within. Then Patty Quigley jumped out of the vehicle. The massive guy behind the wheel exited next and moved to the rear of the vehicle.

That's when all hell broke loose. Bullets decimated the vehicle. The occupants scrambled for cover. Mick-Mac couldn't tell from which direction the onslaught came, but the sheer volume and rapid succession of gunfire indicated more than one shooter. He flattened himself on the ground, his muddied body camouflaged in the dense muck.

At last, the fireworks ceased, the only sound the quickening rain slamming the massacred SUV. He needed to move. The barn was obviously out of the question. The route to the cabin was too far and too open. If he could make it to the lake, he'd be shrouded in the inky water and could make his way back to—

Fire tore through his right bicep. The impact flipped him onto his back. The churning clouds high above unleashed their wrath, pummeling his face with their needle-sharp arsenal. He sensed movement to his left. Heavy footsteps closed in, the *thwuck-thwuck* sound heightening as they grew nearer. *Get up, Mick.* Closer. *Thwuck-thwuck.* The darkened silhouette loomed over him, more ominous than the malevolent sky backdropping it.

The murky shadow stood frozen, as if studying him. *He thinks I'm dead.* The shadow shifted. A deafening *click* interrupted the unremitting sizzle of the rain as it slammed the ground around him. Sheer desperation shook him from his reverie. In a last-ditch attempt, he swung his good arm out and connected with his attacker's mud-caked boot.

The man came down hard, the rifle harmlessly expelling its lethal dose into the blurred atmosphere, a split-second flash-bang lighting up Mick-Mac's peripheral vision long enough to catch a glimpse of the man as he crashed down on Mick-Mac's legs. The man, now weaponless, fumbled for purchase on the viscous ground, writhing atop Mick-Mac like a greased pig.

The two men thrashed about in a maniacal mud wrestling match, a vision Mick-Mac would have found comical if it weren't for the bone-shattering pressure on his neck. His opponent, way out of his weight class, clamped a crushing hand around the cop's neck like the locking jaw of a lion on its hapless prey.

Mick-Mac struggled for breath, clawing at the immovable vise cutting off his life supply. He squeezed his eyes shut, a burst of red penetrating his eyelids. His will to fight diminishing as the vise clamped tighter. Then he saw her. Marnie. Not the shattered doll splayed on the sidewalk in front of a 7-Eleven but the hypnotic beauty full of vivacity and grace. He reached out to her, longing to touch her one more time. Inches from her slender, delicate fingers. His strength draining, he grasped for her.

The spectral hand retreated without warning, unwilling to accept him into its lifeless embrace. The melodious voice of his beloved brushed his ear. *Fight, Mickey. Fight.*

Back in the land of the living, the pressure on his lungs intensifying, the heavy weight compressing his body heightening, the maelstrom around him deafening. The blood vessels in his engorged eyes felt ready to burst, set to spew their viscous contents in a violent and gruesome explosion. Then he spotted it. Right there in front of him.

With all the remaining strength he could muster, he snatched up the axe. With limited mobility, he thrust the head of the axe upward into his enemy's face. The man released a piercing scream and the pressure around Mick-Mac's neck waned, then subsided. The man recoiled, giving Mick-Mac just enough freedom to slip out from under him.

Clutching the axe with his one good arm, and thankful to be a southpaw, he swung the weapon. The axe sliced through the dense air in a glorious shimmery arc, ending its descent with a dull *thwack*. The man, confusion settling into his steely eyes, grasped in vain at the axe that lay buried deep in his skull. His eyes honed on Mick-Mac's, blinked in rapid succession a few times, then froze in a serene gaze. His lips curled up ever so slightly into a smirk, likely an involuntary reflex, or perhaps the realization of accepting that the eyes gazing back at him had gotten the last laugh.

The weight of the axe pulled the man down with an uneventful splat. Mick-Mac clutched at his throat, willing air back into its passageway, gingerly examining it to ensure everything was still intact. When he felt somewhat confident no permanent damage had been done, and his labored breathing became steadier, he rose on spindly legs.

He slogged through the thickening sludge, uncontrollable shivers racking his battered body. The agitated lake loomed before him yet felt light years away. With each sluggish step, a new pain introduced itself. At last, he reached the lake. He let the waves lap at his shins for a moment. Then he slipped into the shroud of the murky water and made his way toward the cabin.

CHAPTER FIFTY-SIX

"You actually do look like Rambo," Joe said. "Or maybe the Terminator."

Glen laughed and tossed a pistol to Joe. Joe turned the piece over in his fingers and said, "Seriously, bro? What am I supposed to do with this? Throw it at them?"

"Listen, Joey," Glen said. "I've seen how you handle a firearm. You're more likely to shoot yourself. Besides, you're staying here."

"Like hell I am," Joe spat back. "I'm the one who got us into this mess in the first place."

Glen, his hulking body armored up, got up in Joe's face. "Listen, this is what I'm trained for. It's what I do. And it's my fault that Rebecca's involved in this mess." Glen pointed at Blazer. "Besides, I need someone to look after the mutt." Blazer, tongue lolling lazily, tail on autopilot, let out a muffled yelp.

Joe felt his entire body inhale. Even when the chips were down, he couldn't pull out a pair of aces. "So, I'm supposed to just sit here twiddling my thumbs with this vicious attack dog as my protection?" Blazer's tail stopped mid-wag, as if he'd taken the comment personally.

"These are trained killers out there, Joey," Glen said, agitation stirring in his face. "This goes way beyond a couple of two-bit thieves. We're talking about Dominic Guierriero's team."

Joe laughed. "Yeah, I've dealt with his men once before, remember? They couldn't even hit me when I was hanging off the side of a roof. Besides, going out there alone is suicide."

"He won't be alone."

MacAvoy stood in the open doorway, a bloody, muddy mess. He looked as though he'd been to hell and back.

"Mick!" Glen said, his recent nemesis now his comrade in arms. "Where the hell have you been?" He wrapped the smaller man in a tight embrace. "I owe you, man," Glen said. "Big time."

MacAvoy plunked heavily into a chair. "That you do, my friend. That you do." He looked at Glen. "I saw Rebecca."

Glen's body shuddered. "Is she okay?"

MacAvoy nodded slowly. "Yeah, she and the Three Stooges are holed up in the barn out back. I took out one of the ninjas."

"Where?" Glen said.

"By the woodpile. Oh, and there's another one plastered to the side of your house."

Joe looked at his brother. "That must've been that noise we heard."

"Okay," Glen said. "So those two and the one I took out makes three. Our odds are getting better."

"How many of them do you think there are?" MacAvoy said.

Glen shrugged. "Best guess, six or eight. Or maybe fifty."

"Fifty minus three," MacAvoy said. His eyes looked maniacal, as if he were ready to go out there and take on the other forty-seven. His eyes shifted to Glen. "So, what's the plan, boss?"

"Well, my main mission is getting Rebecca back," he said. "And if anyone gets in my way, God help him." He gave MacAvoy a once-over. "Mick, if you're planning on helping me out, we'd better get you strapped up."

Glen led the way, leaving Joe and Blazer watching from the sidelines. Before heading downstairs, Glen glanced back at his brother. Joe didn't have to say a thing. The look of contempt burning through his eyes said it all.

CHAPTER FIFTY-SEVEN

"Get Frankie T on the line," Dom Jr. said. Diego nodded. His chest felt taut, as if something were violently tugging on the muscles, gnawing at the bones. The interior of the car seemed to be closing in on him, a giant unseeing hand slowly crushing him.

He'd never been a fan of enclosed spaces, and right now, with the wind and rain hammering the vehicle, blotting out the world, he was suffocating. He clawed at his neck, loosened his tie discreetly, for fear that Diego might sense any weakness. That fear of being exposed as anything less than a pillar of strength trumped all others. But claustrophobia had pulled into a close second.

The fear began when he was a small boy, maybe nine or ten, and it had shadowed him ever since. A harmless game of hide-and-seek. That was the culprit behind the years of sheet-soaked nightmares and avoidance of elevators, tunnels, airplanes, crowds, and ice chests. Especially ice chests.

It had been an ideal summer day, the kind you could put on a postcard. Perfect for a picnic. And so, Padre and a few of his associates, with wives and kids in tow, headed out to a private villa high up in the mountains, with vistas that extended for days. While the adults told ribald stories and sipped colorful drinks from fancy glasses, the kids splashed in the nearby swimming pool.

"I'm bored." The announcement came from Mateo, a stocky mean-looking kid with thick eyebrows that resembled two fat, black caterpillars that had crawled on up on his face and set up camp right there above those beady eyes. "Let's do something fun."

"Like what?" said Paolo, a wiry kid with hair that didn't know which way to go. Paolo was the polar opposite of his brother Mateo, quiet and sensitive. Nicky liked being around Paolo. He could let down his guard with Paolo, and that made him feel safe. With Mateo, Nicky was always looking over his shoulder, waiting for the much larger boy to shove a spider in his face or throw him off the side of a cliff.

Mateo hopped out of the pool. "I dunno. Something fun. Adventurous."

Two other boys Nicky didn't know shrugged and joined Mateo poolside. Paolo hesitated before giving in to his brother's icy glare. The girls all shook their heads in disdain. They despised Mateo and made no effort to hide it.

"What about you, Guierriero?" Mateo chimed in that sing-songy voice that everyone hated, yet no one dared to imitate. "Or are you chicken shit?"

The girls, who had been singing some annoying nursery rhyme, stopped mid-chorus. Their gazes fell heavy on Nicky's shoulders. He especially felt the weight of Bianca Conti's eyes. Bianca. A girl who made him feel funny, but in a good way.

"So, are you coming?" Mateo's shadow loomed large, blotting out the sun.

Bianca smiled and returned to singing that droning, nonsensical tune. Nicky reluctantly joined the other boys. He thought to ask Padre if it was okay, then decided that would look lame and subject him to endless teasing from Mateo. His father's spirited roar echoed through the hillside. His mother, looking more beautiful than ever, tossed back her head and joined the rest of the adults in laughing at whatever hilarious tale Padre, the master storyteller, was regaling them with.

A nudge from Mateo turned his attention back to the boys. Nicky snatched up his t-shirt and sneakers and bounded toward the forest with the other boys. The forest was thick, but enough light penetrated the majestic pines to avoid tripping over an uprooted tree or boulder. After a few minutes of trekking, the forest split open, revealing a worn pasture.

Nicky glanced around. Sunlight bounced off glints of metal, ricocheting around the boys. Shielding his eyes, he spotted a few rusted old cars and trucks, broken-down pieces of furniture, an upended stove, discarded clothes and litter tossed about as far as the eye could see. He wondered how all this junk had wound up in this field, tucked in the middle of nowhere. Especially the imposing black pickup truck that looked much too large to have navigated the dense forest surrounding it.

"Cool!" Mateo yelled. He climbed atop a mountain of rubble and said, "I'm king of the hill!" The other boys followed suit, climbing and jumping and squealing with laughter.

Nicky was peering inside a termite-ridden wardrobe closet when Mateo yelled, "Hide and seek! Paolo, you're it."

Paolo, compliant as always, turned his back and started counting. The boys scattered. Nicky contemplated his options. Inside the wardrobe, crawling with insects or behind a large, elegant sofa he suspected had once graced the sitting room of a magnificent home like his. A shove nearly sent him sprawling.

"I've got the perfect hiding spot for you," Mateo said. "C'mon!"

Nicky followed him with hesitation, clambering over heaps of wood and trash and treacherous tangles of corroded metal. Mateo pointed eagerly.

"What is it?" Nicky said.

"It's an old ice box, dummy."

Nicky stared at the decayed chest. It reminded him of a coffin. "Is it safe?" he said.

Mateo grinned. "Of course, it's safe. Look, there's no lock on it." He was right. The lock appeared to have rusted off long ago, leaving only a thin metal latch.

"I don't know," Nicky said.

Ready or not, here I come!

"Hurry up," Mateo said. "He's coming. Or are you chicken shit?"

The words slammed Nicky. He hated Mateo. The bullying. The name-calling. The way he made Nicky feel small, like one of those bugs crawling around in that old wardrobe. "No, I'm not chicken shit," he said defiantly and hefted himself into the old box.

The blackness was suffocating. The air was thick, hot on his skin. He heard muffled laughter that sounded light years away. He waited. The laughter dissolved. Now only silence. And darkness. He fumbled in the blackness for the hasp that opened the door. At last, his trembling fingers connected. He tugged on the latch and pushed. The door didn't budge. Again. Spindly legs tickled the back of his neck. Then his legs.

His screams echoed inside the box, his coffin. He imagined thousands of spiders skittering over his body. He screamed louder, slammed his fists against the door. His lungs hurt, as though they were being sucked into the deep caverns of his body. He tried to release a puff of air, to inflate his lungs that felt as though they were crumbling up inside him.

At last, a calm settled in. He stopped screaming. His fists stopped pounding. His lungs stopped fighting. He lay still in the black void, resigned to his fate. He thought about how mad Mother would be that he'd dirtied his new swim trunks. Then he thought of Padre, holding his dying baby girl in his arms. Her floral swimsuit not dirty at all, but brilliant and shiny.

Padre's voice, distant yet clear, reassuring him that everything was okay. His eyes snapped open. Padre's face, a mask of horror, gazed down on his son. *Nicky, you're okay now. You're safe. I've got you, son.*

Padre stood beside the old ice chest, cradling his son in the shelter of his arms, weeping softly as he had one summer day not so long ago with the little girl in the sunflower-dotted swimsuit, water dripping soundlessly off her tiny, lifeless body.

"Boss."

Dom Jr. was back from the confines of that old chest to the constricted space of the luxurious car. But this coffin had a way out. "What is it?"

"Frankie T is on the line," Diego said.

Boss. Frankie T's voice was crackly but audible.

"Frankie, what's going on?"

We've got three men down.

"Three men d—who?"

Enzo. Angel. And—

"And who?"

Paolo.

Dom Jr. squeezed his eyes shut, holding back the tears that would force their way out no matter how tightly he squeezed. Paolo. The boy who he'd trusted like a brother. Paolo. The boy who had led Padre to the old ice chest. The old ice chest with a stick jammed into its metal latch, sealing it shut. Paolo. The boy brave enough to denounce his evil brother. Paolo. The boy who had grown to be the man who would lay down his life for a friend.

He wept. For Paolo. For Padre. For his baby sister. Then rage took over. It shook him, engulfing him with a power that rattled his bones.

Boss? You there?

Dom Jr.'s voice was steady, firm. "Take those motherfuckers down now. Every last one of them."

PART FOUR

Endgame

CHAPTER FIFTY-EIGHT

"So, what now?"

Patty released a heavy puff of air, hoping it was mighty enough to bring the precarious ceiling crashing down on Rufus's fat, glistening head. "How the fuck am I supposed to know? We have no car and we're trapped like rats in here."

Katie sat down on a square of hay, squeezing her sodden body with trembling arms. Rebecca cowered nearby. Patty surveyed the dank barn. It reeked of old horse shit and mildewed wood. Brittle bales of hay lay haphazardly about the ruinous space. A decomposing baler lurked ominously in a shadowy corner. The cavernous structure shuddered violently against the tempest that beat its heavy fist with mad fury.

She considered her options. As much as she'd wanted this to play out with her standing over Cowboy's pleading, pathetic face before extinguishing it, that opportunity no longer seemed to be on the table, thanks to the big fucking wrench Little Dom had tossed into the ring. No, the priority now was to get as far away from this battleground as they could.

With the bullet-ridden SUV no longer a viable option, they needed a Plan B. The shiny red pickup truck would do nicely. Patty was sure Rufus could hotwire anything with four wheels. They'd take along the sweet little thing as insurance and dump her somewhere once they were free and clear with the money.

The money.

"Rufus, go out there and get the money," she demanded.

Rufus grunted. "Are you kidding? There ain't no way in hell I'm going out there naked. Give me one good reason why I should."

Patty balled up her fists, sucked in her face, and said, "You want a reason? How about I give you four million reasons?"

"I'll go." The near whisper came from Katie.

"No, sweetie," Patty said. "It's too dangerous out there."

"But it's not too dangerous for me?" Rufus screamed over the hammering around them. He thrust a finger at Rebecca. "Why not send her?"

Rebecca shrunk into herself. "Great idea, genius," Patty said. "You think we let her go she's coming back? Not a chance."

Katie pushed herself off the hay bale. "Let me do it, Auntie. We've come too far to lose it all."

"I said no." Patty's voice was steady, calm. Firm. "The big lunk here is gonna get that sexy pickup out there fired up and then we, along with our four mil and change, are getting out of Dodge." Movement beyond the cracks in the wall to her right. "Someone's out there." The cracks of light shifted again. "Get up in the loft," she whispered. The trio gazed at her dumbly. "Now!"

Joe felt helpless. Blazer sat at attention before him, as if waiting for his marching orders. "Sorry, pal," Joe said. "Looks like we've been benched for the season." Blazer's tail swept the floor soundlessly.

His whole life, he'd been shrouded in the oversized shadow of his brother. And now, the shadow had swallowed him up completely. While Glen and his new best bud were out there basking in the limelight and kicking ass, he was relegated to sitting this one out. He should be used to it at this point. After all, he'd mastered the art of sitting on the sidelines his whole life. The kid who always faded into the back of the classroom, praying not to be called on. The teen who watched silently from the wings as his best friend stole the girl of his dreams away at Homecoming dance. The man who'd allowed countless colleagues to clamber over him on the corporate ladder.

No more.

He snatched up what arsenal remained on the table and looked at Blazer. "Come on boy, let's show them who's badass." The dog hesitated and slowly approached Joe. Blazer's ears went rigid. A low growl escaped his mouth, his eyes alert, his nostrils flaring.

"What is it, boy?" Then he heard it. Someone was in the house.

He backed up slowly, brushing against Blazer, who stood stock-still. Something cold pressed into the back of his neck. Joe stumbled forward, moved to raise the gun that hung limply in his fingers.

"Drop it."

The piece clattered to the floor. Blazer stood to his right, emitting a low growl but otherwise motionless. Joe straightened his tired body and turned to face the man. He didn't look like a killer. In fact, he looked like someone you'd pass by on the street and toss a friendly nod.

The man, stocky yet fit, smiled as he studied the quivering mess on the other side of his gun barrel. At last, he said, "So, you're the infamous Joe Campbell." He pursed his lips. "Thought you'd look a little more impressive."

Joe wondered why he was still standing. Why this guy hadn't already put a bullet between his eyes. What the guy said next gave him his answer.

"Wait'll Dom gets a load of you." He let out a raucous laugh. Blazer growled. The man swung the gun in the dog's direction. Blazer winced, lowered his snout in defeat. The man cocked the gun.

"Don't," Joe said. The man turned his gaze. "He's harmless. Just look at him."

The man laughed again. "Yeah, quite the attack dog you've got there. Looks even more pathetic than you."

What had Glen said? *He may look like the friendliest, most harmless mutt, but he's also trained to protect to the death.* Then he'd said the attack word. Something foreign. French, maybe? *What was it? What's the phrase?*

The man poked him in the chest with his piece. "Let's get moving. There's someone who's very eager to meet you, Mr. Campbell."

What's the attack code? No, it's not French. Italian, maybe?

"I said move!" The man's amiable face had morphed into that of a snarling beast.

No, not Italian. Spanish? Yes! Spanish! A common phrase. One he'd heard before.

"I'll say it one more time, and then I'm going to put a cap in your knee. MOVE!"

Qué pasa! That was it. He was sure of it. Or was he?

Joe heard the gun cock. "Qué pasa!" he screamed.

Blazer was on the guy before Joe could blink. The mild-mannered mutt was ravenous, pulling the man to the floor with a heavy thud. The gun rocketed from the man's grip, skittered across the floor. A blur of fur and flesh spun before Joe, the man screaming and thrashing about as the dog tore angrily at his flailing limbs.

This was one time that Joe was happy to be relegated to the sidelines.

The carnage lasted a couple of minutes, the man slowly winding down. At last, his screams now pitiful sobs, the man seemed reserved to his fate, like a fly struggling to escape a cobweb as the menacing spider moves in for the kill.

The sobs stopped. The man's crumpled and tattered body motionless. Blazer shook him a few times, then looked at Joe as if seeking approval.

"Good boy," Joe said, still stunned by the bloody heap on display before him. Blazer's tail wagged vigorously. He brushed his cold snout against Joe's tremulous hand, sending a slight shockwave up Joe's arm.

Joe sat on the floor, Blazer's head lazing on his leg, for what seemed like hours. When, at last, his legs signaled him they had enough strength to stand, he rose. Blazer trotted blissfully behind him as he moved to the kitchen sink. He splashed a healthy dose of icy water on his face and straightened his spine. Reinvigorated, he turned to the multilingual dog that had saved him from a fate worse than death and said, "Alright, Blazer, let's go get your dad!"

CHAPTER FIFTY-NINE

The footsteps below them moved then paused. Moved then paused. Methodically searching the barn. Patty could feel Katie's trembling body pressed sharply into her side. Rebecca resembled a mannequin, frozen in fear. *Is she even breathing?* Rufus crouched like a testosterone-fueled wrestler ready to take on his opponent.

The air in the loft hung thick and heavy like a sagging clothesline after an unexpected rain shower. Water bled through a decaying roof that looked ready to throw in the towel and come crashing down on them. The space was barren aside from discarded bales of hay that looked like they hadn't seen the light of day since the Nixon administration. A large square door was carved into one wall, Patty guessed for hoisting the bales up into the storage space. A thick wrought iron latch sealed it shut.

The footsteps stopped. Nothing but the rhythmic patter above their heads. They listened for the footsteps to resume.

No movement. Rufus shrugged. Then the realization slapped Patty in the face.

The man was on the ladder. Patty motioned to Rufus, did an *itsy-bitsy spider* movement with her fingers. Rebecca, realizing the situation, dissolved further into the darkened shadows, her face etched with terror. Rufus, with nothing but his bone-crunching hands as weapons, positioned himself for the inevitable attack.

The first thing Patty saw was the nose of the gun. She recognized it immediately as a Beretta M9, a semi-automatic sidearm pistol popular in military circles. Lightweight and compact enough to easily handle and conceal, yet lethal enough to get the job done. Dominic had trained Patty to shoot using a Beretta, explaining that its automatic safety features prevented accidental discharge. "After all," he'd said, "I can't have my number one girl blowing a toe off those lovely feet." At the time, the sentiment had been endearing. Now it only made her cringe.

The gunman let out a heavy grunt and hefted himself onto the top rung of the unstable ladder. Before he could react, Rufus flung his massive body at the man. Their tangled bodies seemed to hang in the air, as if tethered by some unseen force, then vanished in a blur. A sickening crash followed.

Katie let out a half scream and propelled herself toward the loft's edge. Patty yanked her back and crept forward. The two men lay side by side on the cold, weather-beaten floor. Bales of hay rested leisurely to either side, as if they'd scattered to avoid a collision. Rufus writhed in pain, the impact taking a heavy toll even with his extra padding of muscle. Patty's eyes searched hungrily for the Beretta.

Rufus tried to pull himself up into a seated position, fighting the semi-conscious state he appeared to be in. The other man lay still.

"Rufus, get up," Patty called from above. The big lug's head lolled around, as if seeking the source of the voice. He tried again to sit up, then crashed down, cupping his watermelon head in massive hands.

Patty turned to her niece. "Katie, I'm going down. You stay put."

Katie grasped her aunt's arm tightly and said, "Auntie, you can't."

Patty released her and said briskly, "It'll be okay. Now promise me you'll stay here." Katie nodded dumbly. Patty shifted her gaze to the woman who pushed herself further into the shadows. "And keep an eye on that one."

She heard stirring as she maneuvered her way down the rickety ladder. She needed to find that gun. Reaching the last rung, Patty stepped with trepidation onto the rustic floor. A low moan behind her. Patty spun around, expecting the gunman to be front and center, gun leveled at her. The man was just as she'd last seen him, immobile, his lights clearly knocked out. Rufus struggled once more to pull himself up. Patty grasped for purchase and with everything she had, hoisted the big man to his knees. His wits slowly returning, Rufus, with help from a woman less than half his size, stood on wobbly legs.

Patty smiled and said, "I thought we'd lost you there for a second, big guy." Rufus smiled back weakly. Then his eyes went wild.

Patty was jerked back violently and carelessly tossed aside like an unwanted doll. Her head slammed against a thick wooden beam, probably the only thing keeping this dilapidated wreck of a building from crashing down. The two men came in and out of focus, their bodies performing a brutal, spasmodic dance. They crashed into a tall stack of bales. The compressed blocks, which Patty decided looked like oversized versions of that shredded wheat cereal Katie loved so much, scattered like cockroaches in daylight.

The two men, both dazed and unsteady, exchanged punches in what looked like a poorly choreographed fight scene from a cheesy Steven Seagal flick. Then she spotted it. Right there beside a discarded hay bale. The Beretta. Ready for the taking. Patty shook off the bees buzzing around in her head and made a desperate move for the gun. She ignored the visceral grunts and sickening sounds of bone connecting with flesh, her sole focus the hunk of metal just out of grasp.

As her fingers brushed the cold metal, a guttural cry broke her steely determination. Katie's head hung over the loft's edge above, her face twisted up in horror.

"No!" she screamed. But she wasn't looking at Patty. Patty's eyes followed those of her niece's and then she understood the sheer panic in Katie's eyes. The gunman, a rusted pitchfork clenched firmly in hand, loomed over Rufus.

In a last-ditch attempt, Patty lunged for the Beretta. Gripping the pistol as Dominic "The Skinner" Guierriero had so patiently and lovingly shown her on that warm day in a sun-dappled meadow dotted with brilliant bursts of poppies, she took aim.

As the man's powerful arms raised the menacing weapon, Patty released her own deadly dose. The bullet tore into the man's back. His body went rigid, then tottered and collapsed in a heap, the pitchfork tossed carelessly aside.

Patty, gun still glued to her grip, stumbled toward the two men. Katie's piercing shrieks signaled she was too late. She stood over Rufus, his unblinking eyes fixed on her, his mouth open in a silent scream. His neck released a torrent of blood, marring the intricate inkwork Patty had always detested. Now, up close, she appreciated its beauty. Patty realized with horror that her barrage on the henchman had also put one square in the neck of her oafish sidekick. Rufus was, as Dominic would say, collateral damage.

Katie's screams had reached a crescendo, the jarring sounds of anguish reverberating through the cavernous space. Patty, wanting to console her, yet also wanting to cease that godawful screeching, tucked the Beretta into her jacket and ascended the loft.

She wrapped her arms around the convulsing body of her niece, tenderly stroked the girl's hair. Abruptly, she stopped.

"Where is she?" She pushed herself back, face to face with the blubbering Katie. "I said, where is she?"

Katie quieted, her lips still trembling, and glanced around.

The door behind them swung open, the unrelenting rain tearing through the gaping hole. Patty stared at the ages-old pulley protruding from the structure, at the rope that danced maniacally in the torrent. Their bargaining chip had literally gone right out the window.

CHAPTER SIXTY

Joe stood before the scene of the carnage. Blazer tucked himself close, brushing Joe's leg. The decimated SUV looked as though it had been to war and back. Bullet-riddled metal. Shattered glass. Anyone inside surely couldn't have survived the onslaught. He approached the vehicle with hesitation, praying his brother's girlfriend wasn't in the mangled heap.

Glen's brilliant red pickup was curbed beside the wreck. It was largely intact, though signs of collateral damage were evident in its marred body and spider-cracked windows. Joe peered through what had been the black SUV's rear window. No sign of Rebecca, or anyone else for that matter. A heavy arsenal was strewn about in the rear of the vehicle. Two large black bags were tucked among the weapons.

He reached inside, his fingers dancing across the lethal pile of steel, coming to rest on one of the rugged canvas bags. He fumbled for the zipper and peered inside.

A loud crack from the barn sent him stumbling back, slipping in the thick muck. Blazer, ears on high alert, took refuge behind the woodpile nearby. Joe, unsure of which direction the gunshot had come from, followed the dog's lead. He peered out from behind the soggy stack of wood, cut with precision by the ever-meticulous Glen. Then he gazed back at the wounded SUV and began to formulate a plan.

Rebecca realized her window of opportunity was a one-time offer. With Katie distracted by whatever was going on below them, it was now or never. She moved stealthily toward the beckoning door. The screaming and mayhem on her back, she reached for the wrought iron latch securing the door, tugged on the sliding pin. It didn't budge.

Years of dampness and lack of use seemed to have fused the metal together. Blocking her only means of escape. She fumbled around in her pockets for something to unwedge the pin. Her phone might have done the trick, if it hadn't been confiscated earlier by the crazy bitch howling behind her.

Her fingers wrapped around a cylinder. A cigarette lighter. Glen had begged her to quit for months. Although she'd cut down significantly, and had convinced Glen that she'd quit cold turkey, she stole an occasional fix when she couldn't curtail the urge. She'd felt guilty about the ruse, a betrayal to the man she loved. But the events of today indicated he had a few skeletons of his own, much bigger skeletons than a nasty little habit. If they made it out of this alive, there'd be a serious come-to-Jesus discussion on the agenda.

But now was not a time for doubt, accusations, or anger. She needed a plan. Quick. She recalled an expression Glen used from time to time when a situation arose without a clear solution. *Just MacGyver it!* he'd say, in reference to a television show in which the hero could seemingly get out of any dicey situation with a Swiss Army knife and a roll of duct tape.

Without either at her disposal, the lighter would have to do. She flicked the gadget, hoping the light wouldn't distract Katie from her tantrum. She ran the flame along the rusted bits of metal, praying for success. Wrapping her hand in her sleeve, she tugged at the heated metal pin. Nothing. It was hopeless. She'd fare better with the duct tape. At least with that, she could silence the piercing wails that thrummed in her head.

She applied more heat, tears stinging her cheeks. Tugged. Movement. Not much, but it gave her something she desperately need right now—hope. More heat. More tugging.

At last, when she thought all was lost, the metal pin slid loose. She glanced back, yet to be detected. But she knew time was running out. As gingerly as she could, Rebecca pulled on the heavy door. The rush of wind and rain was deafening, outdone only by the screams of Katie twenty feet away.

A pulley system was rigged to the exterior wall of the barn, with a thick rope looped around it. The rigging was ancient but appeared to be in working condition. She gripped the coarse rope, gave it a sharp tug. It seemed stable enough. Only one way to find out.

She swung through the opening, half-expecting to plunge to the ground a good twenty feet below. The rope held. She began her descent, the screams of her captor dissipating in the storm.

Joe had just secured a couple of sidearms to his body when he heard someone approaching. He pressed himself against the SUV and steadied one of the pistols he'd confiscated from the doomed vehicle. Had he even checked to make sure it was loaded?

Footsteps slogged through the coagulated mud, heavy breath keeping cadence. The spitting rain fogged his visibility, but his ears worked just fine. The intruder was nearly upon him. A shadowy silhouette emerged from behind the SUV. Joe made his move.

"FREEZE!" he screamed over the tumult, gun cocked and ready just like Glen had taught him.

A clipped squeal escaped from the woman standing before him.

"Rebecca?" Joe said incredulously, staring at the sodden and disheveled woman. She blinked a few times, studying the stranger with a gun trained on her head. Her expression conveyed a range of emotions, the two principal ones being terror and confusion. "It's me, Joe. Joe Campbell."

Rebecca blinked a few more times, either out of bewilderment or from the deluge slamming her face. "Joe?" Joe nodded and smiled. "Could you aim that thing somewhere else, please?" she said.

Realizing he still had the gun trained on her, he lowered his arm. "I'm so sorry," he said. Rebecca smiled and threw her arms around him.

"Nice to finally meet you, Joe Campbell."

"Likewise," he said.

Rebecca's smile drizzled away. "Where's Glen?"

"I'm not sure," Joe said. "I think with Mick."

"Mick?" The sea of confusion had washed back in.

"Never mind," Joe said. "It's a long story. One I'd love to tell you over a beer sometime. But right now, we've got to get you somewhere safe."

Rebecca pointed to the barn. "The crazies are in there," she said. "And all hell is breaking loose."

"How did you get away?" Joe asked.

Rebecca smiled again. "Long story. One I'd love to share over a beer sometime. But right now, I've got to get you somewhere safe."

Joe decided he liked this girl already. Sense of humor, even under duress. For all his poor decisions over the years, Glen had finally gotten it right. He reached out a hand. Rebecca took it. "Let's get the hell out of here while we can."

CHAPTER SIXTY-ONE

Dom Jr.'s patience had been stretched beyond its limits. It was about to snap. And when it did, God help anyone in the crosshairs.

"Diego, get Frankie T on the line. Now."

"Sure boss—oh, here he comes."

Frankie T emerged quickly, as if his hair was on fire. He hopped in the front passenger side, shook off the raindrops that had collected on his head like a swarm of bees. At least he'd had the good sense not to jump into the backseat. That was Dom Jr.'s sacred space.

Frankie T took a moment to catch his breath, then said, "They're all dead."

Dom Jr. sighed. "They'd better not all be dead, Frankie. Did I not specifically say Campbell comes to me alive and kicking? I did say that, didn't I, Diego?"

Diego, ever the company man, nodded and said, "I believe you did, boss."

Frankie T shook his head spasmodically. "No, you don't understand."

"What don't I understand?"

Frankie T's body shuddered, seemed to collapse into itself. "When I said *they*, I didn't mean *them*." He released a guttural sob. "I meant *us*."

Dom Jr. let the words settle in for a few moments. Then he said, "You're telling me my so-called dream team couldn't handle a bunch of two-bit amateurs?" He studied the back of Frankie T's head, locked in place. When he got no answer, he said, "I must have heard you incorrectly, Frankie. Diego, did I hear him incorrectly?"

Diego, stock-still and professional, said, "No, boss, I believe you heard him correctly."

"Look at me, Frankie," Dom Jr. said, his voice soft and steady. Frankie T didn't budge. "I said look at me, you mother-fucker!" Frankie T's head jerked to the left. Dom Jr. had seen the look before. The look of stone-cold terror. "And what do you suppose we should do to remedy this situation, Frankie?"

Frankie T, reduced to a blubbering child, grabbed his head in his hands and said, "I think we should get the fuck out of here!"

Dom Jr. nodded slowly. "You think we should get the fuck out of here, do you?"

"Y-y-es, boss," Frankie T stammered.

Dom Jr. turned his gaze to the faithful Diego. "Diego, Frankie here thinks we should head on home. Maybe we can stop on the way and get him some dry clothes and a warm meal. What do you think, Diego?"

Diego said dully, "I don't think that's a good idea, boss."

"Nor do I," Dom Jr. said, with the calm of a baby drifting off to sleep. "Nor do I." With that, he raised the gun that had been resting on his lap and fired. Frankie T jerked violently forward. His head slammed into the windshield, the glass spidering in all directions.

Uncustomary of Diego to challenge him, his driver said, "I know he deserved that, boss, but we're already outnumbered here. Would it have been better to deal with him later?"

"Loyalty, Diego," Dom Jr. replied. "Without loyalty, you have nothing." Diego nodded. "And sorry about the mess," Dom Jr. added. "I know you like to keep a neat house."

"That's alright, boss," Diego said, his body ramrod straight.

Dom Jr. patted his driver on the shoulder and said, "We'll get you a new one tomorrow."

"Yes, boss."

Dom Jr. pushed open the car door, the slantwise torrent hammering his face. "Come on, big man. Let's you and I end this thing now."

Diego didn't say a word, only nodded slowly and exited the vehicle. The two men, locked and loaded, pressed their bodies into the surging tempest and moved with purpose in their step.

CHAPTER SIXTY-TWO

"There they are," Rebecca said, pointing to her right. Joe could make out two shadowy figures moving through the blur. Sure enough, it was Glen and Mick. Joe grabbed Rebecca's hand, and they sprinted toward the duo.

Glen spotted them and barreled forward, swallowing up Rebecca's small frame in a tight embrace. They clung to one another like long-lost lovers meeting again for the first time in decades.

"I hate to break up this beautiful moment," Mick said, "but we've got a couple of live ones up ahead."

Glen, Rebecca, and Joe all turned in the direction Mick was pointing. Patty and Kate, each struggling with a large bag, made their way to the boathouse.

"Okay, listen up," Glen said. "Joey, I want you to take Rebecca to the house. Mick, you're coming with me."

"No."

"Joey, I'm not messing around. Do as I say—"

"No." Joe stood firm. "No way."

Glen threw up his hands. "I get it, Joey," he said. "We're all in this because of you and yada yada. I get it. I really do. But you're in over your head here."

"That may be true, Glen. But I'm not backing down. I'm taking back my life right now. Are you with me or not?"

Glen opened his mouth to speak, but Joe's eyes made it clear anything he said would fall on deaf ears. Exasperated, he said, "Okay, baby brother, have it your way." He looked at Mick. "Mick, get Rebecca to safety." Mick nodded and gripped the woman's arm.

Rebecca recoiled. "Glen, you can't go in there," she said. "You don't know what you're up against. That woman is crazy."

Glen smiled and said, "But we've got the upper hand, babe. Because the Campbell boys here are both bat-shit crazy." He looked at Joe. "Ain't that right, Joey?" Joe smiled and nodded. "Now, please get safe."

Rebecca, realizing this battle was futile, shook her head and stormed off toward the cabin. Mick wished them luck and headed off behind her.

Glen turned to his brother. "You ready to do this?"

Joe raised the gun he was toting and said, "Readier than I've ever been in my life."

"Grab the money, Katie." Patty surveyed the arsenal in the SUV and grabbed what she could carry.

Katie grunted. "These bags are really heavy."

Patty grinned. "Now you know what four million dollars feels like. Here, give me one. Now, let's get moving."

They moved swiftly toward the boat dock, the unrelenting rain pressing a firm hand on them with every step.

"There it is," Patty said. "Come on. We're almost there."

The door to the boathouse slapped violently back and forth. They dragged their heavy cargo inside, and Patty slammed the door. The precarious structure provided little shelter from the gale, but at least Patty could see what was in front of her.

"What now?" Katie said.

Patty glanced around. "Keys. We need keys."

"Why would anyone leave keys out in the open?" Katie said.

"Look around, kid," Patty said. "There ain't a soul within two miles of this place to waltz in and steal a boat now, is there?"

Katie shrugged, strands of hair plastered to her pretty face. Her eyes lit up. "There!" she said, pointing at a wooden box attached to a wall.

"Bingo!" Patty said. She fished inside the box. One key. Two boats. She hoped it was for the slick red number, though she was doubtful. If she had a beauty like that, no way she'd leave a key for the taking, miles from civilization or not.

"Let me see if I can get it started," Patty said. Katie nodded and plunked down on the heavy bag at her feet, looking as though she were about to nod off. Patty headed for the racing boat, angry waves lapping at its glossy physique. She boarded the unsteady vessel, nearly losing her footing on its slick bottom. Tried the key. No go. Guess they'd have to settle for the Whaler.

She instructed Katie to get the bags on board and turned the key, praying the old tub would start. It kicked in without fail, as reliable as that old Toyota she'd clocked in two-hundred-thousand miles and change on. Now she just had to figure out how to drive this damned thing.

"STOP!"

The voice boomed over the tempest, sending Katie tumbling to the floor. Patty turned and what she saw shook her to the core.

———

Dom Jr. pointed the gun at the two women in the Boston Whaler. One of the women slipped and fell. The other turned toward his voice.

They stared in stunned silence at one another. Then Dom Jr. said, "Patty?" as if questioning what he was seeing. It took a moment to process. Then he said, "What the fuck are you doing here, Patty?" Then he remembered the tape recording left at his Padre's slaughter. How it mentioned Charlene. And the pieces started to fall into place. "You killed my father? *You?*" He steadied the gun.

Patty raised her hands slowly, shook her head. "No, you've got it all wrong, Dominic," she said. Was that fear in her voice? "It was Campbell. Joe Campbell. That's your man."

"Then what are you doing here?" he asked. "Let me guess. You just happened to be vacationing out in the middle of nowhere and stumbled upon the man who killed my Padre?"

Patty stood motionless, speechless.

Dom Jr. shook his head. "Are you telling me this is one of those 'hell hath no fury like a woman scorned' situations? That you killed him because he didn't want your battered old body and decrepit face? Is that what all this is about?"

"He killed my mother!" The woman who'd fallen rose to her

feet. "Your piece of shit father killed my mother!" The young woman fell against Patty in a crumpled heap, her body convulsing.

Dom Jr. smiled. "Ah, you must be Charlene's girl. Katie, is it?"

The young woman turned and lunged in his direction. He leveled the gun at her. Heard a rifle cock to his left. Two men stood shoulder to shoulder, their sights set on Dom Jr. and his trusty sidekick.

Dom Jr. laughed. "Let me guess. Joe Campbell, I presume?"

CHAPTER SIXTY-THREE

Joe's pulse thrummed in his ears. His head felt as if it were full of cotton. He couldn't think clearly. He had his gun trained on a notorious gangster and yet he felt frozen in place, completely numb, unable to feel the cold metal in his hand. His brother's voice nudged him.

"Drop the guns, assholes," Glen said stonily.

Without warning, Dom Jr. and his henchman lifted their weapons in unison like synchronized swimmers. "I'd say we have a bit of a situation here, wouldn't you, Diego?" he said to the man beside him. The man nodded without flinching.

"Listen, Mr. Guierriero," Joe said, trying to quell the dire situation. "I had nothing to do with your father's murder. It was her." His eyes rolled to Patty. "And her." He gazed at his wife and his emotions boiled over as his mind relived that moment when he'd realized he'd been played.

Guierriero, his guard unwavering, looked at Joe. "And how did you get mixed up in this sordid little affair, Mr. Campbell?"

"They set me up. Patty and—" He paused. "And my wife."

Guierriero laughed. "Your wife? Well, isn't this priceless? What's next? Is this jarhead beside you Patty's bastard son?"

Glen scoffed. "No, I'm just the bastard who's gonna send you to see your dear old dead daddy."

Joe watched with horror as the rage built up in Guierriero's eyes. The man's body tensed, his trigger finger twitched. Glen's remark had set him off, and all hell was about to break loose.

"HEY!"

Out of nowhere, Mick appeared, double fisted, his beads set on the two gangsters.

That was when all hell broke loose.

CHAPTER SIXTY-FOUR

Rebecca paced the room. She felt helpless. Unable to do anything. Unable to see anything behind the blur of the storm. She'd searched for a phone, a laptop, any way she could reach out for help. Blazer brushed her leg. She ruffled the fur on the big dog's nape, her only sense of solace.

Who was this enigma she'd fallen in love with? She'd always suspected he might be hiding something but never imagined it to be anything that would put her in danger. The Glen she knew was kind, nurturing, protective and above all, loyal. She'd never been the jealous type, never sensed infidelity. Oh, she knew the temptations were there. Wherever they went, she could feel the eyes of a thousand women searing the man on her arm. And yet, his eyes never wavered.

Lately, she'd sensed he had wanted to tell her something, to open up, maybe about their future. And now, she was left wondering if there was any future at all. How did she even know this mess had anything to do with Glen? Those women had seemed fixated on his brother. A brother she really didn't know a thing about.

Glen had mentioned him, expressed sadness over the distance that had pushed them further apart over the years. And yet, by all accounts Glen had shared about his brother, Joe Campbell appeared to be an average, ordinary man. But appearances can be deceiving.

Blazer stood by a door, slightly ajar, moaning softly.

"What is it, boy?" The dog's moaning heightened, his tail sweeping the air. He nudged the door with his nose, pushing it open further. He began to pant rhythmically, his steely gaze moving from the door to Rebecca, then back to the door.

"Is someone down there?" A sense of dread crept up her spine like an army of ants. Could one of the gunmen be down there? She edged toward the door, her mind telling her to flee. But where could she go? The real danger lay outside. Or did it?

She spotted a gun on a table by the sofa. How had she missed that when she'd reconned the room earlier? She picked it up, studied it. It appeared to be loaded. But she knew about as much about guns as she did about Joe Campbell, which was next to nothing.

Blazer pushed the door open a few more inches. She gripped the gun the way she'd seen done on TV and the movies and moved toward the door. She flicked on a light switch. Steps descended to a concrete floor. The basement. For all the occasions she'd been here, she'd never considered there was a basement. Glen had never mentioned one. But why would he?

Rebecca descended the stairs, each step bringing her closer to potential danger. Blazer's hot breath behind her quickened, then suddenly he brushed past her and bounded down the stairs, nearly sending her toppling. The big goofy dog stared up at her, grinning, body moving in cadence with his tail, as if to say, *Come on down, nothing bad here.*

The fear that had gripped her waned, leaving her with a slight feeling of unease. She stepped forward. As her foot landed on the cold concrete, she hesitated, waiting for something to happen. For some demon to jump out at her like in a horror movie. Instead, only silence.

She glanced to her left. A long narrow hallway tapered into darkness. To her right, a large steel door. A walk-in freezer, perhaps? Blazer stood before the ominous door, gazing intently at the oversized latch. Rebecca edged toward the door and tugged on the latch. It wasn't cold, as she had anticipated. Maybe it wasn't a freezer after all. The door yawned open and what she saw was beyond anything she could have predicted. She let out a gasp loud enough to alarm Blazer. She entered the room, the deafening thrumming of her heart beating soundly in her head.

CHAPTER SIXTY-FIVE

Patty saw her window of opportunity and knew she wouldn't get another. As the four men squared off against one another, it was as if they'd forgotten she and Katie were here. It was now or never. She turned the key, and the Whaler lurched forward.

Joe's finger trembled on the trigger. He could feel the tension coming to a boil. He sensed something in Guierriero's eyes, in the oh-so-slight shift in his stance. It was going down. His mind told him to pull the trigger. Kill or be killed.

The rev of an engine abruptly froze the scene, as if a director had yelled *CUT!* All eyes moved to the diverting sound. The Boston Whaler shot from the gate, a plume of water churning in its wake. A quick succession of shots rang out, bullets tearing into the boat's hull. Glen grabbed Joe by the collar, jerking him to the ground.

The assault continued, a barrage of lead shredding the boat's worn façade. And yet, for all the damage inflicted upon it, the boat remained afloat. Tom Campbell's story of the unsinkable Molly Brown had been right on target. The boat lolled in place for a moment. Then a brilliant flash lit up the bleak sky.

When the first bullets hit, Patty and Katie hit the deck. Patty felt a sudden pain in her right arm, as if she'd been shot with a supersized needle. Katie screamed and her body coiled up into itself. Patty spotted a large canister. She realized too late what it was. A bullet tore through the gas tank, and a brilliant light erupted around her.

"Katie!" she screamed. "We need to get off the boat!" The gunfire had briefly ceased, but she knew another round was imminent. She hit the accelerator, and the boat lurched forward. Despite the precipitation slamming them from overhead, the fire spread with a vengeance.

"We need to jump, Katie!"

Katie nodded. Then her eyes shifted to her right. "The money, Auntie," she said, pointing toward the black bags, the flames creeping up quickly. Patty shook her head, screaming that it was too late, there was no time. Katie lunged for the bags.

Joe watched in awe as the burning boat sped forward through the storm, his wife and Patty frantically flailing about. Then an orange glow filled the sky as the boat exploded.

CHAPTER SIXTY-SIX

Mick-Mac had just gotten Dominic Guierriero's attention when the Whaler lurched forward, diverting his attention. As Guierriero and his partner unleashed a barrage on the departing boat, Mick-Mac assessed his options.

He spotted Glen and Joe taking cover behind the Master-craft. He crouched and moved slowly toward the enemy. As he approached, their attention locked on the Whaler, he took aim. That was when the world exploded.

The reverberation knocked Guierriero and his man off their feet. The flash was blinding. It was time. Mick-Mac surged forward, guns locked and loaded, descending on the shaken men. He heard Glen yell something indecipherable. Then, without warning, Guierriero's henchman was up.

At first, Mick-Mac felt as though he'd been punched in the chest. Then pain seared through him. He came down hard, the gun carelessly slipping from his grasp. Breathing became difficult, then impossible. Heavy eyelids slammed shut. He tried to open his eyes, to escape the blackness. At last, he gave up the struggle.

Blackness. Silence. An overwhelming feeling of peace. And then he saw her. Marnie. Waving goodbye as she mounted her bicycle and rode off into the morning mist. She turned and smiled and then was engulfed by a blinding light. Mick-Mac's instinct was to shield himself from the radiant glow. Instead, he embraced it and let it swallow him up.

CHAPTER SIXTY-SEVEN

Chunks of lead pierced the Mastercraft's slick torso, marring its beauty. Glen pushed his brother behind him, shielding Joe with his impressive size.

"Stay here," Glen said firmly.

"What are you going to do, Glen?"

Glen smiled. "What I do best, Joey." He crouched and moved toward the enemy. Joe thought to stop him but knew it was in vain. Glen had always lived by his own set of rules, and he wasn't going to change now.

"Diego!" Joe heard Guierriero yell. He'd spotted Glen. Joe lunged forward, searching for his brother in the crossfire. Glen charged forward, unleashing his fury. Diego took the brunt of his wrath, doing a spasmodic dance before crashing to the ground. Guierriero was quicker to react, diving for cover.

Joe rushed toward his brother. "Glen!" Glen's head swiveled toward Joe. He motioned for Joe to get back, anger in his eyes. A loud *crack*. As if in slow motion, Glen's body writhed, and he was down. Joe's gaze met Guierriero's, an emotion far beyond rage burning behind his dead eyes. Guierriero took aim. But this time Joe was quicker.

"It's over, Guierriero!" Joe said, adrenaline working overtime. He unleashed his own fury. Guierriero clutched his shoulder and disappeared into the windswept shadows.

Joe looked down at his brother. His eyes were glazed over, his body limp. This man, who had seemed invincible, unstoppable, unsinkable like that damn Boston Whaler, was mortal after all. Joe's body deflated. At last, he released the ball of pressure that had built up inside him for days, coiling itself around his innards. His body heaved. And then he wept.

Dom Jr. had underestimated this small, insignificant man. His bicep throbbed. He applied pressure to the oozing wound and was suddenly overcome by a raging tempest flooding into his body.

With the powerhouse brother out of the picture, it was time to finish this once and for all.

For Padre.

Joe dragged his brother's weighty body to the shelter of the sleek boat he'd envisioned them cruising along Lake Winnipesaukee in when this was all over, rekindling what they'd once had. Once they were shielded, he released his brother's muscled arms from his grip. They fell soundlessly to the rain-soaked planks. Joe, exhaustion at last overtaking adrenaline, slumped to the floor.

A groan. Probably the wind. Again. He glanced up, wiping a mix of rain and tears from his eyes. Movement. Were his eyes playing tricks? Then Glen's body shifted.

"You're alive!" Joe cradled his brother's sturdy head in his hands. Glen opened his eyes. He grinned then grimaced and clutched his side. Joe lifted his brother's shirt, surveying the damage. He breathed a sigh of relief. "Looks like it's just a flesh wound," Joe said.

Glen winked and said, "Sometimes, those hurt the most. Shouldn't have given Mick my Kevlar." He groaned and said, "Help me up." As Joe reached for his brother, Glen's expression darkened.

Joe looked in the direction of his brother's upward gaze. Dominic Guierriero Jr. stood over them, his face twisting into a grotesque grin.

"Looks like your dumb luck has finally run out, Joe Campbell," he said and trained the gun directly between Joe's eyes.

"Listen, Guierriero," Joe said, noting the tremor in his voice. "I was set up. You have to believe me."

Guierriero looked blankly at him and said, "I no longer care. Now where's the money?"

Glen groaned as he shifted into a seated position. Then he pointed out at the raging lake that lapped with ferocity at the dock. "Out there," he said and grinned. "In a million pieces with your girlfriend and my boat."

Guierriero laughed. "Girlfriend? That bitch was nothing but trouble from the day my father met her." His smile turned to an angry slit and his eyes darkened. "And now, my friend, it's time we say goodbye." He waggled the gun from one brother to the other. "Eeny, meeny, miny, moe—"

Joe squeezed his eyes shut and steeled himself for the blast. He'd once heard your entire life flashes before your eyes when death is imminent, but the only images that flashed through his mind were of Patty and Kate. And how they had played him so well. Then his thoughts flashed to Glen and how their rekindled friendship had been so short-lived. And an overwhelming sense of loss and sadness flooded through him.

Thwack.

He opened his eyes. Dominic Guierriero, Jr., his jaw dropped as if it were on a hinge, eyes protruding grotesquely from their sockets, was still, his frozen arm poised to fire. The razor-sharp arrow jutted out of his neck, a thin trickle of red sliding down his thick neck. Guierriero stood like that for a long moment, the mouth and eyes unmoving, the gun in his hand unwavering. At last, he crashed loudly to the dock.

Then she came into view. Rebecca. Poised like a pro with the sleek crossbow. She let the weapon fall to her side and surged forward through the rain.

"Are you okay?" she said, gazing with horror at Glen's blood-stained shirt. She threw the metal contraption aside and knelt beside him.

"I'm fine, baby," he said. "Just a flesh wound." Then his eyes zeroed in on her. "What the hell was that?"

Rebecca shrugged and said, "I spent a lot of time at my granddaddy's farm in Kansas when I was a teenager. Not much else to do in Kansas when you're fifteen. And if you think I'm good, you should see my grandmother."

Joe laughed and said, "I'm not so sure I want to. In fact, I'm a bit terrified of you right now."

Rebecca brushed a sodden strand of hair from her face. "Well, anyway, you're welcome."

Joe reached out and hugged the petite woman who had just saved his life. Glen threw an arm around her too and they kissed. Joe felt a momentary pang of jealousy but quickly brushed it aside.

"Can I get in on this lovefest?"

Their attention turned to Mick, looking like he'd been through a war—which, in a sense, he had. "Mick," Glen said, looking happy to see his new friend alive. "Good to see you among the land of the living."

"If you hadn't given me that vest, I don't know where I'd be right now." Mick winced and massaged his chest. "Knocked the breath out of me and I may have a cracked rib or two, but it sure beats the alternative. Thanks."

Glen nodded, then said, "Did you see my girl?" He pulled her close, beaming with pride.

"Pretty impressive," Mick said. "I might have a spot for you on the force."

Rebecca shook her head and said, "No thanks, Mick. My days of shooting anything other than a game of pool are over."

Joe laughed. Then his gaze moved to the lake. He recalled his first meeting with Kate, a woman who had once been as charming as Rebecca. Something slapped his arm.

"You okay, Joey?" Glen said, apparently sensing his brother's dejection.

Joe nodded slowly, feigning indifference. "Yeah, yeah, I'm fine."

"Damn shame about the money, though," Glen said. "I wonder how much it was?"

"Four million," Rebecca said. Glen gave her a puzzled look.

"When I was stuck in that car, that's practically all they talked about." She looked at Joe. "And maybe a little about you."

Joe put up his hands and said, "Never mind, I don't want to know." Then he looked at his brother and his face cracked open in a grin.

"What?" Glen said.

"What if I told you that money wasn't on the boat?"

"But we saw them with the bags."

"Suppose the money wasn't in the bags."

"Then where would it be?"

"In the back of your truck."

Six surprised eyes met Joe's. Then Mick said, "I don't understand."

"Well," Joe began. "When I was trapped out there by the barn before I ran into Rebecca, I found the bags of money in the back of the SUV. So, I hauled them over to your truck and dumped the contents into your truck. Then I filled the bags from your nicely stacked woodpile. I guess when Patty and Kate made their getaway, they didn't think to look inside."

Glen slapped his brother on the shoulder hard. Too hard. Joe winced. "You are something else, brother," he said. Glen glanced around. "So, if my math is correct, there are four of us, so a cool million each."

Mick shook his head. "Glen, I think you're mistaken. There was only one million, which I came upon before the cavalry rode in—which, by the way, will probably be soon. You may live miles from nowhere, but I'm sure that explosion was seen from across the lake."

"But, Mick," Glen said. "You can start fresh, live easy."

"Naw," Mick said. "I wouldn't know what to do with that kind of money. I'm a simple guy. Being a cop is all I know."

"Mick—"

Mick cut Glen off and said, "Listen, you three need to get out of here. I'll take care of the rest. Who knows, maybe there'll even be a promotion in it for me." He winked. "After all, I just singlehandedly took down Dominic Guierriero Jr.'s killers."

Glen tried to argue again, but realized it was in vain. "Now let's get a move on before I shoot you with that thing," Mick said, pointing at the glistening crossbow by Rebecca's feet.

CHAPTER SIXTY-EIGHT

"You wanna run that by me again, Mick-Mac?" Eddie Diaz glared at Mick-Mac with a mix of contempt and suspicion.

Mick-Mac sighed and prepared himself to retell his story—his fictional story—knowing Eddie would be looking to punch holes in the slightest inconsistency. In his version, Joe, Glen, and Rebecca were never on the scene.

Together, the foursome had run through every possible scenario, punching their own holes in their fictional story. Joe pointed out that they needed an explanation for the body that had clearly been mauled by an animal. That was an easy one, Glen had explained. He had seen his share of wild dogs, bobcats, and even a mountain lion during his time here. Rebecca's car had to disappear. Getting her car dislodged from the muck took some effort, but they'd managed. Luckily, the heavy rains washed away much of the evidence, but they'd painstakingly wiped down any surface that might be stamped with a suspicious fingerprint.

"Like I said," Mick-Mac began, "I got an anonymous phone call from a woman telling me she had knowledge of the hit on Guierriero and gave me this address."

"Who was this woman?"

"I have no idea. Her voice was muffled. In hindsight, I believe it was Patty Quigley."

Diaz glanced down at his notebook. "Quigley. The woman you said was driving the boat that blew up."

"That's correct."

"And the woman you said killed Dominic Guierriero in the hit at the bar."

"Correct. She admitted to it, and to the murder of Mitch Wasserman."

"Joe Campbell's coworker."

"Yes."

"Why would she kill Wasserman?"

"My theory is that she went to this Joe Campbell's office for some reason and this guy happened to be in the wrong place at the wrong time."

Diaz sighed. "Why Joe Campbell? How does he figure into this?"

"It appears Quigley and Campbell's wife, who it turns out are related, plotted a scheme to pin the hit in the bar on Joe Campbell."

"So, you're saying this Campbell guy was an unwitting pawn in this plot?"

Mick-Mac nodded, hoping his retelling was in sync with what was scribbled in Diaz's little black book. "Yes. Kate Campbell admitted that she'd helped her aunt set up her husband. But she insisted that was her only part in the scheme. She said it was Patty Quigley who masterminded the murder of Dominic Guierriero."

"Sounds like this woman was a regular old Jezebel. But why would she throw her own aunt under the bus?"

"Well, when Guierriero's son has a gun pointed at you, you're likely to spill your guts. Kate Campbell was terrified. She was attempting to escape in the boat but Guierriero and his henchman had them pinned down. Maybe she thought by coming clean, she could save her own skin, even if it meant sacrificing her aunt's."

Diaz thumbed through his notes. "But she didn't, did she? So, how did Guierriero end up with an arrow through the back of his neck?"

Here's where Mick-Mac and the trio had to get creative. They'd dragged Rufus's body from the barn, put the crossbow in his hands. "That big lug with the crossbow was in love with Campbell's wife and when it looked apparent Guierriero wasn't going to let her go, he fired. Then his henchman unleashed on the boat and it caught fire then exploded. I saw it all unfold from my vantage point."

"And then what?"

Mick-Mac nodded. "The guy who took out the boat spotted me and took aim. But I was quicker."

"And then you took out the last man standing, according to your statement."

Mick-Mac nodded, relieved to be nearing the end of the story. "That guy with the crossbow reloaded and had a bead on me. So, I took him down too."

Diaz frowned, the fabrication apparently lining up with his notes. "Well, you're a regular old Jason Bourne, aren't you,

MacAvoy?" he said with venom. "I mean, you singlehandedly took out Guierriero and his posse."

"No, I didn't say I took them all out. You might want to recheck your notes, Eddie. Quigley and her crew had a hand in that."

Diaz looked to the sky, a calming blue, the storm having passed an hour or so ago. "And how do you explain the mauled body?"

Mick-Mac shrugged. "A wild dog, perhaps?"

Diaz sighed loudly, frustration etched into his face. "You realize we'll be checking all your claims, including your firearm."

Mick-Mac nodded. *And you'll find it all adds up.* He had Glen to thank for that. This enigmatic man ran through the scenario as though he were directing a play. Mick-Mac got the feeling he'd done this before. Glen pointed out that the bullets found in some of the bodies Mick-Mac had shot in their fairytale version wouldn't match Mick-Mac's gun, the only gun he had arrived on scene with.

That's where the bunker came into play. Realizing he was outnumbered, and outgunned, he'd taken cover in the cabin, stumbled upon the bunker. Hence, the additional weapons in his possession.

Mick-Mac's battered body signaled it needed some rest. And a stiff drink. "Are we done here, Eddie?"

Diaz nodded reluctantly. As Mick-Mac turned to leave, Diaz said, "Just one more thing."

"What's that?" Mick-Mac felt his heart skip a beat. Had they overlooked something?

"If Joe Campbell had no part in this bloodbath, then why are bodies strewn all over his brother's property? I don't get the connection."

Mick-Mac's heart nestled back into place. "Kate Campbell was seeing her husband's brother behind his back," he blurted out.

"She what?" Diaz said incredulously.

Rebecca had come up with that one. Obviously, the address would be tracked back to Glen Campbell, brother of Joe Campbell.

"Kate Campbell knew this location. Knew how isolated it was. She'd been using Glen just as she'd used her husband. She must have known he wouldn't be here." Mick-Mac swept his arm around their surroundings. "If I wanted to lure Guierriero for an ambush, what better place than somewhere remote, somewhere I knew like the back of my hand."

Diaz shook his head. "How could you know Kate Campbell was having an affair? Did she confess to that too?"

Mick-Mac laughed. "Of course not. I found handwritten notes in the cabin from her to Glen. Mostly silly little love notes. I've already pointed those out to the team." These notes were, in fact, written by Rebecca, Kate's handwriting style dictated by Joe. If an in-depth analysis were to be done, which Mick-Mac doubted, the authenticity of these notes could come into question.

Diaz shuffled his feet in the hardening mud. "So, this was all about money?"

Mick-Mac shrugged. "Isn't money usually the motivator?" Then he added, "Especially when it's a million bucks."

Diaz nodded, though skepticism still sat stubbornly in his eyes. "Well, it appears the Campbell brothers have vanished into thin air, doesn't it?"

Mick-Mac shrugged again. "Looks that way. Like I said, I've never laid eyes on either one of them." A surge of pain shot up his spine. "Now are we done here?" he said, no longer containing his anger.

Diaz tucked his notebook into his jacket pocket. "For now," he said. "But I'll be watching you, MacAvoy."

Mick-Mac smiled. "And I'll be watching you watching me, Eddie." He walked toward the cabin, ignoring the flashing lights and the adrenaline-fueled techies running about, clearly excited to be working a case that was bound for the front page. Probably a book deal and Netflix series to boot.

"Hold on."

Mick-Mac groaned and turned toward Diaz. "Eddie, you said we were done."

"Just one more thing that's eating at me. Why would Patty Quigley call *you* to tip you off?"

Shit. He hadn't thought of that. *Think fast, Mick.*

The lie continued. "Well, here's my theory." *Okay, Mick, what's your theory?* "So, I suspect that Patty Quigley and Kate Campbell came here with the intention of killing Dominic Guierriero, Jr." *Good start. Keep it coming.* "And that big oaf with them, the guy with the crossbow, was their patsy. They were setting him up to take the fall." He looked at Diaz, who appeared to be buying the lie. "Think about it, Eddie. He owned the joint where the hit took place. And why wasn't he on that boat with them as they made their getaway?"

Diaz nodded slowly. "You have a point. But if money was the motivator, why leave it behind?"

Mick-Mac nodded. He was getting better at this lying game. "I thought of that myself. My guess is that they couldn't get back to that SUV to grab it. I mean, did you see that thing? It looked like it had been to hell and back."

"That it did. But why you? Why contact *you*?"

Mick-Mac shrugged, conspiring his next lie. "I don't know. Maybe she found out I was working the Wasserman case and thought she could somehow tie that murder to Joe Campbell too."

Diaz didn't seem to be buying this last bit he was selling. But he looked defeated and exhausted. "Okay, that's it for now," he replied without emotion. He'd already said that once before. Mick-Mac needed that drink. He turned to leave again.

"Hey, MacAvoy!" Eddie's booming voice slammed Mick-Mac's back. *Are you kidding me?* He groaned and spun around. "What is it, Diaz?" he spat, his patience having long left the building.

Diaz, now taking on an air of curiosity, said, "What do you make of that bunker in the basement? It's really something."

Mick-Mac threw up his hands. "Sure is. Took me by surprise too. Maybe this Glen Campbell guy was one of those crazy conspiracy nuts who thinks the apocalypse is coming."

"Maybe," Eddie said, shaking his head. "I guess when we find him, we'll know."

Mick-Mac nodded, waved, and turned away. *But you never will*, he thought, and his face cracked into a smile.

EPILOGUE

A muted watercolor landscape of purples, reds, and yellows played out on the day's waning canvas, the fiery orb lessening in intensity as it slid into the Aegean Sea, its shift almost over. Joe polished off the last of his beer and let the gentle breeze massage his face. He spotted his brother heading his way.

Glen, donning his customary uniform of tank top, board shorts, and flip-flops, plunked down beside him at the seaside bar and said, "We're good to go, Joey." Glen was referring to the license for their new tour business, Trailblazer Excursions. The bartender approached, a curious look on his face as he studied the brothers.

They got a lot of that these days, Joe with his deformed ear and his brother with a conspicuous scar adorning his shorn skull. While Glen's wound made him look tougher than usual, Joe's grotesque cartilage only made passersby look with revulsion. He'd eventually go under the knife to repair the disfigurement. Until then, he'd let his hair grow to mask the mutilation.

Joe signaled for a refill and said, "What'll it be, brother?"

"I'm good," Glen said. The bartender, sneaking one last glance at the impressive scar, nodded and was gone.

"Shouldn't we be celebrating?" Joe said.

"Yes," Glen said. "And we will. I'm just gonna grab a quick shower." The smell of sea water and fresh sweat clung to his brother's tanned and toned skin.

"Where's Rebecca?" Joe asked. Although initially shocked and angered by Glen's secret life, she'd softened and seemed to be adjusting well to her new lifestyle. Which was a pretty damn good lifestyle.

"She's at her beach yoga class with her new best friend," Glen said. The friend Glen was referring to was Blazer, who seemed especially protective of Rebecca since their ordeal nearly a month ago.

Joe's cell buzzed. "It's Mick."

"Tell him I said hello and to get his ass over here for a visit," Glen said before heading off. Joe nodded and picked up his phone.

"Hey, Mick."

"How's the weather over there?" Mick said, a hint of exhaustion edging his voice.

"Couldn't be better," Joe replied. "So, how's life in the big city?" Joe had heard of Mick's recent promotion. And his role as lead on the search for Joe Campbell and his brother, which Glen found hysterical.

"Busy," Mick said. There was a long silence. Then he said, "They found partial remains in the lake."

"Is it Kate?" Joe said with a mixture of anger and sadness.

Despite the betrayal, a part of Joe still loved her. He'd tucked these feelings away in the depths of his memory bank, but every so often they crept back to the surface.

"Too soon to tell," Mick said gravely. "The body was burned beyond recognition. Forensics is on it. They're still searching for another body, but so far they've come up empty." Sensing Joe's anguish, he changed the subject, his voice suddenly alive. "Looks like you're in the clear for the Guierriero murders," he said. His tone dropped again. "But you're still wanted for questioning in the murder of Mitch Wasserman."

Mitch. The poor miserable bastard. Despite his personal loathing for the man, Joe still had pangs of guilt over his death, usually in the dead of night when his mind was abuzz with destructive thoughts.

"Well, you know where to find me," Joe said with a slight laugh. Though nothing about the situation felt in the least bit amusing. "So, Glen wants to know when you're coming for a little R & R."

A long pause, followed by, "One day." Another pause. "Anyway, I'll let you know when I hear more on the DNA results."

They exchanged friendly yet awkward goodbyes. Though Joe knew Mick would never roll over on them, he also sensed the deception left Mick with an uneasiness that bore deep into his soul.

The bartender slid a drink in front of Joe. "Excuse me," Joe said. "I didn't order this."

The bartender smiled and said, "It was sent by the lady over there." He nodded toward the back of the outside bar, the tables jammed with locals and tourists alike, enjoying the balmy evening air.

Joe scanned the faces. "What lady?"

The bartender, a look of puzzlement washing over him, shrugged and said, "She appears to be gone." Joe was about to press him for more information but a fresh-scrubbed young couple, probably honeymooners, signaled and the man disappeared.

Joe scanned the crowd again, his heart in his throat, then gazed at the concoction before him.

Do you mind my asking what a Sidecar is?

It's Cognac with orange liqueur and lemon juice. I've never been much of a Chardonnay girl.

Panic seized Joe, sending shockwaves through his body. Had Kate survived the blast? Or was this just an odd coincidence? Even if she were alive, how would she find him?

Because you talked about wanting to chuck it all and live by the sea in Mykonos on many occasions, Joe, that's how.

The sun had tucked itself under the watery cover of the sea and tiki torches lit up the night. Joe threw some money on the bar and rushed out onto the balmy beach, stumbling through the white pristine sands toward his bungalow.

As he approached the house, he saw the dim glower of lights. He'd find Glen and Rebecca sitting on the veranda, wrapped tightly in one another's arms staring out at the night sky, Blazer curled contentedly at their feet.

To his horror, he found something else.

Rebecca and Blazer were nowhere in sight, but Glen was. Out on the veranda. With a gun pressed to his head.

He stared at the woman on the other end of the weapon, back from the dead. Back with a vengeance.

"Hello, Cowboy." Patty Quigley smiled. A malicious smile,

seething with hatred. She nodded to a chair that ~~...~~ them "Please, sit."

Joe, helplessness snowballing over him, complied. "~~I~~ just want to —"

"Silence." Her tone was calm yet forceful. "You no lo~~nger~~ call the shots."

The sight of Patty had been a shock. But what stunned Jo~~e~~ more than seeing her was the realization that the charred body pulled from the lake was his wife, the woman he'd once thought he'd grow old with. "How did you—"

"Find you?" Patty said, the sinister grin stretching her face. "Let's just say my little Katie told me everything," she said. "I mean, seriously Cowboy, of all the places you could disappear to, you pick the place that you bored Katie with over and over?"

Because I thought you were at the bottom of a lake in a million pieces.

Patty scoffed. "You know how many times Katie told me she had to listen to your stories about living the simple life here in Mykonos, pretending to show interest in your stupid pipe dreams?"

Joe's eyes met his brother's. There was no look of fear or panic. Only one of resignation. So, that was it. In the end, Patty had gotten the better of him. Game over.

"Let Glen go," he said. "You can do whatever you want with me, but he has nothing to do with this."

Patty laughed, pressed the gun firmly into Glen's skull. "Oh, I plan to do whatever I want with you, Cowboy," she said. "But first you're going to watch your brother die. Just like I had to watch Katie die."

Stalling and hoping for some miracle to turn the tide on the situation, Joe said, "How were you able to escape and not Kate?"

367

A new emotion washed over Patty's face. Sadness. If he could tap into her anguish, maybe she'd let her guard down.

"The money," Patty said flatly. "I told Katie we had to get off that floating graveyard before it blew, but she looked first at me, then the bags of cash. And made her decision." There was a long pause. Then she said, "But she did it for me. She wanted me to have a good life."

Glen let out a loud snort, the first noise he'd made since Joe had arrived.

"What are you laughing at?" Patty said, twisting and grinding the shiny metal into Glen's temple.

He grimaced and said, "There was no money in those bags. That bitch blew herself up over a pile of seasoned firewood." He laughed louder.

Joe tensed, realizing his brother's arrogance was escalating the situation. If Patty had let her guard down, it was now standing at full attention. Glen had poked the bear. And the claws were out. Joe noticed a colorful flash to his left.

Patty's face twisted up in rage, hatred seeping through every pore. The flash of color reappeared. Rebecca. In a vibrant beach coverall. Bouncing toward the veranda, Blazer trotting happily beside her. He tried to get her attention, to signal her to turn back. But her mind was in the clouds, a pleasant smile illuminating her sun-kissed complexion.

"Hey, Cowboy." Joe's eyes shifted back to Patty. "Want to know what Katie's last words were to me?"

Rebecca moved with purpose, now merely steps from danger. Joe shook his head, regret coursing through his veins.

"She told me she loved me," Patty said. "So, Cowboy, any last words you want to say to your brother before I make a mess of this lovely space?"

Rebecca suddenly paused just out of eyeshot to Patty and Glen, catching Joe's desperate gaze, confusion freezing her in her tracks. Instinct took hold of Blazer. He stood stock-still beside a perplexed Rebecca, tilting his head slightly, his steely eyes locked on Joe's.

"I said, any last words?" Patty's voice shook Joe from his stupor. He looked again to Blazer, the dog's high-alert gaze scorching him.

He moved his gaze slowly to meet Patty's. "Just two," he said.

"Yeah, Cowboy, what's that?"

"*Que pasa!*"

CPSIA information can be obtained
at www.ICGtesting.com
Printed in the USA
BVHW071515021022
648430BV00001B/2